HIDDEN
IN A
DECADE

For the residents of
Audrey Stirley Court

Jules.c. Hillyer
(on behalf of the author)

HIDDEN IN A DECADE

ANN HILLYAR

Matador
9 Priory Business Park,
Wistow Road, Kibworth Beauchamp,
Leicestershire. LE8 0RX
Tel: 0116 279 2299
Email: books@troubador.co.uk
Web: www.troubador.co.uk/matador
Twitter: @matadorbooks

ISBN 978 1788037 341

British Library Cataloguing in Publication Data.
A catalogue record for this book is available from the British Library.

Typeset in 11pt Aldine by Troubador Publishing Ltd, Leicester, UK

Matador is an imprint of Troubador Publishing Ltd

ANN HILLYAR

Born in Eltham, London, in 1938, Ann took up nursing at St Mary's Hospital, Paddington before her marriage to a BP Oil executive with whom she had four children. Much later, divorced and independent, she lit up her second partner's non-fiction story with compelling personal experience, then produced a unique self-help guide called *Everyman The Pilgrim*. Today that partner uncovers material of hers written prior to her illness and passing in 2011, a key novel in which she shows what may lie hidden in our lives – yet for our wellbeing must be made conscious.

As her close partner for thirty years I dedicate this book to its author whose noble life I was privileged to share, but who passed on before I could recognise and admire her sensitive skill here in leaving a light for our world to follow.

My thanks go to Cressida Mattei for her crucial help in preparation of this volume, also to Linda McVan for her supportive advice.

And not least, due credit must go to skilful artist/illustrator Elaine Gill for her front cover depiction of Maples.

CHAPTER ONE

Mrs Pope cycled slowly up the long, twisting driveway to the house. It was hot in the late May sun and she began to wish she hadn't bothered with a coat. She hated to admit it, but even at her age her mother's words still rang in her ears every time she left home: "Make sure you take a coat with you. It might rain." But then mother had always been the pessimist. She shrugged off the negative thoughts which that parent always seemed to evoke, and began to look about her. The old sit-up-and-beg bike creaked and rattled beneath her substantial weight, but she was used to the noises and they didn't spoil enjoyment of the scene spread out in carefree abundance.

It must have been ten years since she was last here. Although she had often cycled past the iron gates on her way from the village, she hadn't bothered to stop and look. She was amazed how a decade of neglect could allow nature to have its way. The drive was hung over with lilac bushes, their heavy racemes of scented purple blooms swinging off old twisted branches. Butterflies fluttered over the flower heads. Her country eye recognised small tortoiseshells, red admirals and orange tips. Entwined through the lilac, honey suckles had climbed towards the sun; a sound like muted machinery came from bees hovering around the flowers. Roses, long past pruning, were budding again and the ground between the bushes was covered by fading bluebells, cow parsley and of course the ubiquitous nettles. Mrs Pope could remember a time when two gardeners had worked daily here keeping the grounds in apple-pie order, but the country woman in her preferred it overgrown. Nature was following her own design – no longer forced to conform.

This thought led Mrs Pope to recall her own life with Charlie, her dead husband. Ten years had also passed since his death, she realised with a small jolt. He had liked conformity; had liked everything in its proper place. She knew she didn't miss him. She enjoyed doing things her way – slap-happy some called it, but she didn't care. Let them think what they liked. She couldn't even see his face now – no hint of his features was reflected in her two sons. They both resembled her.

It had been a cold, loveless marriage, a union she had been egged into by her mother who was fond of saying: "A woman shouldn't be left on the shelf." There had been no passion in it – either love or anger. Sometimes when Mrs Pope settled down in the evening to watch one of her favourite 'soaps' she couldn't equate the threshing coupling of two people with the quick assaults on her body by Charlie. Did men and women really experience such depth of feeling? It was on television, therefore she decided it must be true.

As time had gone by she and Charlie seemed to live in separate worlds, hardly speaking. She had found him dead in his armchair one afternoon, and the only tremulous reaction as she had stood looking down at him was one of relief. She wore conventional black for the funeral but all the way through the service she was saying to herself: "At last I can have the cottage for my very own." Doris had hugged the thought to her.

Her musings were abruptly halted after she rounded the corner of the driveway and the house lay in front of her. It was a Queen Anne mansion, with three floors built from soft red brick. Once it must have held an aura of romance and life, fun parties would have been celebrated, generations of children would have loved it, but now years of neglect gave it an air of sadness. The paint around the elegant high windows was flaking, the pointing between the bricks was crumbling, and tall pine trees hung over the roof breaking up the hot sunlight. The house cried out to be lived in again. The large front door, with its pretty fanlight, was set back under a rounded, tiled porch approached by shallow steps, flanked by overgrown shrubs on either side. Doris dismounted and stood back to take a proper look. The unaccustomed length of the cycle ride had induced perspiration, but still a shiver ran down her spine as she stared at the closed windows. She hadn't experienced that frisson for many years; indeed, not since she had last been employed as a cleaner at this house by its then elderly reclusive owner.

Involuntarily giving herself a mental shake she recalled the estate agent's instructions. He had stopped her in the village street about a week ago and said heartily: "Mrs Pope, how are you?" She nodded at him, knowing he did not care one way or the other. A mischievous idea occurred to her that she could be bloody-minded and bore him with a long tale of her arthritis – that would teach him a lesson. However, she refrained, simply looking at him. The agent, Mr Barker, hadn't even noticed the pause. He'd been too engaged in a show of waving to the bank manager who crossed the road in front of them. Doris's sharp eyes didn't miss much. 'Pompous twit', she thought, and waited. Mr Barker turned to her again, hardly seeing the ordinary little woman standing in front of him.

"You used to clean up at the house called Maples didn't you?"

She assented.

"Well," he continued, "we've finally managed to let it to a family on a year's lease, renewable of course. A very *good* family," he emphasised with practised snobbery. "Mr Latimer has taken early retirement from the Navy and is now a business consultant."

The triumph of finding a tenant connected with the business world seemed to ooze from him. As far as Doris was concerned the business world could be operating on another planet and she was already bored, but prepared to wait. A cleaning job was obviously going to be offered and the money would be useful. Perhaps she could earn enough to consider renewing her bedroom curtains? The irony that *she* was engaging in a business contract being lost on her, she realised Mr Barker was still talking. Doris heard him say: "… Call at the office in the next day or so and collect the key. We can discuss wages then."

The key referred to was now in her shopping bag. Doris pushed the cycle round to the back door and took the bag off its handlebars. Meagre sunlight penetrated through the tall trees which bent towards the house as if trying to protect its very fabric from further harm. The path was slippery with dark green moss and she almost missed her footing. Bicycle propped safely against a wall, she put the key into the lock which had become stiff and rusty.

"Someone might at least have thought about doing a bit of oiling!" Doris muttered. She struggled to turn the key and at last, determination to obtain entry won the day, giving her wrists unusual strength. The lock snapped back. As it did so she recalled the lay-out of the house, and remembered that some furniture had been left covered in dust-sheets because the beneficiary of the estate had never taken up residence. This explained why the house was unsold. The door resisted on its hinges, but as she pushed it open the sickly smell of damp and decay wrinkled her nostrils. Any unpleasantness was quickly forgotten, however, while she stared at the sight in the kitchen. Dust and cobwebs were to be expected, and

ANN HILLYAR

both were thick in evidence; what made her stand stock still
was the clear fact that someone else was using the kitchen –
and recently!

Doris blinked at the used plate and mug which, together
with two open cans, stood in a small patch brushed clear of dust
on the kitchen table. A chair had been pushed so hastily aside
it had fallen over. Whoever it was must still be in the house.
Tense, her heart pounding, Doris listened.

The grating rattle of a window being opened somewhere
within the house broke the spell. A picture flashed into her
mind of French windows in the morning room overlooking the
back garden. The intruder was making good his exit that way.
For a woman of her bulk Doris moved surprisingly fast over
to the kitchen window. She stood, peering through the dirt-
encrusted panes, anxious over the lanky figure of a man who
was just visible retreating into the trees.

On safer ground now, she hurried down the hall and
opened the door of the morning room. More evidence of
recent occupation showed itself in the shape of a camp bed with
sleeping bag and pillow neatly folded at one end, redolent of
an institution. Doris scarcely registered this fact, her attention
caught by the open French windows. A swift inspection showed
the catch had been forced and, with a smug expression, she
banged them firmly shut.

Leaving the house by the way she had entered, Doris locked
the door behind her, and pedalled quickly away. Equilibrium
regained, her fertile imagination was already busy elaborating
the tale she would tell her cronies at the 'Over 60's Club'. Doris
had no scruples about embroidering the story in her favour,
already hearing their 'oohs' and 'aahs' of admiration at her
coolness under pressure. Mr Barker would have to be informed
and it was his responsibility to notify the police. He would also
have to find an extra pair of hands if the house was to be made

5

habitable in time for the Latimers, much as it annoyed her to share the wages.

Meanwhile, the unknown man had stood among those trees to observe that little currant bun of a woman trundling off down the drive. He had vaguely recognised her.

"Damn! Damn!" he berated himself. "How could I have been that careless?"

He had only been living in the house for a week. Ten days ago he had still been in psychiatric hospital – that 'awful place' he slid into when depression closed over his mind. This last time he had summoned all his courage to discharge himself against medical advice. Determination filled him to face the memories of shame and self-loathing which rose in his throat, threatening to choke him whenever he thought of Maples. Good God, at thirty-five it was time to pack away his childhood.

Right now, the immediate problem was to remove all traces of his presence from the house. If he knew anything about the local constabulary, once they realised the bird had flown he doubted they would look much further afield. 'Only a passing tramp – most probably harmless enough', they would decide, and snap shut their notebooks. But where could he hide? Maurice's mind flew rapidly round the garden. The rose arbour with its summerhouse came mentally into view. His mother had been in the habit of sitting in there and he had never been welcome. The thought of using it freely gave extra spice to the idea. He moved with easy familiarity through the unkempt grounds, soon finding the small wooden den. Although it was half hidden by leggy, semi-wild roses, the obscurity they offered met his purpose admirably. His spirits lifted as he went inside.

A rush of hot, dry air hit him and he coughed slightly.

The noise disturbed a fat spider who ran back hastily behind two faded deck-chairs – both looking for all the world as if their owners had just gone for tea. There was even a book lying on the bare floor-boards. Bending, Maurice picked up its yellowed pages which still managed to reveal the aspiration of a long dead poet. Absentmindedly he tucked it under one arm.

The hideaway was expedient he decided, and a stream that bubbled through the garden was conveniently close. It only remained for him to clear his meagre belongings out of the house, a bit of legwork at which he then beavered away in mechanical vein. But the transfer was soon made and, true to his forecast, a couple of hours later heard the sound of a car coming up the drive. With distinct lack of enthusiasm a young policeman climbed stiffly out of the driver's seat, yawning widely. One sharp push from his hands opened the French windows and he disappeared from view. He emerged after two minutes, fixed a flimsy padlock on the casement, and without even a glance in the direction of the garden reversed the car and sped away.

Maurice smiled: he had gauged the reaction of officialdom correctly. He was sitting on the grass outside the summerhouse, legs hunched up under his chin, but with thin arms clasped tensely round them because while the engine's harsh sound faded, private reaction to his roots was far more turbulent. Thoughts of regret, bitterness at years wasted, battered him with dreary monotony. Why had he allowed so many opportunities to slide away from him? He should have insisted on going to art school, not been bullied by mother into studying law – studies upon which he had finally closed the books after a miserable first year at university. To his shame he had been used to blaming his weak father for dying when Maurice was fourteen; used to pretending that, had his father lived, he would have spoken up for his son – been a friend to the lonely boy. That particular game of 'Let's Pretend' had run its course. The unpalatable truth had to be faced: that timidity and impotence were his father's only companions. Maurice experienced an unaccustomed flash of pity for that wretched man, but he had come here to confront his own limitations.

As night fell he released the catch on another downstairs window and was in the house again. The light from his torch searched round the room – mother's study. Within these walls he had suffered his worst humiliations. Her desk had been in front of the window, her back to the light; not for her the luxury of idle glances over trees and flower beds. No, she had sat obdurate, fastidiously reading every page of his school report while he stood waiting, heart thumping – not with fear but with hate. The hard-backed chair set before the desk was not for him to sit on, only to be bent over while her upraised voice and arm vehemently emphasised his many apparent deficiencies.

Maurice's thoughts went back to his recent arrival at Maples. The fifty mile coach trip from hospital having tired him, he had rested for a couple of days. They had been spent coming to terms with the unnerving experience of living inside his childhood home again; an experience terminated by the unwelcome interruption of the village woman. Each room he had wandered into was full of shadows and echoes that seemed to twist and distort like cloudy miasmas in his mind. He caught the odd whispered snatch of conversation but the more he strained the less he could hear. The dusty floorboards in the hall outside the study showed evidence of his pacing to and fro. Many times he had paused with his hand on the door knob, convinced he could hear her querulous voice calling to him. As a boy the sound had grated unbearably on his nerves; he used to try to blot it out by clamping his hands tightly over both ears but never quite succeeded. He couldn't ever recall her being soft and motherly, although he supposed she must have been on occasions.

Now that he was in the room it appeared much smaller than he remembered, despite being empty. Of course, he was now six foot instead of five foot – but that wasn't the true reason. He had outgrown her – not just physically but emotionally and mentally. She had shrunk and withered. He shone his torch round, looking for some evidence of her existence. There was none. Nothing at all. Not even a tiny scrap of paper. He laughed suddenly: a harsh sound lacking mirth. She never had been able to reach him inside; and at last she was gone, cold in the churchyard. He was a long, long way from being healed but he had begun the journey. Maurice let himself out of Maples and slipped into the darkness.

Six weeks later the Latimer family moved in.

The twins, Joanna and Ian, were thirteen but small for their age and totally different in appearance. Joanna, marginally the eldest, had dark, curly hair, brown eyes, clear skin and – unusually for her age – a poise and assurance which sat naturally on her young shoulders. Like her mother in looks, she was a close runner-up for charm. By contrast, Ian was a shadow of his sister's vivacity. His self-effacing personality viewed the world through light blue eyes set in a narrow face. His parents seemed to find his approach to life exasperating, and made little attempt to disguise the fact. Ian's sensitivity, exemplified by his love of sketching and interest in nature, was without doubt at variance with his parents' more earthy pursuits. He definitely felt the odd man out in the family and, in quiet moments, wondered if he had been adopted. Often bored at school, Ian would gaze out of the window dreaming that he was the son of an artist who refused to acknowledge him. The master's sharp voice would bring him back to earth again, at least for a while.

His father and mother were dissimilar characters yet, as is often the case, a well-matched pair. Derek Latimer was mean-spirited, his heavy frame outlining a weakness for the flesh-pots. A naval man, his promotion through its hierarchy had been impeded by personal failure to handle men under his command. Quite shrewd enough to recognise his limitations he took early retirement with a commander's pension, whereupon the role of financial consultant suited him better. Clients felt respect and trust for his acumen with their affairs, but almost all disliked the man whose smile never reached his eyes. Latimer cared little or nothing for this fact and was content with his life.

His wife was a hard as nails featherbrain. Love – if such an emotion had ever existed between them – had long since evaporated. In her more honest moments Susan Latimer did admit to herself that she was in awe of her husband, even a little frightened, but he provided a useful meal ticket which she exploited to full advantage. In return she made an excellent hostess, so their marital arrangement suited both partners. Susan Latimer did feel maternal warmth towards her pretty daughter who utilized this soft spot to full advantage, much to Ian's disgust. In his eyes there wasn't much to choose between the trio for unpleasantness: each in their different ways made him seem small and silly. At heart however he knew this was untrue – somewhere inside he felt bigger than all of them.

Time spent at boarding school therefore came as welcome respite for him. Both children attended so-called 'good' preparatory schools. Naturally, one that put emphasis on academia had been selected for Joanna, while a minor establishment of indifferent quality was considered sufficient for Ian's needs. This was a crammer totally bereft of imaginative teaching where, for inflated fees, the boys could be kept out of their families' way. Ian felt stifled. He longed to draw, to paint, but this wish was rejected as an unnecessary adjunct for growth into manhood.

Mid-July was dry and hot, generous for an English

summer. Throughout the first week of the children's holidays Ian mooched round the house and garden, continually being admonished by Susan. Joanna, in her infuriatingly organised way, already had two friends to stay; both ghastly girls in Ian's opinion – forever shrieking and giggling. When he met them their eyes slid over and past him as though he didn't exist. He decided he hated them. His mother was absorbed in showing off the three girls to the local smart set at the tennis club and her car spent most days running up the hill to the village. Ian thought the car as obsessed with social climbing as its driver. Continually left to his own devices he would pack his artist's pad and pencils into an old rucksack, make thickly spread peanut butter sandwiches for lunch, grab an apple and set off for the day whistling cheerfully.

Initial exploration of the grounds revealed them to be far more extensive than first realised. A jobbing gardener had recently cut some extra-long grass close to the house and the rough shape of a lawn emerged, thence quickly dotted with garden furniture by Susan. The rest of the gardens were left delightfully untouched and tangled. Ian loved the way the sun gleamed through the leaves to dapple the cool areas of shade, and light up the head of a profusely flowering purple clematis which had carelessly wound its way among the branches of a young silver birch.

He would sit by the stream happily watching shoals of minnows flashing through the crystal clear water, and occasionally reach down to stroke one. Sandwiches promptly eaten to appease hunger, he would either make a quick sketch of the scene or lie upturned on the warm grass, dreaming while time drifted by. When the sun had moved westwards he would turn to drag his feet home. Painful experience had taught that not one of its occupants would be even mildly interested in his day. They were all too absorbed in their own affairs. To be fair to them, at least they didn't pretend. Ian's bête noire were motley aunts and uncles who had descended on the Latimers through the years, feigning admiration for him. Once he had made the stupid error of showing a sketch to a plump aunt who, because she collected expensive paintings, he mistook for an art connoisseur.

"How sweet, how clever of you," she breathed at him.

Then she had turned to his father: "Such an unusual hobby for a boy, don't you agree Derek?"

Latimer had moved uneasily in his chair and said something along the lines that he would "probably grow out of it".

That decided matters for Ian. Never again would he show his work to any member of the family, and he would not "grow out of it". Once dinner was over he would run up to his room and lie on the bed, chin on hand, and look at the day's sketches. They were good. His heartbeat would quicken and a rare flush colour his pale cheeks. He wasn't boasting; just acknowledging his talent, one he longed to develop. An idea had been buzzing around his head that he must go to Art College. Perhaps he could win a scholarship? But where to apply, and how? Long after he had heard his parents come upstairs and the plumbing noises had finally subsided, he would be awake puzzling over the imponderable questions. One thing was certain: he was on his own in the quest.

One morning, wandering in a different direction, Ian found the path becoming more impenetrable each step he took. Brambles tore at his skin and clothes and he was grateful that his mother paid little attention to his appearance. She probably wouldn't notice the ragged tear in his jeans. With a final effort he was clear of the undergrowth and found himself in an open space, in the middle of which was a small wooden summer-house. Roses grew over it – indeed roses were everywhere – but Ian only had eyes for the structure. This could provide an ideal bolt-hole from the girls on rainy days.

Half expecting to find it locked, he was surprised how easily the door gave way. Once inside he soon detected that someone else had been there. The windows were festooned with spiders' webs, and dust lay everywhere except for one corner which was quite clean. Ian could see small tufts of wool snagged on the rough floor-boards as if a blanket had been dragged over them. Such was his pleasure at finding the den, however, that he didn't spare a thought for the previous occupant. Swirls of dust and an acrid smell made him cough; fresh air was needed if he was to avoid one of his wretched asthma attacks. He hurried outside carrying an old deck-chair he had found, and sat down.

"This is great," he congratulated himself. "A real hide-out, a camp. No one will ever find me here. I can really call it my own."

To remind him of his discovery he made a quick sketch of the house, ate his sandwiches and decided to continue exploring. The door safely shut, Ian pressed on down another path, a strange impatience urging him to hurry. The track became narrow and once he tripped over hidden tree roots. He couldn't explain his haste; after all, he had been along similar paths on the other side of the grounds. He only knew this experience was different.

The path appeared to be leading somewhere, yet at the same time nowhere – so to emerge into clear sunlight made him blink before being brought up sharply at a low fence which Ian deduced must be a boundary between Maples and the field visible on the other side. In the distance a small herd of cows chewed the cud; on the skyline the village church tower stood out in relief against the blue sky. All Ian's attention however was riveted upon the sight of a small white tent, with its flap tied back, set up about sixty yards to his left.

The tent was in the shelter of trees close to the fence. 'Just a camper', Ian surmised, and was turning away when a man came in view carrying an artist's easel and a camping stool. These items were placed facing the view of the church, followed by a second stool which Ian could see was to hold watercolours and brushes. He was enthralled while the man sat on the first stool and began to paint.

Half an hour sped by.

The man cast a glance over his shoulder a couple of times seemingly aware of being observed, but finding no one he continued his work. Ian had never seen an adult look so relaxed and absorbed. In his experience most grown-ups were jerky and impatient, especially his parents. His mother's hands were always restless – touching her hair, her clothes, the ornaments on the mantelpiece, plumping up cushions. She was not a peaceful person. And yet here was this man using his hands in a controlled manner. Suddenly Ian could wait no longer. In his eyes he had found a real artist and he must talk to him. Habitual shyness overcome, he climbed the fence and started off down the field.

CHAPTER TWO

Startled by the movement Maurice looked round to see a young boy hurrying towards him. Crestfallen he waited, wondering what to say to the lad. He was irritated by this interruption to a painting which had begun to show promise. Furthermore, children were an unknown quantity to him; he felt awkward in their company, while acknowledging their vulnerability in a hostile adult world which, for the most part, treated them either as toys or nuisances.

The boy stopped in front of him and Maurice looked down into his face. Two sensitive people stared at each other, both equally tongue-tied. Ian broke the silence, words tumbling out in his anxiety for information.

"Could you tell me how to become a real artist? How to get to art school? How to win a scholarship because I won't have any money and I'm not going to ask my parents for help?"

He broke off, amazed at his effusiveness. His innermost hopes were exposed to a complete stranger. He had never spoken in such a way to anyone in his whole life.

Maurice was taken aback. The questions were totally unexpected. Closer inspection of the boy revealed a thin, eager figure, holding tightly onto an old rucksack while trying to look at the painting on the easel. Maurice took a deep breath and relaxed. He wasn't under threat from this soul.

"You really want to know, don't you?" he probed gently.

Ian looked at him, unaware of the pleading in his eyes.

"Well," continued Maurice, "I only went to art school for a short time, but I think I know where to start making enquiries."

A déjà-vue sensation swept over him as he spoke. An echo of half-remembered thoughts from twenty years ago. He remembered, too, the patient teacher of the art therapy class he joined during one of his many long stays in hospital. The gentle old man had recognised Maurice's natural ability and had done all in his power to encourage him. Even on his days off he would visit Maurice to help give life to a painting, or bring a book with him on the lives of the great painters. When this mentor died Maurice had felt sharp grief for the first time in his life, such kindness and dignity being rare in his experience.

He was brought back into focus by the boy's voice saying:

"Thank you. Please find out all you can."

Ian was in front of the easel wondering how the watercolour's 'magical' quality had been achieved in such a short time. A fairly mundane scene had been lifted onto another plane by the subtle charm of soft colours. Maurice stood quietly to one side and waited. Ian sighed and looked at the man.

Maurice spoke: "You're obviously an artist yourself."

Ian felt his face redden at the words, but his hands moved instinctively to his rucksack. To quell their trembling he stuffed them deep into his pockets.

"You've some of your work with you?" Maurice had correctly interpreted the movement.

Ian nodded, his mind still in a whirl.

"Would…would you look at them and…tell me?" His voice faded away. He was unsure what to do. This artist's opinion of his sketches would be invaluable, but if he should reject them, however tactfully, the ensuing disappointment would be unbearable.

Maurice sensed his dilemma, and to give the boy time to

recover spoke in brisker, more prosaic tones. "By the way, my name is Maurice Caton and yours is…?"

"Ian Latimer."

"Do you live in the village Ian?"

"No. I live over there." Ian waved a hand vaguely behind him. "My parents rent the house called Maples."

The unexpected reply jolted Maurice. He knew the house was occupied, his few sundries having had to be found other quarters in a hurry; but it seemed odd somehow that this boy should be sharing his old home. Since his mother's death his financial affairs were handled by an old-fashioned firm of local solicitors. The modest legacy left to Maurice by his father had just about been exhausted, and in order to augment his slender income the lawyer suggested renting Maples to suitable tenants. Although Maurice could see the practicality of this idea, he wanted no part in the materialistic world of money, which had always been a closed book to him. He had therefore left instructions with the solicitor to act as he thought fit. Of course, he knew of the clause in Mother's will stipulating that the house must not be sold until twenty years after her death. It was as if she still wanted control over him from beyond the grave, Maurice thought with grim humour. But she couldn't prevent him letting the house.

For most of his adult life Maurice had kept well clear of Maples and the village; but on this visit, having forced himself back to face his shame, he had wanted to remain close by while he assessed his reactions. It hadn't been difficult to persuade the neighbouring farmer to let him put up a small tent. The man didn't connect the tall, bony stranger with the skinny boy seen around the big house many years before, Maurice preferring to keep it that way.

"Do you like the house?" Maurice abruptly asked Ian. Suddenly the answer was important.

"No.. not much. Hardly at all." Ian scuffed his plimsolls against a clod of earth, his eyes fixed on the small cloud of dust formed by the movement. "It's unfriendly somehow and too big. But I really love the gardens. They're smashing." His face lit up. "I spend all day in them, exploring. And I've found a proper den where I can make a camp and hide from my awful sister and her friends. I love drawing the gardens too."

He realised he was talking too quickly and felt silly and babyish. The man's face looked stern and forbidding; he reminded Ian of one of his school masters, old Chambers, whom all the boys naturally nicknamed 'Potty'. With Potty you never knew which way he was going to jump. Ian stared at the grass again and waited for what seemed an age.

Had he been able to read his new friend's thoughts he would have been surprised. To Maurice the resemblance between himself and Ian at the same age was uncanny. He would have reacted in identical fashion. His agile mind was busy weighing up the various possibilities as to why they had met. He squinted at the boy, whose head was now bent over his bag, hands fumbling with the buckles: then the bag was open. Ian pulled out the precious sketch pad and handed it to Maurice in silence.

The pages rustled slightly in the breeze as Maurice turned them. The gardens he knew intimately were faithfully reproduced in front of his eyes. There was talent here, considerable talent.

Ian's nails scored into his palms while he eagerly watched for reaction.

"I think you know they're good, don't you?" Maurice said softly, and Ian's eyes lit up with pleasure and sheer relief. "Let me hazard a guess," pursued Maurice. "Your father and mother don't consider that being an artist is a suitable or lucrative occupation? In fact, for a boy it's a bit sissy – not a proper job. Am I right?"

"Yes! Yes!" Ian was almost shouting in an outburst of emotion. "My father laughed at them. I hate him. I hate him! I don't show them to any of those horrible people in that horrible house." Tears came and his voice choked. His nose started to run, and he fumbled for a non-existent handkerchief.

"Listen Ian," Maurice spoke gently, handing over one of his own. "I truly understand how you feel, more than you realise. Come and see me again soon and we'll have a long talk. Meanwhile I'll find out all I can for you. Now blow your nose and wipe your eyes. I'm on your side – remember that. But for the moment I must finish this painting before the light changes. You understand don't you?"

Ian nodded, still not trusting his voice. With a deep sigh he turned back towards Maples.

From then on Ian dropped into the comfortable habit of visiting Maurice. They would sit outside the tent, mugs of coffee to hand, and talk on subjects dear to both their hearts: art, music, nature, and people. Unsure of themselves initially, overtures of friendship were tentative because neither wanted to risk rebuff. Each had been hurt in the past by being too open, too eager in the company of others.

Then came the day, an important watershed for Maurice, when he felt relaxed enough to lower his defences in front of Ian. He told of his boyhood at Maples and a little, just a little, about his mother. Ian had a struggle to understand the depth of emotion expressed by the older man, but felt corresponding tugs of sympathy and paid full attention.

As one summer day melted into another, Maurice almost felt he was receiving a blessing – that his pain had been noticed by someone unseen. In return, he wanted Ian to walk free of the shadow that had dominated and nearly ruined his own life. He became a man with a cause. Ian had to be saved from the toxic shame inflicted by thoughtless, selfish parents, and Maurice's heart told him it lay in his power to help his young friend. But Lord, he really didn't want to relive painful memories, re-open old wounds, not at the very moment he was starting to relax at long last.

Then a panic attack threatened him and he had to breathe deeply to release tension. His stomach twisted into knots and the palms of his hands were sticky with sweat. At last the anxiety lessened and he started to think more calmly. He forced his mind back in time to one of the many group therapy sessions he had endured in mental agony while in hospital. One counsellor in particular had made an impression on him. Although he couldn't recall her name, he could see her young earnest face, framed in a mass of untidy brown hair, and hear her soft Welsh lilt.

About ten patients were seated in a circle listening to the girl explain the term 'toxic shame' which apparently could be the root cause of their many assorted problems. As usual he was in deep despair, quite unable to value his own worth, and more than ready to clutch at any straw. Perhaps an answer to his low opinion of himself lay in her words. In simple language the therapist told the group that while healthy shame is normal human emotion which keeps us informed of our limits, toxic shame makes us believe that our very being is flawed and therefore we feel defective as a human being. Quite enormous energy is expended in building up a false self to hide the one we believe is flawed, to cover the pain. Often the pain is so great that it has to be transferred onto someone else by shaming them.

The men and women in the room split up into two groups and began to talk among themselves. It emerged, Maurice discovered to his amazement, that toxic shame was a common, if hidden, problem. Indeed, he felt it was the closest definition of human bondage he knew. With growing horror he realised his own father and mother had transferred their toxic shame to him. And Ian's parents were engaged in that very practice; it was a chilling form of abuse handed down from father to son, mother to daughter and so on. Ian had to be made to understand the facts, and this, Maurice vowed, he would do.

On starry nights Maurice would lie in his sleeping bag, hands behind head, his mind exploring a diversity of ideas. Answers to his enquiries about different scholarships for Ian had slowly filtered back, courtesy of the G.P.O., to a 'poste restante' in the village. Impatience with people who were slow to respond to any kind of request was tempered, on this occasion, by the knowledge that most colleges would be on summer vacation. It came as a pleasant surprise therefore to receive a friendly, helpful reply from one of his old college professors explaining all the numerous 'ins and outs' necessary for qualification.

'Maybe', thought Maurice, 'I could provide financial help for Ian and thereby get rid of all the wretched form filling. After all I can afford it, but folk are damned touchy about taking money'. He never could understand this attitude. For Pete's sake, what was terrible about accepting money offered as a gift? Still, he could anticipate difficulties lying ahead with the Latimers and he was the last person to add to Ian's problems. On second thoughts maybe he could act as a secret benefactor, rather along the lines of Magwitch in 'Great Expectations'. He chuckled aloud, and fell asleep.

★

Meanwhile Ian was in blissful ignorance of Maurice's schemes. To him this man was a trusted friend and he experienced complete ease in his company. Maurice never talked down to him, and always listened to Ian's views in passive silence. The boy felt himself to matter, felt that he belonged to this world of art and sensitivity upon which Maurice had opened the door.

Then the inevitable happened.

Parochial gossip began to fly round the village. What were this man and young boy doing together every day? The man's interest could mean only one thing and everyone knew what *that* was, my dear! Their small, petty minds took up the theme and tried to tarnish what was pure and altruistic. Of course, Susan Latimer came to hear in a not-so-roundabout fashion. Many who didn't care for her airs and graces made sure of that. Shocked, she told her husband. Not stopping to consider his actions or their consequences, Latimer got in his car and drove like a bat out of hell to the field gate.

Dusk was nearly complete, and hurrying across the uneven ground he could see the light from a hurricane lamp hung outside the tent. Maurice was seated on a hummock, facing the trees, enthralled by the throbbing evensong aired by a blackbird. He hadn't seen or heard Latimer's approach from behind him, but was soon aware of strong hands grasping him roughly under the shoulders and hauling him to his feet. Startled and caught off balance by surprise, Maurice twisted away from the painful fingers and spun round to face his adversary.

A hard eyed, florid man, head jutted forward, was spewing out filthy accusations, whisky-laden breath making Maurice flinch. The man kept trying to grab him again, though Maurice ducked and weaved, his comparative fitness keeping him well out of reach. The two moved round each other like wary animals.

Suddenly to Maurice, his opponent embodied all the injustices he had endured in the past. An almost unbearable tension snapped, and out lashed his right fist. The blow caught Latimer squarely in the face sending him sprawling on his back.

Consumed with rage Maurice stood over him, filled with an overwhelming urge to kick the slumped body. On the brink however his innate sense of fair play asserted itself, and his breathing eased. His hands pushed hard in his pockets, he moved away from the man he guessed must be Latimer, and stared up at the night sky. Control of the situation had moved into his court. Seconds afterward Latimer scrambled onto all fours, cursing and swearing. Maurice looked down at the flabby figure with contempt. Like most bullies Latimer cringed back muttering: "Leave me alone. Get away." Maurice stood and waited in silence while the other staggered to his feet, swaying from side to side.

"Oh for God's sake man, sit down," said Maurice harshly, impatient with this display of childish behaviour. "I'm not going to touch you."

Latimer lowered himself down gingerly on the grass, his bleary eyes trying to focus on the tall figure he could just distinguish in the dark.

"Now listen to me Latimer. It's high time you learnt a few home truths. First of all I'm not, and never have been, a homosexual. Your son has the talent to become an artist, so I've been giving him the encouragement he deserves and yet lacks at home. We're friends, although I don't expect you to understand that. Secondly, I'm your landlord."

Latimer's head jerked up at the last words and he stared at Maurice, who pressed home the point.

"My name is Maurice Caton and I'm the owner of Maples. As your landlord I instructed my solicitor, Hartley Staples, to make enquiries into your background. His subsequent report contained some rather unsavoury information. To begin with, you left the Navy under a cloud, although the incident was hushed up – the usual closing of ranks. But there was talk of mental bullying of a junior rating. Am I right?"

From the angry tide sweeping across Latimer's face Maurice knew he was, and carried on relentlessly.

"Well, in my book that didn't make you a bad financial risk as a tenant. In fact, I thought you and Maples suited each other. But after you moved in I decided to have further investigations made into your character. My informant discovered you'd been party to some wheeler-dealings, in addition to some tax dodges. The kind of thing that wouldn't go down at all well with your clients, or your fair weather friends at the golf club. I believe you're quite proud of your status in the community and would probably hate to lose it. Also, you'd hate word to get around that you're not what you appear to be on the outside. Eh?"

Maurice surprised himself. He hadn't realised he could slip into the role of blackmailer without compunction. His taunts about the shady deals had been a complete shot in the dark, but he had the correct measure of his man. Maurice was far more worldly wise than many gave him credit for; indeed, he often thought he was far more practical than many materialists who accused him of being the opposite. One glance at Latimer's frightened face told its own story. Coldly Maurice took full advantage.

"Unless you scotch these disgusting insinuations about Ian and myself – and I don't doubt you're quite clever enough to think of a way – then I'll make sure the appropriate authorities come to hear of you. It would pay you, Latimer, to be more honest and above board in your financial and private life from now on. For a so-called intelligent man *YOU* are a bloody fool. I think I've made myself crystal clear. Now damn well get out!"

Sweaty and shaky, Latimer stood up and stumbled off across the field to his car. Maurice suddenly felt weak at the knees but almost ninety-nine per cent sure those right words would be dropped in the ears of the rat pack that made up most of the village. He was to be proved correct.

★

Ian knew nothing of the scene that had transpired in the field. Relief at being ignored for several days by his father was tempered by the unpalatable knowledge that autumn term was looming. Prep. school was behind him and public school was the next hurdle. Piqued at having to accompany his mother to the school outfitters, he was surly and uncommunicative on the return journey. One glance at the set profile of her son in the passenger seat made Susan sigh, and in that moment she gave up for ever any attempt to understand him. Thoughts of her popular daughter restored some pride in her maternal abilities, although she had a more than sneaking suspicion that a couple of years from now would find Joanna a handful.

Back home Ian raced upstairs and pulled on his jeans, anxious to pour out his woes to Maurice. At thirteen Ian epitomised the self-centredness of puberty: it never occurred to him that his friend may have problems of his own.

Maurice had spent most of that day pacing up and down the field, railing at his inadequacies. The control he had demonstrated after the fracas with Latimer had sharply focused his mind. With shame he remembered only too vividly times past when he had let slip a chance for dignified behaviour, simply because he had felt the underdog, unworthy. Retrospection exposed broken relationships, unfulfilled talent, and ill-spent money. The anger inside lacerated him. He was crying, stabbing at the air with clenched fists. Blinded by his tears, he stumbled over a tree root and fell heavily, bruising his left knee. He didn't care. He wanted to hurt himself. Gradually his sobs lessened. Emotionally spent, he felt comforted by the sun's warmth on his back, the smell of the earth, the movement of insects in the grass.

Tension seeped out of his body into the ground, and for

a fleeting moment he caught a sense of the rightness and wholeness of life. He rolled onto his back and idly followed the trails of high white clouds, spreading across the sky. Each one was different; each one made its own peculiar pattern. Unexpectedly he recalled quiet words spoken by the only therapist he had truly respected. Her name was Margaret Willis, a vague looking middle-aged woman, big hearted with a mind to match. One day he had been sunk in depression even more than usual. He just wanted to die in the quicksand that gripped him. He had been blaming his mother, his father, his school – anyone or anything he could transfer pain onto.

Margaret had leant towards him, and taken his trembling fingers between her hands. She spoke softly:

"Remember, Maurice, *you* create your own reality. No one else does it but *you*, and only *you* can alter it. This applies to everyone. Other people are not to blame for our reactions to circumstances. You have to alter your attitude from within and take responsibility for your thoughts."

He hadn't answered but the phrases had struck home. Now their true significance was clear. If he could change his behaviour once, then he could do so again. His choice of attitude in the present could affect both past mental images and future reactions.

A plethora of ideas raced through his mind. He had his artistic talent. He wasn't interested whether his work sold; he simply needed to paint, to create a thing of beauty. It was important to stay close to Maples, and he had already thought of a way to achieve that aim. The fact that he was different from the small-minded folk of the village didn't bother him; in fact he took a perverse delight in the knowledge. Ian's friendship was valued above everything else, and he knew he could guide the boy. Ten years from now the freehold of the house passed to him. Perhaps he could open an art school? The ghost of his mother was growing misty and shapeless; her influence appeared to be floating off and away.

Before this positive mood had time to evaporate he jumped to his feet, barely aware of the pain in his knee. Quickly he sluiced his face and hands, pulled on a jacket, and almost jauntily set off for the village.

Meanwhile, Ian hurried down the path to the field, concern for Maurice now nagging. The weather would turn inexorably colder and to camp then was out of the question. But where could Maurice go? Where would he live? Friends and family appeared to be non-existent in his life. Secretly Ian considered this an enviable state. His relatives seemed to produce, at regular intervals, another smelly baby to swell their ever growing numbers.

"Please, please," Ian beseeched out loud, "don't let him move too far away. I couldn't bear that."

He climbed the fence, hot and thirsty after running, and the disappointment of an empty tent made him feel almost physically sick. It seemed imperative to have immediate answers. Where could Maurice be? He was always here. Moodily kicking a stone around, Ian kept his eyes fixed on the gate as if he could conjure his friend out of thin air. Minutes dragged by. Then, there he was, strolling down the road from the village. Ian's excitement pounded across the field, almost colliding with the wanderer at the gate.

"I thought you were never coming!" Ian was shouting in relief. "Where've you been? I wanted to talk to you."

Maurice was taken aback at the warmth of the reception, and, although touched, didn't know what to say. He was unused to handling another's emotions. To cover his embarrassment he lay a clumsy arm over the boy's shoulders and they walked back to the tent. Coffee was brewed and drunk in silence following a ritual by now familiar to both. Maurice was the first to speak:

"Tell me what's troubling you, Ian."

"It's everything... I don't know where to start. Everything seems to be happening at once. I don't want to go to my new school. I'll hate it...I just know I will. I don't want to leave you. I want things to go on as they were. And what will you do? Summer is ending. You can't stay on in the tent – you know you can't. I hate everything – everything's spoilt." Much to his consternation he began to cry.

Maurice busied himself clearing away the coffee mugs and waited for the pent-up emotion to spend itself. The boy blew his nose and started to apologise for being silly. Maurice interrupted:

"Never say sorry for crying, Ian. There's nothing sissy about it. Cry as much as you want. It's good for you. Tears are a healthy safety valve. Western society – in its so called wisdom – has coined the phrase: 'Big boys don't cry'. Ignore it and them. Do what you feel like. However, to somewhat change the subject. Do you want to hear my news?"

Ian was staring at his feet but nodded.

"First of all, the little problem of my winter quarters is solved." Maurice couldn't quite keep a note of self- satisfaction out of his voice.

Ian glanced up at the change of tone. The usually solemn man was practically smirking while he continued:

"When I was a boy most of the villagers ignored me – probably thought I was rather odd being such a loner at that age. I never had school friends to stay at Maples. Mother never encouraged visitors to the house." A sarcastic sneer had entered his voice. "There were no children living locally whom she considered suitable companions for her precious son. I became used to amusing myself. I spent most days sketching and reading rather like you. In many ways my childhood was similar to yours, Ian, except I was an only child. Anyway, one or two of the villagers were kind to me, especially the lady who ran the general stores. On Saturday mornings during the holidays, my father and I would walk to the village to buy my weekly sweets from that little shop. It was one of the few times I can recall when we seemed like a normal father and son – simply enjoying each other's company, laughing and talking together. But we both knew 'she' was back at the house, waiting like a spider in a web to bind us tightly to her…"

Maurice's voice tailed away. Ian saw that his face muscles were taut and set except for a nerve twitching in his right cheek. The boy had sense enough to remain silent and, after a short pause, Maurice took up his tale again:

"Today, I remembered that the shop keeper used to let one or two rooms in her house, and I kept my fingers crossed that she still did. Well, to cut a long story short, she'd hung up her 'landlady's hat' several years back. The really good news is that she's prepared to wear it again for me. Mrs Denning – that's her name – is a widow and I think she'll be glad to have company in the house. Her cooking talents can be admired, and judging from the aroma wafting from the kitchen I shan't be stingy with my praise. It's ages since I tasted home cooking! In return I can do odd jobs for her in the house and garden because the rent asked is peanuts."

Ian registered surprise at the phrase, 'odd jobs', and Maurice grinned.

"I'm a darn sight more practical than most people give me credit for. Not all artists are head in the clouds dreamers, young Ian!"

He pretended to cuff Ian's ears and the boy laughed. He could tell Maurice was excited by the day's events and he liked the effect on his friend. It was good to see him relaxed. Maurice went on:

"Mrs Denning is happy to let me have an empty room

on the first floor. Its main attraction is the large bay window which lets in plenty of good strong light, and there I can set up my easel. I can't remember if I've told you before but I've got several favourite bits of furniture in store. It's quite some while since I last saw them, but I know there's a comfortable old wing armchair, a small oak bookcase, a couple of lamps and a round Wilton rug. There may be one or two other items I've forgotten about but they'll do for starters, although I'll need a bed of course. Once they're arranged, and some of my pictures are on the walls, it should look jolly cosy. D'you know Ian, I'm really looking forward to having a place I can call home. Since my main meal is to be with Mrs D, the rest of the time tea and a sandwich will suffice. I should be able to get down to some serious work. How does it all sound to you?"

"Gosh, that's smashing! And now you won't want to move away for a year or two will you?" Ian's voice sounded wistful.

"I'll be here when you want me," Maurice assured him. "I've no intention of going anywhere. In return you can start your new school with good grace. Oh, I know only too well how school seems a complete waste of time, and on the whole 'they' have made it so, I agree. But you can turn the situation to your advantage, Ian."

Far from convinced, Ian pulled a face. Before he could lodge a protest, Maurice chipped in first.

"You told me you saw a jolly well equipped art room and that the master seemed easy going and friendly. Well … make use of those two salient facts. You'll have to pull out all the stops if you want to win a scholarship. They don't grow on trees – they're like gold dust. You'll need all the help you can get, believe me. Be yourself, be natural, and you're bound to make two or three firm friends so that life won't be too grim."

Now that Ian looked somewhat mollified, Maurice decided it was politic to rest his case.

"How'd you like to give me a hand packing up this damned tent," he queried, "and starting to move my stuff, such as it is, over to Mrs Denning's house? There isn't anything heavy. It will probably take me two or three days to arrange for the bigger items to be sent over, but if we get our fingers out we should have everything in place before you've got to start a new term."

They set to work with a will, and it wasn't long before Mrs Denning was opening her front door with a tea and chocolate cake welcome.

CHAPTER THREE

Maurice was whistling under his breath. Overall he was content with his life, apart from one shadow which he kept well behind him.

Once again it was a summers' day, but fifteen years had passed since that other summer when he had begun lodging with Mrs Denning. Nostalgia stirred deep within him whenever he thought about his cosy room, and the life he had enjoyed. A slow restoration of self-respect, a belief in his capabilities, a gentle healing, had taken place under that kind lady's roof. His work had taken on a warmth and maturity which reflected those inner changes. His landscape paintings had sensitivity and depth to them that made the onlooker catch his breath. The world he painted was on a higher level of reality, seeming to draw you into the canvas so that trees, rocks, the very flowers quivered and vibrated around one. You and nature were unified: there was no separation.

Commercially he became a success. Within a few years a new Maurice Caton painting was quite collectable. Amused but quietly chuffed by this development, he still took small interest in his financial affairs. An accountant was hired to mind all such matters.

This particular morning, however, his mind was on other considerations. He looked about him. It was an elegant street he was strolling down, a city street of Georgian houses treated with the respect they deserved by their owners. The wide front doors gleamed with brass fittings, and the bow windows were exquisitely proportioned.

Maurice's step quickened. He checked in his pocket to make sure he had the invitation card. He really didn't need it and he knew the words by heart; he simply liked to know it was there. It merely stated: 'You are invited to the Latimer Gallery on Tuesday, August 28th at 11 a.m. R.S.V.P.'

He stood stock still for a moment, almost overwhelmed by tenderness and pride. His abrupt halt caused a comely young woman, who had been walking behind, to collide with him. Maurice apologised and she smiled appreciatively. Her eyes took in a tall, slim, quite handsome man in his early fifties, thick curly hair going grey, dressed in a well cut suit and highly polished shoes. Maurice chuckled to himself. By now he was used to women finding him attractive, and although he enjoyed their company, he had always been celibate and had no intention of changing. For him, life was less complicated that way.

Marriage had beckoned him once and he had almost responded. The girl had been intelligent, attractive and remarkably unpossessive. Most men, he realised, would have jumped at the chance. But, when out of her company, questions had kept bothering him; questions he felt unable to answer. Did he want feminine clutter in the bedroom, in the bathroom? Did he want meals at set times each day? Did he want someone to know where he was going whenever he left the house? He loved long, solitary walks at night. The world asleep was a quieter, freer place unhampered by noise and he found his thoughts ranged far and wide. He could not envisage a wife being content with that situation! The replies he had earnestly sought kept returning:

'No'. He knew he valued his solitude too much, therefore with some regret on both sides they had parted.

All such thoughts dissolved upon reaching a house which exhibited a discreet sign announcing 'Latimer Gallery – Oil and Watercolour Paintings'. He moved back on the wide pavement looking up at the words. This day, this occasion, meant so much to him: the culmination of a dream. The scene before him blurred as memories returned…

He had of course kept his promise to Ian and stayed with Mrs Denning, at ease with the comfortable bachelor life it afforded. Ian's talent had duly flowered and the day finally came when he rushed up the stairs two at a time, bursting into Maurice's room with news of the hard won scholarship to Art College. The two old friends, never demonstrative, stared at each other, Ian now as tall as Maurice. Their eyes were on a level and the look of sheer delight and pride which passed between them said more than any words.

Ian had little contact with his mother and sister by this time, so only Maurice and the school's art master really understood and shared the exaltation of his achievement. His father had died from alcoholism two years before, the death scarcely coming as a surprise to family and acquaintances. Since Latimer's dressing-down with Maurice, all his bravura with clients had deserted him. Whisky became an insidious friend. One had only to observe the slack mouth, the shaking hands, the unhealthy tinge in his cheeks, for the truth to be painfully evident.

Ian had thought him pathetic. Disgust erased all last vestiges of filial affection as he watched his father's once smart suits be replaced by stained shirts and crumpled trousers. Maurice, having been rock-bottom himself, felt twinges of pity for the shuffling figure. He recognised self-loathing.

No tears were shed at the lonely end.

The scholarship prize ushered in two happy and productive years for Ian. His burgeoning talents surprised even himself.

College life was made the sweeter by a small coterie of friends, and vacations were spent mainly in Maurice's company. Indeed, Mrs Denning automatically set an extra place for dinner when Ian was home. Then came the terrible day of the accident.

Even after all these years every moment of that day seemed to be etched on Maurice's mind like a series of cameos. It had been Joanna Latimer, displaying finer feelings never before hinted at, who had come to Mrs Denning's one frosty winter morning. Without dramatisation or hysteria, she had told of Ian being horribly injured by a hit and run driver. The previous evening he had been crossing the road on his way back to college in the company of friends, when car headlamps blinded them in the darkness. The pain and anxiety etched on her features had been mirrored by Maurice. His world seemed shattered for ever.

He had walked over to his window and stood looking down at the garden, his hands gripping the sill. His mind seemed to be floating in space, detached from the rest of him. But the artist in him noticed cloud patterns in the rime on the grass. Pale silvery blue fingers stretched out across the lawn; tears blurred the scene and the fingers wavered and became indistinct.

It was Joanna who drove him and her mother the twenty mile journey to a hospital near Ian's college. Maurice had sat on the back seat, frozen in silence, watching the lights of oncoming cars. Was one of them the car that had almost destroyed Ian? Maurice felt suffocated by overwhelming hatred and desire to hurt, to strike back in return. The three of them sat, unified by suffering, in an impersonal hospital waiting room, desperate for news: any news. The door had opened and a doctor's tired voice was saying: "…the operation is over; Ian has come through; early days yet but he's young etc., etc…" Maurice let out a sharp breath and began to live again.

…These were harsh picture memories and he was pleasantly

returned from them by bustle in the city street. Maurice glanced at his watch. It was just past eleven o'clock. Guests were walking up the steps leading to the house where the open door beckoned.

He joined them, and entered a spacious, airy hall. Inside, a social gathering was in full swing, its catering staff adroit at balancing trays of drinks with consummate skill. Taking a proffered glass, his eyes sought a familiar figure. Despite his height, it was impossible to see over the heads of people who moved through the hall and reception room. Lord, how he detested crowds with their incessant monkey-chatter; small talk bored him. The undulating babble was not loud enough however to eclipse a clear, young voice:

"Maurice..Maurice.. I'm here.. down here. Speak to me!"

His left trouser leg was being tugged. He looked down blankly. A small girl, about four or five years of age, stared up at him. With a warm smile creasing the lines round his eyes, Maurice bent and picked up the child, settling her comfortably in the crook of his arm. This was Esther, the apple of his eye, only child of Ian and his wife, Yvonne.

Unused to the ways of children, Esther had nevertheless enchanted and delighted him from the first moment he had seen her curling baby fingers round his. Her innocence aroused in him the paternal instinct to protect. She had been born out of a love match, and he wanted to keep that love wrapped round her like a mantle. Fair haired and beautiful, Esther's blue eyes matched her soft dress.

Precious indeed were the hours when Ian and Yvonne entrusted her to his care. He would take the little girl on bus rides, considering this a more civilised, stylish mode of country travel than the cramped nether-world of a car; it also enabled him to give his young companion undivided attention.

The bus would swing along between views over high-banked lanes, most seats crowded with country folk smiling and nodding at these two who seemed in their eyes to be the archetype father and daughter. Maurice was oblivious of the glances; he and the child were absorbed in each other's company. She had a sturdy, compact figure, and whenever the bus discharged them at their destination her short legs kept pace with his longer stride. The world to Esther was magical, a wonderland, and her excitement quickened his own aesthetic imagination.

Some days they would explore the still overgrown gardens of Maples. Maurice had come into his full inheritance five years before, and he deliberately left the untamed areas almost exactly as they were the day Ian first found them: a lush jungle. A little judicious pruning kept the worst excesses under control, but that was all. Esther was enchanted with the summerhouse and would play there happily with a 'make-believe' family. Maurice would lie back in one of the deck-chairs, smoke his pipe, and review lazily the course of his life. The whole Latimer family had been responsible in diverse ways for the changes that had taken place, both to and in him.

He was a rather different man from the shy, insecure person Ian had met in the farmer's field all those years ago. Confidence in his ability as an artist had increased his self-worth and he was now more ready to tolerate the shortcomings of others, as well as his own. Esther would talk to her 'family' and he would watch with affection, smiling when he thought how surprised his mother would have been at the sight of a small, dungaree-clad girl playing in the summer-house. Poor Mother, he mused, how she had let the sweet moments of life slip by.

…An amused-sounding voice broke his reverie and jolted him back to the present day.

"A penny for your thoughts, Maurice!"

A slim young woman stood in front of him, and Maurice

regarded her with pleasure. Her open face was composed of calm, regular features with eyes of identical blue to her daughter's – a face that in her later years would probably be described as handsome. Maurice greeted her warmly:

"Why hallo Yvonne. I'm rude not to have found you before this. Young Esther managed to track me down. I've been in some sort of dream ever since I got here. Must be going round the bend or something."

Yvonne stood on tiptoe and lightly kissed his cheek, noting tell-tale signs of fatigue under his eyes.

"I was beginning to wonder where you were. Thought you'd forgotten us!"

She made a face at him, pretending to be annoyed.

"Mea culpa! Mea culpa!" chanted Maurice, trying to look suitably chastened. They both laughed, comfortable in each other's company. Privately Maurice thought she was the best thing that could have happened to Ian, and often marvelled at the caprices of life that turned misfortune into blessing.

"I can see you've got your hands full with Esther." Yvonne remarked. "Hope she's not too heavy for you. You look a bit tired today."

Maurice looked at her more closely. Did she suspect something was wrong? A most perceptive woman was Yvonne, and he wanted to keep his troubles to himself – at least until after the safe launch of the Gallery. But her head was bent towards the child almost asleep in his arms, and her fair curtain of hair obscured any expression. The truth was that she and Ian had certainly begun to discern illness in their friend; the lines in his face looked deeper every time they saw him. However, they kept their own counsel. He would tell them in his own good time.

"This is quite a day, eh Maurice? Mind you, I don't think you've even looked round yet!" Ian had quietly come up behind the trio and Maurice gave a guilty start. He knew Ian was joking but that didn't prevent him feeling annoyed with himself. What was the matter with him today for Pete's sake? He turned to Ian. Once again that subtle communion, ever present from their first meeting, flowed between them in a smile. Ian was wearing a dark grey suit and crisp white shirt, an empty right sleeve neatly folded into one pocket.

"Hand that imp back to her mum and come with me."

He put an arm round his wife's waist and gave her a quick squeeze.

"I want your absolute honest opinion of the whole layout." Ian's voice couldn't disguise the obvious pride and excitement he felt about the whole venture. "I'll lead the way if you like."

Yvonne, cradling her sleepy daughter, watched the two men move off together. Another, lesser woman might have been jealous of the profound relationship between her husband and the older man. Indeed, when these two were in each other's company her presence seemed to be forgotten, albeit unintentionally. For a time they needed no one else. But right from the start of the young couple's romance they had made a pact to be completely open and honest with each other: absolutely no secrets.

So of course Yvonne knew the story of Maples, how Ian and Maurice had met, and all the drama that followed. She understood their fellowship and loved them both all the more because of it.

The friends entered a cosily enticing room, created by Ian and Yvonne's skilful blend of decor, flowers and drapes. The walls were painted pale green – a perfect background for the gold frames of the pictures. Table lamps dropped soft pools of light in corners where sunlight failed to reach. Large bowls of white roses from Maples' garden stood on every available surface, their fragrance filling the air with sweetness. Maurice couldn't fault a single thing, even if he had wanted to.

There were about a dozen people in the room, moving from picture to picture, catalogues in hand. The hum of their conversation didn't intrude at all; it added to the air of friendliness and warmth. Maurice knew that the price ticket on each frame, discreetly glanced at by enquiring eyes, was modest by today's standards. He and Ian wanted it that way. Any money earned here was used for Maurice's project at Maples, and Ian took a small commission to support his little family in the snug flat upstairs. In spite of his frugality, Maurice still felt guilt at someone paying for what had given him pleasure to create.

Recognition of him as the artist began to cause a stir in the room and self-consciousness took hold. He disliked being stared at and was thankful it was a rare occurrence. A sideways look at Ian noted that the younger man appeared relaxed, acknowledging the appreciative smiles from potential clients. Always aware of Maurice's moods, Ian stopped to give him a quizzical stare. The lad's own thin features were alight with enthusiasm. He was in his element.

They were standing by one of the bow windows which overlooked the street. Velvet curtains were looped back on either side, serving to emphasise the beautiful proportions. A shaft of sunlight moved across Maurice's face exposing dark circles under his eyes. Ian was startled by these obvious signs of tiredness, and unease mounted which he tried hard to conceal, while knowing the difficulty of this because the man could read him like a book. Had Yvonne been right in her diagnosis after all? Had her nurse's training detected something? Was their friend ill? Ian pushed the thought out of his mind. It was selfish he knew, but his carefully constructed life must not be spoiled. Everything had to be perfect – especially today. He attempted a weak joke.

"For the sleeping partner in this venture old chap, you certainly fit the part this morning. What's wrong? You've hardly uttered a word."

"I'm really sorry Ian.. it's just that my mind seems miles away." He clapped a hand to his forehead. "God knows what's the matter with me. Simply everything you and Yvonne have done for the Gallery is marvellous. Truly it is. You both deserve the success I feel it's going to be. A lot of damned hard work has gone on behind the scenes – I know that. But you know *me*. Miserable old bugger that I am, I always look forward to socialising but when it comes to the crunch.. well.. I can't think what to say to people. You're much better at that sort of thing than me."

Ian let out a small sigh of relief – this he could cope with. In spite of an aura of casual sophistication he still sought Maurice's approval. Childish though it was, it mattered: no use trying to deny the fact. He *needed* to achieve. Years of being talked down to by his parents had worn a deep groove in his psyche.

He had felt unworthy – still did at times if he was honest. Moreover, the irony of the present situation was not lost on him. He used to be filled with contempt for the business acumen displayed by his father, yet he was exhibiting the same flair. Had Latimer senior handed it down in his genes?

Ian had stared at his own reflection while shaving that morning. Thank goodness no other resemblance was obvious. Despite that, he regretted his father could not be at the Gallery's launch to witness his success; not because he cared a fig for him, he didn't, but just to show off his abilities. Not an attitude to be particularly proud of, but a realistic one.

Maurice gave a small embarrassed laugh.

"I know you'll think me rude but I'd like to get back to Maples if you don't mind. I seem to be tired. Must be all those late nights trying to finish a painting in time for the opening."

For the first time in their long companionship each knew

the truth was being delicately skirted. There was an awkward silence, broken by Maurice.

"Look old fellow, this isn't the time or place to go into what's bugging me. This is your red letter day – yours and Yvonne's. Come to lunch at the weekend. Bring Esther too of course. We can talk properly then."

"I understand," responded Ian, touching him lightly on the arm. "We'll be there I promise. Would you like Yvonne to drive you home?"

"Good Lord, no.. I wouldn't hear of it.. today of all days!" Maurice held up a hand as Ian opened his mouth to protest. "No. No arguing. I'll catch my usual bus."

Ian and Yvonne stood together at the front door watching Maurice go down the steps. At the bottom he turned, waved cheerfully, and set off down the street. With heavy hearts his friends turned and went back into the Gallery.

The bus trundled its familiar route. Maurice sat back, looking without seeing at the scenery. A line from an old song came into mind: 'There's no place like home.' Corny but true for him, however; that fact couldn't be denied. What made it remarkable was his award of the accolade to Maples: the house he had loathed and only wanted escape from years before. Now he looked forward to, relished even, the shelter it gave.

Lost in thought he hadn't realised his destination was reached until the driver, who knew him well, twisted round in his seat and called down the aisle: "Your stop Mr Caton." Maurice thanked him and alighted by the gates Doris Pope had once passed through. These days another Mrs Pope cycled up the drive to clean – a daughter-in-law of that other doughty female. A further twist of fate he noted.

The wrought iron gates moved smoothly open and shut, and he began to stroll up the path; still overgrown, but comfortingly, with none of the sinister shadows from boyhood. The early afternoon sun was warm on his face. Pausing, he took off jacket and tie, undid his shirt's top button and rolled up the sleeves. That felt much freer; he hated the confines of formal clothing which he only donned under protest.

He rounded the corner and there stood the house. Although structurally unaltered, there were subtle differences. The building had come to life; it had found heart and warmth. Maurice fervently believed that houses, like people, needed love in order to develop fully. Maples beckoned to him like a welcoming friend. The sash windows were open, the front door stood ajar, and from somewhere within a piano was being played. He could faintly hear the dreamy strains of a Chopin nocturne. A feeling of peace and atonement stole over him, while tense muscles relaxed. It was good to be back. Despite only having been away for a few hours, in an odd way much had happened to him under the surface.

The paving stones leading to the rear were no longer slippery with moss, and the smell of damp and decay was replaced by the wholesome aroma of fresh baking. Two women, chatting idly, looked up in surprise at his entry into the kitchen. The older of the pair had a soft, country voice, a dumpy shape, her cheeks flushed from the heat of the Aga. This was Christine Pope. The other figure was tall and slender, casually dressed in slacks and blouse, worn with timeless elegance. The sort of girl to turn most men's heads. This was Joanna Latimer, Maurice's right hand at Maples.

"I'm that sorry Mr Caton," flapped Christine, "tea in't quite ready yet, since we didn't think you'd be back s'soon. But I can bring you and Joanna a tray outside if y'like?"

"That Christine, I would like. In fact, I can't think of

anything I'd like better at this moment," conceded Maurice, knowing that "a nice cup of tea" was Christine's stock answer to most problems. He often wondered how it would feel to have such a simple attitude to life. He turned to Joanna but, from somewhere down the hall, a phone started to intrude.

"Don't worry Maurice," said Joanna, "I'll take that." She moved with quick, light steps towards the hall, and soon she could be heard talking, an undercurrent of laughter in her voice.

Suddenly feeling superfluous, he wandered out of the kitchen. The old stone flags outside the door were warm and mellow in the sun. The tall trees had been well pruned back and the patio was in sunlight for most of the day. A large round wooden table and comfortable wicker chairs encouraged everyone who stayed at the house to drop into the easy habit of eating meals alfresco. When some of the undergrowth was being cleared, several large terracotta pots and urns were unearthed and planted to overflowing with lobelia, geraniums, busy lizzies, petunias and nasturtiums. The bold mix of colours gave a Mediterranean spiciness to the area which was quite irresistible, both for humans and insects.

Maurice flopped down in one of the chairs and almost immediately Christine appeared with a loaded tea-tray. He stood up to take the burden just as Joanna came back, smiling broadly.

"That was Martin on the phone," she announced. "Apparently the powers that be are more than pleased with results here. And – now for the good news – they might be persuaded to part with a bit more loot. Martin's a skilful arm twister! Anyway he's wining and dining me tonight, so I'll find out more then. Hey, that cake looks good. I'm starving."

Maurice smiled affectionately at her. He liked watching Joanna's deft, swift movements as she poured tea for them both. Her approach to life was efficient and methodical; his admiration for her grew daily. With healthy appetite she cut two generous slices of fruit cake. Maurice shook his head at the proffered plate, but Joanna's small white teeth made short work of her portion.

"Hey! How'd it go at Latimers, Maurice? I rang Ian earlier to wish them luck. He understood we couldn't both be away from here. Still, I did feel a bit mean not being there. And you're back earlier than expected."

Maurice ignored the last remark in his reply: "Oh, I rather think it's going to be successful. Complimentary words flying about all over the place. Everyone was in their glad rags. Any excuse to dress up." Joanna hid a smile. "You'll hear more about it on Sunday. The trio are coming to lunch. We haven't any students until next week have we?"

Mouth full of the other slice of cake, Joanna shook her head.

"Good.. good," said Maurice, sounding preoccupied. He swallowed the remainder of his tea. "I think a pipe is called for. I'll wander off to have a smoke."

Joanna opened her mouth as if about to speak and then changed her mind. For a moment or two she watched Maurice's retreat to the summerhouse, sighed and hurriedly gathered up the tea things, taking the tray into the kitchen.

"Leave the washing up Chris, I'll do it later."

"Okay, thanks Joanna. If I hurry I can pop in 'n' see Mum afore the kids get back frum swimmin'. She does luv a bit of a gossip now that she can't get out s'much. Nosy ole bag but I'm fond of 'er really. See you tomorrow."

"Cheerio."

Joanna sped upstairs to look in her wardrobe and wash her hair. Martin was special and she wanted to look her most attractive this evening. Humming to herself, she began to run a bath.

CHAPTER FOUR

Maurice moved like a sleep-walker toward the summerhouse, his fingers automatically searching for pipe and tobacco pouch. The ritual preparation soothed taut nerves; and soon, drifts of fine, pale blue smoke wreathed his head.

When he reached the den it was black waves of weakness and nausea that threatened to engulf him. He leant against the door for support. The wood smelt warm, dusty, comforting and durable. Two shiny green beetles were mating by the window, oblivious of his presence. He envied them their thrust at life; he wanted desperately to live. He was frightened by the feeling of losing control. It was only four or five weeks since the doctor had given the diagnosis, but already fatigue was a daily companion. Part of him longed to give in; to sink into a soft bed and never get up again. On the other hand, there was so much he wanted to complete that the strength left in him shouted: 'Fight! Fight!'

He knelt on the grass, tears running down his face. It was such a bloody unfair blow, especially when he was at last making something of his life. He had tasted the sweet fruits of friendship and success and was reluctant to part with them. 'Don't then,' urged his inner voice. 'Share your worries and sorrows with those who love you. You owe them honesty and frankness. They have a right to know and together you will win.' Would they though?

Someone had left the familiar deck-chair outside the summer-house. Exhausted by emotion, he sat down and closed his eyes. Eddies of confusion whirled round his mind; images and half-formed impressions created crazy, kaleidoscopic patterns. Unable to sit still, he stood up and began to pace the lawn. His thoughts flew back in time, like arrows piercing his most poignant moments.

The years rolling back revealed a basic theme of being misunderstood throughout his early years: of having no sense of personal worth and scant self-respect – hardly a surprise when he took stock of school and home life. The educational regime had never been in sympathy with his passionate desire to become a painter, an artist. The staff had reserved interest and encouragement solely for boys with academic promise. Set apart as an oddball, he felt that society made no provision for individualists; its herd mind simply could not cope. Anyone who stepped outside the norm was treated with dismissive contempt. And of course no help was forthcoming from his parents, especially his mother.

For him, like many sensitive souls before and since, adolescence was torture. He stumbled through exams. Hot shame and anger still coursed his veins for meekly submitting to his mother's insistence on law studies. God in heaven, what had possessed him? A year into the hated subject, at least he'd sensibly packed his bags and left for art school, financed with the help of his father's legacy. No: don't lie to yourself; it hadn't been good sense which had brought about the change but the first breakdown. After that, there was no going back to law.

The years following were a see-saw of highs and lows. Living in rented rooms, neglecting himself, he would occasionally sell a painting. That was a high. But the lows pressed in and dragged him down. This period of his life was grey and misty. He had shut off contact with Maples. Often alone, he had felt unlovable, riddled with faults. Nervous collapse became an unpleasant habit. After emergence from the last episode, he made the decision to return to his old home. Perhaps he was clutching at straws, but empty rooms are full of past echoes which, if listened to, might give him a more balanced view of the present. He had felt he owed himself a last try to find self-respect. If the attempt failed, he had resolved to leave the human race. But then had come the day when he had met Ian and life became precious.

Cramp in a calf muscle brought him painfully back to the moment. He glanced at his watch. Heavens, he had been walking around for about an hour. He stretched the stiff leg, wincing as circulation began to return. In the distance came the sound of a car drawing up to the front door and Joanna's attractive laugh as she joined Martin. Tyres scrunched the gravel while the car turned and sped away.

In the silence that followed came the faint tones of a piano. With a start Maurice remembered the young player, Megan Smart. She had been a student at Maples for a year, ever since its doors had been opened for eight young people. All disparate characters, he reflected, but with one common denominator that united them. Each possessed considerable talent – either as an artist or a musician – and each had fought for an outlet for their gifts while living in arid wasteland.

Nevertheless, gifted as Megan undoubtedly was, she still needed to eat. Joanna might be efficient in many areas but cooking wasn't one of them. Caught up in preparations for her evening with Martin, it was unlikely she had provided for Megan's hunger pangs. He put away the deck-chair and made a slow unsteady return to the kitchen. He had surmised correctly – no sign of any supper dish. He went across the hall to his mother's old study, halting outside; even after all this time his fingers still found difficulty in touching the handle. All was quiet within. Resistance overcome, he knocked gently and entered. A thin slip of a girl was seated at a baby grand piano, hands folded in her lap. Although reliably informed by Joanna that this waif was eighteen, in his eyes she didn't appear a day over twelve.

"Megan, how's about some supper? You must be hungry? Hm?" he queried, standing in the doorway. How different the room looked now, he thought, with its flowery wallpaper white paint, and gold brocade curtains. A room to linger in at last.

The girl shot him a quick, surprised look.

"I'm starving," came the brief reply.

"Okay then. Follow me. We'll see what we can rustle up."

Back in the kitchen he made a speedy assessment of the fridge's contents. Bachelor life had trained him to produce simple meals as fast as possible. Fifteen minutes later, two plates boasted an appetising display, and the smell of scrambled eggs, bacon, fried bread and tomatoes reminded both how hungry they were. Megan set the table and for a while they sat in companionable silence. Then, plates stacked in the sink, a fresh pot of coffee brewing, Maurice lit a pipe, leaned back in his chair and regarded this young protégé.

What he saw was a girl whose dark hair hung straight down on either side of her narrow, pale face, the paleness accentuated by her clothes. These were a long black skirt, shapeless black jumper, and on what could have been attractive legs, heavy black shoes which reminded him of ex-Army issue.

"That was a smashing meal, Maurice. Thanks. You're a good cook." Megan's voice was unexpectedly deep and rather gruff.

Warmed by the compliment, Maurice took the chance to open up a conversation.

"You seem to have settled in well here, Megan. You strike me as someone determined on leaving the past behind, and simply getting on with the present. Has living at Maples helped you with this at all, d'you think?"

The girl's head jerked up. She appeared startled, reminding him of a young wild animal catching an odd scent. He kicked himself. Why the hell couldn't he learn to hold his tongue? Unable to stop looking down the years at his own sorry past, he was curious how others coped, but he tried to refrain from emotive probing of the students. However, at times, the desire to know became an intense itch which he couldn't leave alone. In Megan's case he felt he had gone too far for once. Joanna had relayed the girl's terrible home conditions which made his own appear mild by comparison. Because of the abuse Megan had suffered she never went back to see her mother; Maples was her home. The other young people were resident only in term time.

The girl's voice broke into the void:

"Maples has saved my life and given me life."

Tears filled her eyes and Maurice looked away out of the window. Perhaps it was something to do with the 'breaking of bread' together, but he sensed Megan's defences were lowered. The sun was faintly tinting the sky with rose coloured clouds, its rays stretching golden above them. The beauty made his own throat ache. This time of day was always poignant, he mused; with evening came the promise of a new morning, a re-birth, in just a few hours.

"I must go to my room for a while, Maurice," said Megan. "I..I've some reading to catch up on." Her eyes met his briefly and he nodded understanding. He knew only too well that need to be on one's own.

When she had left the kitchen, and he could hear those heavy boots clumping upstairs, he wandered outside and sat on the patio. The sun still had warmth which was soothing on his face. For once oblivious of bird song all around, he pondered Megan's simple affirmation. It had moved him and wiped out any last remaining vestiges of doubt he still held about his aims for Maples. New hope stirred in him about his own future; an inner awareness felt the roots of his illness loosening their hold. His throat constricted again. He wanted, more than he had ever wanted anything in his life before, to be allowed to complete the work he and Joanna had started. 'Our great project', was Joanna's pet phrase; he couldn't leave her to carry on alone. He felt light-headed, like a man reprieved. He recalled how the project had begun.

…Without doubt, Joanna had been the major surprise in his life. Once, if he had thought of her at all, it was to dismiss her as a shallow, flighty teenager. That was until the day of her twin's accident. Within twenty-four hours she had changed from child to woman. While her mother collapsed with strain, Joanna had become gritty and practical. Calmly, without fuss, she adopted the role of his chauffeur, ferrying him daily to the hospital: a forty mile round trip. Thrown into close contact, they talked seriously for the first time. A mutual liking and respect grew. The days following the amputation of Ian's right arm had been terrible, but slowly much that was good and positive unfolded. Two months after the operation Ian had been pronounced fit for convalescence. Since Susan Latimer had abdicated her responsibility, Maurice had suggested Austria, that land of flower decked houses and meadows. The utter calm and purity of its mountains had once gone a long way to restore his own equilibrium. He had wanted Ian to have a chance to share in that same beauty, so for the first time in his life he made a decision for someone else. It was an agreeable feeling. Joanna had booked the tickets, he had paid for them, and they had both seen Ian off at the airport.

In true romantic tradition Ian had fallen in love with Yvonne, his nurse at the clinic, and eventually they married. Ian would grin sheepishly when he recounted this story, saying it sounded too much akin to a Victorian novelette. But he knew himself to be a fortunate man.

Ian's promise as an artist now broken, he had turned his attention to Maurice, deciding to help him find an outlet for his work. Relieved at Ian's positive approach to life, his friend had just shrugged his shoulders and grinned. The painter's usual 'modus operandi' was to finish a canvas, and then stack it carelessly in his overcrowded studio at Maples, where Christine Pope carried out erratic housekeeping. Ian was convinced that a great talent was being wasted. Many folk could gain pleasure from simple contemplation of a Maurice Caton landscape; one or two might even wish to purchase. With a thoroughness which was the hallmark of all he undertook, Ian embarked on a design management course at the local polytechnic. Frequent visits to Maples kept him immersed happily in the milieu of art and artists: a world he loved.

Perceptive Joanna had guessed correctly at Maurice's loneliness after Ian's marriage. Glad to leave London behind at weekends she would drive down to Maples, a house she liked now that its rightful owner was installed. Here she was treated as an equal, not a sex object; a refreshing change after the attitude of many males. She was an intelligent, quick-witted woman who found her librarian's post too routine for her agile mind.

"Give it up then. Change it," had been Maurice's response when consulted. "For Pete's sake, there's no need to set limitations on yourself. At your age the world lies at your feet. Have a good, hard think about which areas of life interest you the most. If you're patient, an answer should come."

Without hesitation she had known the answer.

"People!" she declared triumphantly, eyes sparkling.

"I like people. Always have. I'm interested in what makes them tick. And what's more, I want to get involved with their problems, their hang-ups. I want to go to university and read psychology. Mind you, I'm not sure what I'd do with a degree once I'd got it!" She had run a hand rather agitatedly through her hair, disturbing its usual smooth appearance. Her face was flushed with excitement.

"Hold on. Take a step at a time." cautioned Maurice. "You're leaping ahead. Running before you've learnt to walk. Are you absolutely sure, Jo, that this is what you want?" She had nodded vehemently. "Right then. First things first. Which university do you want to try for? Oxford? Cambridge?"

"London. London University," she broke in. "As you know, I house-share in Wimbledon with those four good friends of mine. The arrangement suits me, suits us all, and I wouldn't want to let them down by leaving suddenly. It's difficult to find the right person to fit in with an established group. And it would be a fairly easy tube ride to the University. I could still come down here from time to time. It would all be marvellous.. wonderful.. I know it's right for me. I can hardly wait."

Joanna's conversations were frequently dotted with superlatives. He tended to ignore them, having grown used to her mode of speech.

"I've got the right number of 'A' levels," she had continued. "Must find out about grants and such like. But Maurice, I wouldn't be able to come down every weekend of course. What will you do?"

He had looked at her in surprise; a déjà-vu had come over him. Some years back her brother had asked that same question.

"I should just about be able to manage," came his dry response, which had fallen on deaf ears. Joanna was already seated at his desk, writing paper in front of her.

Three years further on, she had gained her degree with honours. Her spirited desire to help her fellow man keener than ever, she had joined a psychotherapy course which widely extended her capabilities.

It had been during one of her weekend visits, with the course drawing to a close, that she had started to observe the familiar house and its owner with fresh eyes: what she saw caused her fertile mind to start buzzing. Several weeks later, the two had been sitting up late talking: a habit that suited this pair of night birds. Although it was early summer, the evening had been cool, and a log fire was burning aromatically in the grate. Ensconced in a comfortable armchair, one of a pair on each side of the fireplace, her legs stretched out to the warmth, a pot of Earl Grey tea on the low table between them, Joanna felt Maples was a real home.

"Do you realise Maurice," Joanna had asked softly, "that most of this house is never used? It's positively indecent the way you rattle round here like a pea in a pod!"

She had deliberately kept her voice light and jokey. This was to be the introduction of an idea starting to take shape and form; its reception at best would probably be cool. A glance at her companion showed him relaxed in his chair, eyes half closed, for all the world near to sleep. She was not deceived. He would be alert to every nuance in her voice: this man was an acute listener.

On cue he had straightened up, and given her a quizzical look.

"True.. true," he concurred, "but what do you suggest I do with all this space? Perhaps open a nursing home? I could stack the zimmers in the lobby, like a surrealistic sculpture. Very Art deco. Except I don't think they had zimmers in the '30's."

This deliberate facetiousness gained him much needed thinking time. Joanna was about to probe a sensitive area which was not quite ready for exploration. A charred log dropped in the grate. Leaning forward, he broke it into splinters with the poker. Hot flames sputtered up the chimney, creating the only movement in the room, which was otherwise oddly still. There was a tangible sense of the house beginning a new phase in its history.

"I'm serious about this," Joanna had insisted, her fingers of both hands locked together.

"I can see that. Carry on. I'm listening."

She took a deep breath, unlocked her hands, and plunged in, confidence gained somewhat by his tone.

"Well, I meet many young people through my work who are all screwed up, mixed up – call it what you like. Most come from broken homes, from awful inner city ghettos, they're thought to be bottom of the pile. School was meaningless to them. They nearly all truanted one or two days a week. Can you blame them when lessons bore no relevance to their everyday life? What they needed was practical guidance in coping with the world, not learning a string of useless history dates. Hell, life can be pretty tough and lonely for most of us and we can all do with a helping hand from time to time."

She gave him a quick look, and he nodded abruptly. She ploughed on:

"Our educational system is blinkered, held back by those in authority who lack imagination. I get really steamed up on this point. Small wonder that some kids heave bricks through windows, or swear, or spray graffiti. Their boiling frustration has to have an outlet or they'd explode. But I truly believe there's a spark of creativity in each of us, and often these so called 'drop-outs' are among the most creative and intelligent in society. However, no encouragement: hence the violence – a reaction to the mumbo-jumbo forced down their throats.

"A number of them have been coming to our therapy sessions, and I've discovered that hidden under their bolshy attitudes, at least in a small handful of them, lies a genuine talent for art and music. In other words, here are embryonic artists and musicians with unfulfilled potential. The spark may never get a chance to be ignited. Although they'd dearly love an opportunity to explore and expand their gifts, they would find this hard to put into words, and there's nowhere for them to go. Nowhere. What's needed is a safe, understanding environment to help them develop into rounded human beings with something to offer the world. Something to pass on to future generations. Sorry to sound intense, but I feel strongly about their plight. It's like watching young, caged animals catching the scent of freedom, only to have it snatched away."

Joanna had sat hunched in the armchair, her face inflamed by strength of emotion, hands stretched unconsciously towards Maurice. Acting on impulse, he now leant across and took one of them between his own. The movement startled her, for he was not a demonstrative man. She sat quietly and waited, her case presented.

"What is it you want from me?" he asked slowly.

No immediate reply was offered by his companion. Joanna instead took time to pour tea, tucked long legs up beneath her, and then posed a question:

"Have I ever mentioned Martin to you?"

"I think so."

"He's a super chap, very special," she went on. "You know how some people are? Extraordinarily dedicated to his work with difficult teenagers. He heads a small team of us who are trying hard to help some of them from the ghettos I was telling you about. A pall of despair seems to hang over those tower blocks: they're my picture of hell, Maurice. One boy, Joseph, seems to represent them all. The dice was heavily loaded against him from day one. Father unknown. Brought up, if you can call it that, by his mother who works full-time. He's also black and unemployed. Small wonder he spent most of his time running wild with a street gang in Lewisham. This is where Martin runs a youth club three nights a week, close to the kids' homes, including Joseph's. Through patiently building trust with Joseph – and that has taken some doing – Martin's persuaded him to drop in at the club a couple of evenings a week. Since then he's come under my wing, and I've found out he can draw. Mostly pen and ink sketches of birds and animals. Copied of course, but what does that matter? He's lucky to see more than a few sparrows and the odd cat and dog. But they are beautifully drawn.

"When he first showed me, tears came into my eyes. They made him seem so vulnerable. But I think he has *real* talent, Maurice, and the most important factor is that he *wants* to draw. His creativity transforms him – he becomes a different person, much more gentle. Trouble is, I don't know how to take it any further. You see, he's on probation for theft, like most of the kids. This means he has to have regular supervision. I feel, though that a one to one relationship would be the making of him..." She stopped, her voice sounding ragged and dry.

Maurice's absorption in the account showed on his face. Her words had echoed an idea formulated several weeks before, although he had tried to tuck it back into a corner of his mind. Selfish it might be, but frankly he hadn't wanted his privacy invaded; at least not for a while. The thought had been anathema. Now, however, despite these past reservations, his decision was made. He would agree to the suggestion about to be voiced. He felt sure his hunch was correct.

"Look Maurice, I know it's an awful cheek on my part but I keep thinking about Maples." Its master's face remained impassive. "This house could quite easily be converted into a centre for say six to eight students aged sixteen plus. You're a good teacher. I know because I used to watch you at work with Ian. Perhaps we could advertise for a music teacher. I've taken it upon myself to discuss the legal niceties with Martin, and he said Social Services would have to okay the project but couldn't see them raising too many objections. Quite the reverse. Actually my course finishes in a month or so and I could move in here as a full-time therapist. In fact I'll be looking for somewhere permanent to live…"

Joanna's voice had suddenly tailed off, appalled by her clumsy approach. What had come over her? She had never meant to say all that. How rude and thoughtless to make such sweeping assumptions. Ever since she had known Maurice he had been a loner. Apart from her family, he appeared to have no other friends, or indeed any relatives, and she was expecting, indeed demanding, him to open his house to complete strangers. Her temerity made her blush. What she hadn't known then was the effect her words had produced. Maurice's mind had gone into overdrive: he had already decided which room would make the best teaching studio.

CHAPTER FIVE

A cool breeze ruffling his hair brought him back once again to the present. He shivered, stood up, stretching stiff arms above his head.

'Hmm. Well, we've come a long way since that particular evening,' he said to himself. 'From now on it's the future that's important. The kids' future – Maples' future – *my* future!'

In buoyant mood, he went into the kitchen and opened the door leading to a square, well-proportioned hall. Soft hues from a jug of sweet peas were reflected in a mahogany table, and a grandfather clock ticked melodically. He stood and listened with a heightened sense of awareness. All was quiet and still. There was nothing to jar the senses; nothing here to hurt him. He had the best interests of the house at heart, and felt its spirit acknowledge this care.

He climbed the wide, curving staircase, his hand lightly touching the smooth handrail. On the landing he paused outside Megan's door. Faint sounds within from a radio and rustling paper were the only signs of occupation. He lifted his hand to knock, then let it fall again, entered his own room and walked over to the window. Beneath him the drive rounded gracefully past a ceanothus bush, which was so thickly clustered with deep blue flowers it was impossible to see any leaves. Seven-thirty, but still only hints of evening in the sky – perfect time for a walk. Feeling like a small boy allowed out after supper, he changed shoes and all but ran downstairs en route for freedom.

At the bottom of the stone steps he paused to admire the house. A Virginia creeper, whose tendrils wound their insistent way to frame the windows, relieved the once stark walls. Eight of these windows on the first floor belonged to the bedsitting rooms of Maples' students. It went without saying that once he and Joanna were agreed upon the project, she never doubted her ability to make it work: from that day forward the grass never grew under her feet. She deliberately furnished the bedrooms with only bare essentials, knowing that young people would soon fill them with their own personalities. The morning room, with its French windows, had become an airy art studio, and the piano was comfortably ensconced in the old study.

Maurice let slip a contented sigh, and stepped out briskly. He left the grounds, and set off up the incline to the village. On his right was the field where he had first met Ian. The five bar gate was hanging open on broken hinges, and he watched two campers inexpertly erecting a tent. He smiled. He would always feel warm affection for that field.

Ten minutes later the village came into view. Seen in the evening light it looked quintessentially English. The focal point was its Green, shadowed by some fine old horse-chestnut trees, a few fast-fading pink and white candles still throwing off a faint perfume, and with more than a hint of spiky green cases showing. Here was held the annual village fete and, on September's first Sunday, the gipsy horse fair. This was an occasion for timid souls to keep doors and windows shut while earthy words were bandied around, and rowdy but good-natured barterings were sealed with a smack of hands.

An eclectic mixture of buildings were grouped round the green. By far the largest was that Georgian rectory, a perfect example of architecture for its graceful period. The present incumbent and his wife dreamed wistfully of a smaller, warmer house however, because unlike their predecessors who had private incomes, their rector's stipend made it impossible to heat every room.

Content with life lived simply was Happy Woodgate who, from the day of her birth eighty odd years before, had never moved from her tiny cottage. No one knew her real Christian name, and Maurice was quite convinced that 'Happy' would be engraved on her headstone when the time came: a fitting memorial to a woman who had loved and served her fellow man all through her long life.

Many years ago her father had turned their front parlour into an Aladdin's cave of surprises. On a wooden counter sugar mice lay beside brown shoelaces; shirt buttons were in a box next to succulent raspberries picked that same morning from Happy's garden. When lessons were over for the day, village school children crowded in to buy strings of liquorice or small bags of toffees. Happy would stand beside her old-fashioned till, smiling and nodding. She knew each child by name as she had their parents before them. From the edge of the green Maurice could see her now – a gentle figure moving slowly through her luxuriant front garden, picking blooms for the house, their petals already moist with dew. For a moment he wished he had brought a sketch pad, but saw how impossible it would be to capture her humble wisdom on paper. She welcomed every new birth and grieved for every death in that small community.

Intermingling in hotchpotch fashion with the cottages were the village shops: the butchers, the estate agents now organised by Mr Barker's son, the bakers, the newsagents doubling as the Post Office, the general stores where Maurice had lodged with Mrs Denning, and a tiny branch of Lloyd's bank. A daily bus served the local town ten miles distant, but most folk supported their own shops, perhaps riding in for the weekly market day.

At heart the villagers held fast to the same criterion as their forbears; years of experience had taught that in a small village, dependent on each other for help, it paid to keep on good terms with one another. Most were kindly, with the odd malicious gossip scattered here and there. She, and it always was a she, got quickly cut to size by her neighbours. The majority were strong and healthy; the local doctor was rarely consulted. If they had been asked they would have credited country air and produce for their robust constitutions. Studying this venerable group of cottages, each cheek by jowl with one another, Maurice felt curiously lonely and made an on-the-spot decision to visit John Dean, Maples' music teacher.

The quality of John's playing had once inspired concert audiences worldwide. Many admirers were disappointed when, still riding the crest of that wave, he retired at fifty, but he had never once regretted his resolve. He had bought a house in one of the roads which ran like spiders' legs off the green. Maurice strolled towards it, passing the Globe Inn on his way. This looked old, but had been built by a local brewery just sixty years ago. A tiny 17th century pub, The Swan, tucked away at the back of the village, was the haunt for hardened drinkers. More abstemious folk had, by unspoken consent, adopted the Globe for their general meeting place. A large upstairs room lent itself naturally for monthly gatherings of various clubs that flourished in the community. A smattering of regulars were seated outside, glasses to hand, enjoying the mellow evening, and they smiled at Maurice as he went by. Acknowledging their greetings he was struck, not for the first time, by their total incuriosity about his life. He was in the village but not *of* it.

The road he turned into was narrow and leafy, following the natural course of the stream which meandered through the village, sometimes underground, then reappearing unexpectedly. John's house was the last before true countryside took over. It had been designed by a competent builder in the

1920s and had a homely, durable appearance, although sorely in need of a coat of paint. Its diamond paned windows caught the evening light and winked a welcome. Maurice pushed open the dark green wooden gate and walked up an uneven brick path to the front door, which opened before he had time to knock.

"Well hallo there maestro! Come in, come in," John grinned, standing to one side with an exaggerated bow.

"It's a perfect evening, but suddenly in the midst of all the beauty I felt lonely." Maurice explained, stiffly self-conscious.

"True beauty often makes me restless. It seems tinged with sadness," John responded. "But don't let's stand here. I was on my way to the kitchen to fetch a cold drink – that's how I saw you coming up the path. Would you like one? Lager and lime okay?"

Maurice nodded absentmindedly and followed his friend into the sitting room. French windows stood open, framing a pleasant vista of the small back garden, and a low easy chair had been turned to face this view. The green of the grass coupled with white bush roses grown close to the house created a refreshing sight. A music score and pencil lying on the carpet gave clues to John's industry before interruption. His host pulled another chair over to the windows.

"I'll just get those drinks," he smiled, and disappeared.

Maurice glanced around, impressed as always by the effort of his fellow beings at creative expression. Both John and he were sensitive men, one a musician and the other an artist, each struggling to be true to the highest within them: but there the similarity stopped. The room he was in was a perfect example of this fact. It was almost the entire opposite to its counterpart at Maples. Joanna had once described Maples' sitting room as 'shabbily genteel' – an accurate portrait, agreed Maurice – being cluttered with books and ornaments, armchairs worn but comfortable, dressed in a faded Morris print, table lamps balanced on every available surface, their flexes dangling somewhat dangerously, paintings covered the walls and fresh flowers were everywhere; withal, the log fire begged to be lit, and usually was.

By contrast John's room was austere. The sparse furniture gleamed with polish, everything was in its correct place, and in winter the temperature was positively chilly, the only heating being supplied by an old two bar electric fire which was woefully inadequate. Legend told that John came from humble beginnings, and he certainly still lived in modest style.

It was two years since the friends had first met. Before that they would pass each other in the village with merely the briefest greeting. Then one morning John put a hand on Maurice's arm and stopped him.

"Mr Caton..um..could I call and see you one day? I'd very much like to buy one of your paintings." He spoke quietly, his voice still holding a Yorkshire accent.

"I'd be honoured," replied Maurice with sincerity. Once or twice in a lifetime, if lucky, one meets a person who is good to the core. John Dean was such a person, and Maurice quickly sensed this. However, at the outset of John's first visit both men were somewhat stilted, for by nature each was cautious and reserved. But a delicate water-colour of a bluebell wood in full flower captivated John at once and defences were soon lowered. Equally straightforward in concerns of business, neither demeaned the painting by false pretence over payment. A price was asked and a price was paid. Over the following months a slow growing trust developed between them and Maurice valued the time spent in John's company. It was rewarding experience to converse with a contemporary.

Presently the door opened and John returned, carrying two glasses. They settled themselves before the windows, sipping the iced lager, quiet with their own thoughts, hardly noticing the heavy scents of twilight. In marked contrast to the house, the garden was definitely untidy, but therein lay its charm. In gratitude for an overgrown haven, birds of every kind filled it with movement and song. Bees weaved a stately progress among the tall flowers. Dusk was drawing its curtains on the scene, but now came the moths' turn for their nocturnal dance. Two or three fluttered past the open windows, their manoeuvres appearing to be choreographed.

John let out a long breath and Maurice twisted slightly to look at his companion. He saw a short, wiry man, with pale skin and receding light brown hair, heavily streaked with grey – the kind of man you wouldn't glance at twice in the street; unless, that is, you saw his eyes. They were large and round, deeply set, and an extraordinary light blue. Their colour reminded Maurice of a blackbird's egg, one colour he found difficult to capture on canvas. Their most remarkable quality however, was the depth of kindness and sympathy in their expression. He found these eyes looking at him while their owner said:

"I don't know if I've ever told you this Maurice, but I was secretly delighted when you asked me to be the music teacher at Maples. I'd been lonely – very lonely – since Helen, my wife, died some eight years back. She'd been my strength, my friend, as well as my wife, and although I know folk think me reserved, I wasn't ready to be a bloody recluse. Not yet anyway. We had a child y'know. A little lad. Died just before his second birthday. Dicky heart they said. Didn't seem right somehow in such a little chap. But there we are – these things happen. Helen never really got over it. Anyway what I'm trying to say is this. I've always liked youngsters, like having them about me. My own childhood was poor in the material sense but, my God, mum and dad filled that house of ours with love and laughter. Mum was so warm. How can I describe her? She was simply comfortable to be with. Made you feel you mattered. They both moved heaven and earth to get me to college.

"I truly believe it's every kids' birthright to have a loving home and I've always felt sorry for those that don't. So, your offer was a chance of giving back some of the love I've had. I may be in my sixties but I don't feel a generation gap. When I heard what you and Joanna were planning to do, and that you wanted me to be a part of it – I don't mind telling you, I came back here and did a little dance. I was that chuffed. It beat any concert offer into a cocked hat. Now everything's under way and I can see the difference in those smashing kids. It's like a miracle…"

He broke off and blew his nose. Maurice felt a prickling behind his eyes. It was the longest speech he'd ever heard from John. The two sat in silence. Then Maurice felt John's gaze on him again.

"Here! What am I thinking of? I've been rambling on about myself, yet I had a strong impression that something was troubling you when you came in. Want to talk? Nothing'll go beyond these four walls."

"I know that," said Maurice softly, "and you're right – I do want to talk. But not now. You've helped me more than you know tonight. Look, come to lunch on Sunday. Ian and Co'll be there and we can talk then."

"Thank you. I'd like that." The answer came at once.

Maurice stood up, and John followed him to the front door. As he opened it, he squeezed Maurice's elbow and watched his friend go down the path. With the door shut quietly behind him, John went into his music room. Moving over to the grand piano, he opened the lid, laid his hands on the keys for a moment or two and then began to play.

Events surrounding Maples were gathering apace, however, and the planned Sunday lunch never took place. It was postponed indefinitely.

★

Maurice closed John's gate and turned homeward. The last colours of sunset faded abruptly but, wrapped in his own musings, he was oblivious to the world. He moved like an automaton, his mind sifting John's surprising confidences. How little we know of those around us, he thought; our lives 'touch' – sometimes fleetingly, sometimes for many years – and yet we only see one side of the persona.

Listening to John talk movingly of the death of his young son, Maurice had experienced a degree of empathy for the first time. Although not a parent, he could imagine how that event must have robbed John and Helen of something more than the loss of their child – some part of them had gone too. Suddenly the thought of losing Esther was more than he could bear: in her short life she had already brought joy into his days.

Like touching a sore tooth, he began gingerly to explore John's evocative tale of a childhood that brimmed with love and emotional security. He suffered twinges of envy, much to his chagrin, but forgave himself and wondered instead what kind of man he would have become had his relationship with his own mother been on a different footing. At least he felt he was beginning to understand her more; really she should never have married, but convention probably propelled her: a mistake which spoilt three lives.

Without realising he had arrived, he found himself walking up Maples' drive. By now it was completely dark, but he could have walked the route blindfold. He turned the corner onto the gravel sweep. The house was before him, dark except for a light burning in Megan's room. Joanna and Martin must still be out. Generally after one of these occasions they would bustle in, filling the house with youth and laughter, to make themselves a nightcap.

Unusually for Maurice, he had taken an immediate liking

to Martin. He wasn't in the habit of making snap judgements, preferring to take his time, but would have needed a heart of flint not to warm to this particular man. Martin enjoyed the role of the buffoon, the clown, laughing and joking.

However, beneath the relaxed exterior there dwelt a compassionate, intelligent man of great charm. Women trusted him instinctively on sight – they felt comfortable with him. He was not particularly good looking, aged about thirty something, plumpish, casually dressed; and Joanna palpably adored him.

Forgetting the door was unlocked, Maurice was searching for his key when he first heard the noise. It seemed to come from the direction of the bushes, planted round the base of the stone steps. It had sounded like a faint moan, like an animal, but he somehow knew that this was no animal. Again he heard it – this time a sibilant whisper ending with the sound of his name. His heart started to thud uncomfortably. Images flashed through his mind. Was Joanna lying injured somewhere in the dark? Or Megan? Perhaps she had…? He was stumbling down the four shallow steps when it came again.

"Maurice! Maurice!" Now there was no mistake.

"I'm coming Jo. Hang on! I'm coming." In his haste he missed his footing and slipped. Out from the darkness he felt a hand grip his arm, and he could faintly make out a chalky white face close to his own.

"Maurice, it's me! Help me for pity's sake! Help me!" The features of the face inches from him were like Joanna's, but it wasn't her. It was…

"Susan! Susan Latimer!" he shouted aloud in relief. "But.. what the… What are you doing..?"

The hand grasping his arm moved quickly to clamp over his mouth. He tasted something sticky and salty. The woman half collapsed against him, almost knocking him off balance. They swayed together on the bottom step. He twisted round, grabbed her left arm and draped it round his shoulders, holding her firmly round the waist with his right arm. In this uncomfortable fashion he pulled her with difficulty up the steps. At the top he opened the front door and fumbled until he found the light switch.

Soft though the light was, it exposed a terrible sight. The slender figure, head lolling forward like a rag doll, was clad in dishevelled, blood soaked clothing – red splashes accentuated by a cream dress. With an unpleasant shudder Maurice realised what he had tasted. He lowered the limp form down on the hall chair and took deep breaths to steady himself. Footsteps were running down the stairs, and looking to them he saw Megan. He straightened up and waited.

"I heard such odd noises Maurice," Megan's voice was tight with anxiety. "Are you okay? You look awful!" Her search went past him, took in fully the woman slumped on the chair, and choked back a gasp, hands clenching together – then separating to cover her eyes.

Maurice gently pulled one of her hands down from her face. She winced at the sight revealed.

"Listen to me, Megan," he explained. "This is Susan. Susan Latimer. Jo and Ian's mother. I found her outside when I came back. As you can see there's a lot of blood. I don't know what's happened yet. There must have been a car accident or something. We need a bowl of warm water and some towels. Be quick! I'll move her to the sitting room. It's more comfortable in there and she'll have a chance to rest."

Megan asked no questions. She disappeared in the direction of the kitchen. Maurice's mind had gone into overdrive – detached from his body. He felt icy cold. With effort he managed to half carry, half drag Susan to the sitting room, settle her in an armchair, and switch on a table lamp. Under its light she didn't appear to be injured, despite all the blood – just shocked. She was squirming restlessly and her eyes opened. She tried to speak but he shook his head. Moving to a small cupboard he took out a bottle of brandy, poured a strong measure into a glass, then helped Susan sip it slowly. Her teeth were chattering against the tumbler and she began to shake violently. Grabbing a couple of wool rugs left casually draped over the sofa, he wrapped them round her shoulders, Next the fireguard was removed and fresh logs piled on the still glowing embers. 'Thank heavens the fire's always kept going,' he thought.

He sensed Megan enter the room. She came and knelt by the chair, and squeezing a towel in the bowl, started to wash Susan's streaked face and hands. The woman in the chair had a thin, haggard appearance, her clothes cheap and ill fitting. She was bedecked in necklaces and rings, the gold rings sharply emphasising ugly nicotine stains. She had not worn well. Maurice tried to remember what little he knew of her life after Ian had gone to Austria to convalesce. Jo had kept up a desultory correspondence; Ian had ignored his mother. Vague recollection stirred of Jo reading from a letter about two or three years ago – something about Susan starting a business venture on the continent, in partnership with a shifty friend of Derek's. A common enough story he had thought, and put it from his mind. She had never figured in his life until tonight.

The stiff drink, coupled with the wash, brought Susan more to herself. Struggling upright, she looked with horror at her ruined clothes.

Megan murmured: "Shall I get Jo's dressing gown?"

Maurice nodded. On Megan's swift return with the garment he paced up and down the hall while Susan was helped out of her soiled dress. Deep inside him he suspected this was no accident, that something terrible had taken place. He felt out of his depth and longed for Joanna and Martin's return. When Megan emerged carrying the bundled dress towards the kitchen, he said quickly:

"Don't wash that Megan. Just leave it in the sink. And could you make us a pot of tea or coffee please?"

The girl gave him a quick glance and moved silently away. Aware of gratitude that she wasn't the hysterical type, he took his hands out of his pockets, heaved a long breath, and returned to Susan. She was staring straight ahead, hands gripping the arms of the chair, skin stretched tightly over bony knuckles.

"Got a cigarette?" she asked wearily.

"Sorry, no I haven't. I don't think there's one in the house. Susan, are you actually hurt?"

Without appearing to have heard him, she said in a slow monotone: "I've killed him. He's dead. I know it."

To give both of them time, he enquired gently:

"Tell me what's happened. Was it a car accident? Were you driving?"

He almost heard the answer before it was given.

"No! No! I murdered him!"

Her voice cracked with despair, and she seemed about to faint again. In that moment he glimpsed that common ruse of the detective. You let the other person talk if they wanted to: let them tell their story in their own time. There was no forcing the issue.

He squatted on his haunches to catch the words. Susan's head had dropped forward, muffling her voice:

"He just made me so mad. So flaming mad! I must have been crazy to've ever trusted him in the first place. What the hell was I thinking of? I put ALL my capital in that business. It was a jewellery business. We both knew quite a bit about gems and had opened another shop in this country. It did well for a while. Very well. We made a lot of money. Then the old story. He was fiddling the books and having affairs. Any girl would do. He could be quite charming when it suited him. Despite being middle-aged, women found him attractive – especially when he was spending money on them. I knew about the girls – didn't give a damn one way or the other. But the bastard was cheating me out of my money. That was different. I hate cheats in money."

Maurice remembered how she had been more disgusted by Derek's underhand dealings than by his heavy drinking bouts. He heard Megan return and put a tray down.

The cold voice went on:

"Tonight was the last straw. I found he'd been handling stolen jewels. He was just a cheap fence. He was worthless trash!"

The last words were spat with such vehemence that a trickle of saliva ran out of the corner of the mouth. She threw her head back and, looking at her eyes, Maurice realised she had slipped into a kind of madness. He sat down with foreboding, heavy of heart.

Susan shuddered and continued: "Our new shop was in a town not far from here – not far from Maples. Quite a coincidence, I thought. We'd been out to dinner when he started boasting about being a thief. He was proud of himself. But apparently the police were onto him. He'd had a tip-off from one of his cronies that the police had a strong case against him. He asked me to give him an alibi for a couple of dates. Who the hell did he think he was, asking ME to do that? Who the hell…?"

Her voice rose, sounding shrill and thin. Once again her head slumped on her chest. Megan came forward, and gently picking up Susan's hands began to rub them with her own strong, flexible fingers. The woman quietened and became oddly still at last.

CHAPTER SIX

A car was coming up the drive – from its engine sound a Land Rover. When it was switched off, voices were heard, laughing and talking. Maurice felt weak with relief: Joanna and Martin at last. For a moment he'd thought it was the police. He had been wondering when to ring them, but wanted to give Susan more time before the machinery of law geared into action. Worried, too, about her mental state, he was beginning to feel the effects of shock in his own body. A doctor should be called to examine the woman at least. He got stiffly to his feet and reached the hall as the front door opened and Joanna came in, an aura of health, freshness and excitement buzzing round her. Martin followed.

"Hi Maurice, we've had…" She broke off. "What on earth's the matter? You look…" Martin's arm went round Jo's slim shoulders.

Maurice, in a tired voice, gave the bare outlines. Almost before he had finished she broke impatiently away from Martin, ran to the sitting room, and the two men heard a sharp intake of breath. Martin stood quietly; a solid, comforting presence.

"Have you called the doc yet, Maurice?"

"No. No. I haven't," replied Maurice, distractedly running his hands through his hair. "Everything happened so quickly. Susan didn't seem physically injured – the blood washed off. I suppose I should have done."

"Not to worry. I'll do it. Is his number on the pad?"

"Yes.. should be there. I'll get Megan to make some fresh coffee."

"Megan!" Martin retorted. "Is she okay?"

"She's been marvellous. I couldn't have managed without her."

"Ah – good."

Martin went across to the hall phone and a few seconds later Maurice heard him in conversation. There was a ping as he replaced the handset.

"Chap's out on a case, but his wife'll give him a call on his mobile."

"Mobile?" repeated Maurice blankly.

"Mobile phone. I've got one in the car."

"Aah. I see."

"We'd better go and see how Jo's getting on," said Martin considerately.

Joanna was on her knees, gazing in bewilderment at her mother.

"I don't understand. I hardly recognise her – she's changed so much. She's so thin. Martin, what do you think…?"

Martin helped Jo to her feet, and rubbed a loving hand up and down her spine. "Come and sit down, darling. The doctor's on his way. You all right Megan?"

"Yes, I'm all right," replied the girl. "I'll get us some more coffee."

Martin fetched a hardback chair from beside the desk and sat in front of Susan, whose head was lolling from side to side again, hands twisting together.

"Susan! Wake up Susan," he said in a low, clear voice.

"I'm Martin. I'm a friend of Joanna's."

"You're not the police?" muttered Susan.

"No. I'm not the police. I want to help you. Can you try

and tell me what happened to you tonight? Can you remember what happened?"

Susan moaned and turned her head away, then turned it back again, opened her eyes and looked at Martin's impassive face for a moment or two, and then started talking, her voice appearing more normal.

"Have you a cigarette?"

Martin fished in his pocket and found a crumpled packet.

He lit her one. She took a couple of puffs.

"I killed him! I killed him!"

"Yes Susan. You killed him. But how did you kill him?"

"I shot him. I shot him with my gun!"

Joanna gave a sharp gasp. Martin shook his head quickly in her direction.

"Where did this happen, Susan? Was it near here? Near Maples?"

She nodded. "Yes. Yes. Near here. Not far away." She looked agitated.

Thankfully at that moment Megan brought in a tray of five steaming mugs of coffee. Joanna put an arm round her mother and helped her with the hot drink; some natural colour began to return to her face. They were all grateful for the effects of the coffee – Susan's story was beginning to affect them. For the first time she appeared to be seeing them, and there was a small smile on her face. Maurice and Jo began to recognise the woman they'd known in the past.

"I really do want to tell you what happened. I *must* tell someone," she said in pitiful tone.

"In your own time. When you're ready," responded Martin.

Joanna sat on the floor beside the armchair and held one of her mother's hands. Susan glanced gratefully at her, tears glistening in her eyes:

"We'd finished dinner and left the restaurant. We walked

to the car park. He'd no idea how he'd disgusted me. He looked at his watch a couple of times and checked it against mine. Said he thought his'd stopped. Funny that – usually he couldn't care less about time. Anyway, he suggested going back to my flat above the shop for a last drink, and I agreed. I wanted to find out all I could. I was glad to get in the car. Needed time to think. Once he'd left my flat I thought I could call the police. He didn't live with me and never stayed the night. But I knew him well enough to know he'd try and drag my name into it if I didn't agree to what he demanded. He'd want his pound of flesh, and I'd lose the businesses. I couldn't stand the thought of that. I'd spent years building them up." Her voice began to sound weak and she rubbed a hand across her eyes.

"Do you want to stop now?" Martin raised his eyebrows.

"No. No! I must go on. Just give me a moment."

She swallowed hard and began again… "He knew I'd once lived in the area and I told him I knew a short cut. The car came to a crossroads and I noticed that we were only about half a mile or so from here. I pointed out the road to take to town but got the odd feeling he knew where he was. He drove over the crossroads and a few yards further on suddenly swung the car into a farm lane. I remember saying: "What on earth…?" – or something like that. He turned off the engine and tried to kiss me. I pushed him off. He stank of drink and it made me feel sick. He simply shrugged his shoulders and once more looked at his watch. He began to taunt me. Said only my money had been useful to him. He'd never found me sexy; I was old; he could still get any girl he wanted. He went on and on. I didn't know what to do – he refused to start the car again. I opened my bag to get a cigarette. As I was fumbling inside for the packet my hand touched something hard and cold. It was my gun. I'd got in the habit of carrying it while taking jewels to and from the continent. I had a licence and knew how to use it. Took some lessons. His voice was still going on and on. I couldn't stand it. It had to be stopped. Before I knew what I was doing I'd taken the gun out, pulled off the safety catch, pointed it and shot him. He was still talking when I shot him. Then I shot him again and he stopped. Blood was spurting.. blood was.. I swear I didn't mean to. I swear I didn't…"

There was silence in the room when her voice died away.

No one looked at their neighbour. Cross currents of emotion swirled round the five people present. Maurice's throat felt parched and dry; he was shaking slightly. Over the hush he could hear the slow tick of the grandfather clock in the hall, which gave small comfort.

The hunched figure in the chair began speaking again. Four pairs of eyes stared at her – already she seemed set apart from them.

"I had to get away. I opened the car door, feeling sick, and started running. I knew he was dead. I was still clutching my bag and the gun. I threw them both in a ditch and kept running. I didn't know what to do – where to go. I had to get away from that car and.. and.. from Keith. Then I remembered we were close to this house and thought you, Joanna, might.. might help in some way. I can't remember how I got here. I just crouched in the bushes until I heard footsteps. Oh Christ, what will happen to me? I don't know what to do…"

She was crying softly now. Joanna wrapped her arms round the pathetic figure and cradled her as one would a hurt child. Maurice beckoned Martin and they went out to the hall. Both men were breathing quickly, glad to be out of the emotive atmosphere created by this distraught woman.

"I'll call the police straight away," asserted Maurice. "I know the farm lane she means."

He left Martin to wander up and down the hall while they

were phoned with precise directions where to find that car. At length he replaced the receiver and showed his concern.

"We're a bit out in the sticks here as you know. The nearest police station is roughly fifteen miles away. They reckon it'll take them thirty minutes or more to get here. The area car is tied up with something else. This bloke, Keith, might…"

"Might be injured not dead." interrupted Martin, who had been doing some fast thinking. "We've got to go and see for ourselves. He may be in frantic need of help. The police automatically call an ambulance in cases like this, don't they?"

"Yup. The officer said he would."

"We must hurry then."

"But what about the women? Will they…?" started Maurice.

"Doc's on his way. Jo's sensible and Megan'll be okay. I can see that. Grab your coat and as many blankets that you can lay your hands on."

The two girls having been told of the plan, the men set off in the Land Rover. Maurice got out at the gates, propping a stone against them so that the doctor could drive straight in. Headlights approached at that moment and the indicator signalled a left turn. Dr Wendell's head thrust out of his car window.

"Where are you off to Maurice? I thought my wife said the trouble was at Maples."

Maurice explained, wondering how many more times he'd have to tell the story before his night was over.

"Good idea," approved Alec Wendell. "Remember, if the chap is still breathing, don't try to move him. Just keep him as warm as possible. Good job it's a warm night. You all right?"

He looked keenly at Maurice as he spoke, who said he was. Giving a brief nod, the doctor put his car in gear and hurried up the drive to the house. Getting back in the passenger seat,

Maurice noted with interest that he truly was all right. He experienced none of the usual bothersome signs of fatigue, and was glad to be in action. Five minutes later their powerful headlamps picked out the crossroads, where under direction Martin turned left, and both of them craned forward to find the farm lane.

"Hey, stop! There it is!" exclaimed Maurice. "Damned difficult to see in the dark. How the dickens did this chap notice it I wonder?"

Martin drove on a short distance until he spotted a widening of the verge. By pulling hard on the steering wheel he managed to manoeuvre the Land Rover clear of the road.

He switched off. A blessed darkness and peace enveloped them. An owl hooted close by and they both jumped, nerves jangling, each wondering what lay ahead.

"Got a torch here somewhere. Hope to hell it works. Should do." Martin was scrabbling in the glove compartment. "Yes. I've got it. And it works."

A beam of light flooded the inside of the vehicle and Maurice saw his friend push a mobile phone in his anorak pocket. Climbing awkwardly from the car, he welcomed contact once more with terra firma. He admitted to a feeling of apprehension, having seen death two or three times before but never under violent circumstances.

Quickly walking back to the lane they turned into it, their torch beam picking out the rear of a dark coloured saloon car parked a few yards ahead. Both front doors were open, touching the hedge on either side. They ran up to it, and what was already dawning on Martin as he squeezed his bulky frame between hedge and car, soon stared him abruptly in the face on reaching the driver's seat.

"There's no one here! He's gone!" With this shout back over his shoulder he played the torch around inside more carefully.

"Blood everywhere though. All over the seat and steering wheel. He's crawled out somewhere."

Maurice could see for himself. He felt confused.

"Well, he can't be far away. He must be badly injured with all this blood around. He can't have gone up the lane – the car's too tight a fit with both doors open. His instinct would be to make for the road."

Martin flicked his torch at the bramble hedge.

"He certainly wouldn't have gone that way. The poor bugger must've fallen in a ditch and we missed him."

Back on the road, they searched the ditch and verge for over a hundred yards on both sides and in each direction. No sign of the man.

"I'm bloody well stumped," grumbled Martin, scratching the back of his neck. "He must be somewhere round here."

"Unless.. someone took him," answered Maurice slowly.

"Someone took him…" repeated Martin. "I don't get your.. Aah..penny's dropped."

They started running back to the car. This time Martin torchlit the ground below the driver's door.

"Look, the ground's muddy here. You can see where a body's been dragged out of the car. There're scuff marks in the mud, like shoes have been scraped through it. And..yes., more blood – quite a pool of it – here..behind the offside rear wheel. The body must have been dumped here while whoever it was took a breather. I wouldn't want to drag a body far, I know that.

"So there'd be another car," said Maurice tersely. "Give me the torch. Those heavy showers we had yesterday should have left the ruts pretty wet. Yes! – here Martin. I don't know much about cars but aren't these two sets of tyre tracks?"

"You're right. Patterns are different. No doubt of that. Perhaps this guy, what's his name?… Keith, had arranged to meet someone here. One of his cronies maybe? Susan said he'd looked at his watch a couple of times. And you said it was damned near impossible to see the turning in the dark unless you knew it was there. He must have done a recce beforehand. But where's all this leading us?"

"It means I think that Keith and this accomplice wanted Susan out of the way," replied Maurice. "Even going so far as to wanting her dead, guessing that she wouldn't play ball with them. She must have known too much about them, or they thought she did. It explains why he was boasting to her this evening. He didn't care what she knew then. But for some reason I can't work out yet, Keith couldn't do it on his own. Or wouldn't. He needed help. After all, it's a terrible and drastic step to take. But Susan got him first. She gets away – the other chap arrives, finds Keith either dead or badly injured and manages to get him into his car. But why not leave him where he was? Why go to all the bother of carting him off?"

"Maybe.. maybe Keith was alive and perhaps even conscious," supplied Martin. "After all a flesh wound can cause a lot of bleeding can't it? We were assuming from Susan that she'd fired a fatal shot."

"Yes but.. come on.. just a flesh wound after being shot at point blank range? Hardly likely is it?" protested Maurice.

"I know! I know! But it is possible. Admit that. This chap turns up to find Keith injured. 'Matey' doesn't give a bugger for Keith, who could well have been double crossing him as well as Susan. Seizes his opportunity with his crony in a weak state to find out what he can about the stolen jewels. Bundles him in his car for a bit of arm twisting."

Maurice stared at him incredulously. "Christ! How many detective stories have you been reading?" He put his hands up in the air as Martin started to open his mouth. "Okay! I give in. Anything's possible."

The whole situation was becoming unreal. He was tired and

uncomfortable and Keith's fate seemed remote. He wanted to go home – ideally to bed, although he knew that was a long way off with police questions to answer. This familiar quiet country road which he had known since boyhood would never be the same again for him, now tainted with talk of death and torture. Why did human beings have to behave like barbarians? The hedge and dark sky began to blur alarmingly; he was swaying on his feet. Martin caught his arm.

"Home Maurice. We've both had enough for tonight."

Maurice pointed up the road. "Fat chance of that," he grumbled.

An arc of blue light was approaching, growing bigger by the second; in the dark it was menacing and invasive. The police had arrived and the long night had just begun.

Twenty-four hours had passed; the longest of Maurice's life. It had been a day of contrasts: of light and shade – the pleasure provided by the launch of the Latimer Gallery; the talk with Megan; the concentrated review of his life; the intimate conversation with John Dean; the naked facts of Susan's world with its tragic outcome; the courteous but insistent questions of the police inspector, and finally bed with dawn lightening the eastern sky. He sought escape in sleep but was beyond that stage. After tossing and turning, he got up, showered, and sought the cool benediction of the garden. Kicking off his sandals he sauntered toward the stream, relishing the dew on the grass. A narrow bridge spanned the flow, its wooden rail worn smooth by countless arms leaning over to watch the singing water below. Settling his elbows in a comfortable position Maurice contemplated this gentle scene. The stream never ran dry, no matter how hot the weather; just when at its lowest level, up it would well from source to continually bubble over stones and rocks.

His mind refreshed, he made his way back to the house, sandals swinging from his hands. He filled the kettle and went into the sitting room, pulling up sharply in the doorway. It had lost its feel of home, too full of alien smells and sensations: Susan's heavy perfume, cigarette smoke, tears and harsh words. Impatiently he opened windows, emptied ashtrays, straightened chairs and plumped cushions. Perhaps it wouldn't be too long before life resumed some degree of normality, he sighed. Coffee made, he carried it outside and sat at the patio table where yesterday's cake crumbs were still scattered over the surface. Brushing them to the ground, he watched silently while Maples' tame blackbird ate his fill. The sun was reaching into the courtyard – already he could feel its warmth on his head. Could Susan see the sun from her police cell, he wondered?

He had been secretly dreading the police questions, considering them an invasion of his privacy, but the previous night's episode had been less fraught than expected. The police car had drawn up alongside Martin and himself in that dark lane, and two men had climbed out, donning their caps. Both were fairly short and slight, and from their uniforms it became obvious that one was a constable and the other a sergeant. The facts put before them, it was agreed that he and Martin return to Maples where a detective inspector should have arrived. The lane would be cordoned off and preliminary investigations started. The sergeant had spoken in quiet measured tones, obviously designed to soothe and reassure. Tired though he was, Maurice smiled to himself.

A soft Scottish voice could be heard as they opened Maples' front door, and a man had stood up on their entering the sitting room. It had seemed to take him an age to unwind himself from his chair. The long, almost emaciated figure, was at least 6'4" in height, with a thin face, warm brown eyes, streaks of fair hair brushed smoothly over a balding head, a bony nose bent over a bristly moustache. Maurice put his age at around 40-45 years.

"Good evening gentlemen. Come. Sit down. I'm Detective Inspector Ford. Christopher Ford."

While speaking he had produced a warrant card at which they barely glanced. The three men had shaken hands, then sat on chairs which Maurice noted had been collected from the dining room. Maybe, he thought grimly, these were considered more conducive for sharp answers than reclining comfortable armchairs. The policeman explained that his men had informed him of the disappearance of the shot man. He spoke in clear matter-of-fact tones, the voice registering neither surprise nor concern.

Maurice heard the words but he was looking first at Joanna, then Megan, and lastly Susan. The two girls appeared relaxed on the surface, with Jo seated beside her mother and Megan standing behind them, her hand resting lightly on the back of Jo's chair. Susan Latimer was sitting straight backed, dressed in a blouse and skirt which he recognised belonged to her daughter. Outwardly she looked calm, with her hair brushed and lips outlined in red, but her hands were continually moving, plucking at her skirt's folds, then at the arms of the chair. The atmosphere was explosive with tension.

If the inspector was aware of this – and Maurice was sure he was – then he gave no indication. His eyes moved from face to face. Maurice felt that here was a man who would make a good friend but a bad enemy. The silence, stretched like a taut wire, became oppressive. Ford broke it, addressing Maurice.

"Mrs Latimer has been cautioned," he said – at which Maurice winced inwardly – "and she has made a verbal statement. Miss Latimer and Miss Smart have also briefly given theirs."

Miss Smart? pondered Maurice. Who the dickens?..Oh..

of course – Megan! He'd forgotten her surname, and this momentary bemusement met the policeman's cold regard.

"Mr Caton, I realise you are tired, but if I could have your full attention, please?"

Maurice's face flushed as that coldness continued.

"What I need from you two gentlemen is your brief account of events. A more detailed statement will be taken by my sergeant when he gets here." The inevitable notebook was taken from the pocket of his crumpled linen jacket. "You, sir, are Maurice Caton, and you are Martin Hurst?"

Both agreed.

"Right then, Mr Caton, I'll begin with you if I may. I understand that you are the owner of this house which is run as an art and music school. Good. Now, in your own words simply tell me what happened here tonight."

Maurice told his story, the account sounding wholly unreal to his ears as he progressed. He felt he was believed, but that didn't prevent a mounting sense of unease. Martin followed with his version, during which the front door opened and footsteps squeaked across the hall. The inspector signalled Martin to continue, barely looking up at the man who entered. Maurice guessed this to be the absent detective sergeant and took the opportunity to study him.

He was of average height but appeared shorter, for his head and body were quite round. He brought to mind a roly-poly toy played with by Esther – quite impossible to knock off balance. The man's eyes were small and pale blue, almost hidden in loose, wrinkled skin, and it seemed he had chosen a suit to match as it hung on him in loose folds. His good-natured demeanour perched on the edge of a Windsor chair, crossing his feet neatly at the ankles. When Martin had concluded, the new arrival was introduced: "Detective Sergeant Harry Anderson."

One by one the five participants in the night's drama filed

into the dining room, temporarily in use as a police office, where Sergeant Anderson displayed amazing shorthand speeds.

At last all was done and Susan was led away – a heartrending moment which Maurice, having discovered himself distinctly uncomfortable in the presence of emotional women, had since preferred to gloss over in his mind. The girls had gone straight to bed, and Martin, after a quick nightcap, disappeared into one of the spare rooms. The fact that their long night was now over gladdened Maurice's heart today, like those waters passing happily under his garden bridge.

CHAPTER SEVEN

The sun was well up and domestic sounds came clattering from the kitchen. Maurice drained his last cold coffee dregs, reluctant to face a new day. When he finally entered the kitchen, Joanna, seated at the table, raised her head from cupped hands. The change in her face was shocking; the old lady she would inevitably become now etched there in deep lines. With a small groan he bent and cuddled her to him. For a few moments they remained motionless and silent, then she reached up and kissed his cheek while gently pulling free from his arms, and he could see the young Jo once more.

"I'll make some fresh coffee. D'you want a cup?" She managed a wan smile with the words.

"No thanks m'dear. I'd better try to restrict my coffee intake. I imagine a good deal will be drunk today."

She gave a nod of understanding and fetched herself a mug from the dresser. Maurice moved to the window – the same window Doris Pope had peered through at his disappearing figure many years before: no longer dirt encrusted of course, but with shining panes overlooking the courtyard where several sparrows were quarrelling over the last few cake crumbs. With a sigh he thrust his hands deep in his pockets. At least this familiar cameo made it appear more like any other morning.

He heard water gush into the sink, and turning saw Joanna rub the inside with a cloth – acting as though she didn't know how to stop. Her sobs could be heard over the sound. He turned off the tap, removed the cloth, and perched her on a kitchen stool.

"I was.. I was filling the kettle when I noticed the stains.. the blood stains. That man's blood!" She was struggling to gain composure. "They wouldn't wash away."

Control was completely lost by this time, tears and mucous running down her cheeks, over her chin. He mopped the flow with paper towels, cursing himself the while for not looking in the sink. He should have remembered how Susan's clothes had lain there last evening before removal by the police.

She blew her nose and put a hand on his arm.

"I feel better for that. For crying I mean. Really I do."

Her pallor had been replaced by a more healthy flush and he knew she would now remain steadfast. Quite soon a stranger would have found it impossible to sense anything amiss in the house.

A remarkably spruce Martin was the next arrival in the kitchen, making Maurice only too painfully aware of the twenty odd year gap in their ages. The two young people exchanged a long kiss on the mouth, and Martin's hand slowly stroked Jo's bottom, which together with a lingering glance showed clearly that they were deeply in love. Maurice didn't feel an intruder on the intimate scene. Instead he was absurdly gratified, like a benevolent father. He remembered hearing, in the small hours, Martin's door click open and Joanna's door click shut. He smiled. Somehow it seemed a good omen for the days ahead.

While Jo nibbled toast and marmalade, Martin poured muesli into a bowl, and briskly stirring in milk spoke with the voice of a man used to coping with difficult situations. "We must plan what we're going to do this morning. Top of the list is getting hold of a good lawyer for Susan. Someone who specialises in criminal work. The police are sure to put her up before the local magistrate without delay. D'you know of anyone around here Maurice?"

"Yes, I do as a matter of fact. Geoffrey Staples, the son of my solicitor. I'd heard this was his line of country."

"Great." Martin looked at his watch. "Quarter past eight. D'you have his home number?"

"No. But I can get it from his father." Maurice felt relieved to be of positive help.

"Okay. You get on the blower. Then we must tell Ian."

"I'll do that," interposed Joanna.

Maurice went out into the hall, stifling back a pang of regret that Ian's first full day at the Gallery was to be spoilt. No time to think along those lines. He found Hartley Staples' number and quickly explained to him the reason for the early call. The old man was becoming rather deaf and Maurice had to check his exasperation as he shouted a repeat. The son was a totally different character. He grasped the situation at once and confidently told Maurice to leave it all in his hands. He would alter his morning schedule and visit Susan within the hour.

Through the hall window Christine Pope came into view, puffing across the gravel on her bicycle. A sudden breeze caught at her cotton skirt, lifting it to expose strong thighs. She reminds me of her mother-in-law, thought Maurice, apropos nothing in particular. I wonder why? Do all country women look much the same? He and Christine synchronised their opening of the two doors to the kitchen, and a flurry of wind blew sheets of paper off the table. Squatting under it to retrieve them, he could hear Jo tell the news and watched Christine's toes clench in her open sandals. When he stood up, her honest, rosy- cheeked face had paled.

"Oh Mister Caton, Mister Caton, it's terribul – terribul!" She sounded close to tears. "You alroight? Can I make yer some breakfast?"

"No. No thanks, Christine. Not now. But there is something

you can do to help. Will you look after Esther today? We shall need someone and you're the ideal person."

"Oh, Mister Caton, you know oi'd luv to. I always wanted a little girl but after 'aving my two boys the doctor said I mustn''ave…"

"Yes, yes! I know, Christine," came the hurried interruption. The tale of Christine's disappointment at the lack of a daughter had been heard before and this wasn't the time to hear it again. "Thanks a lot," he added as an afterthought.

"Furst uv all, I'm going to give that sink a good clean," she replied, bending down to find the scourer.

"Then I'll make you all some tay."

Maurice however was only half listening because Jo was returning from phoning Ian. He could tell from her face it had been a strain.

"They're coming straight over," was her only comment, flopping down heavily at the table.

The retrieved sheets of paper were still in Maurice's hand, and he noticed that one piece had been partially covered in writing. Martin took it from him, confessing half apologetically: "My list. My aide-memoire. Couldn't operate without one!"

It was somewhat touching to glimpse this dash of weakness mixed with capability.

Half an hour later, while dejectedly loitering in the sitting room, Maurice heard the familiar scrunch of tyres on gravel, and looking through the window witnessed the arrival of Ian en famille. Knowing Ian in every mood, the hunched shoulders and set expression as he climbed from the passenger seat indicated suppressed irritation. And who could blame him? sympathised Maurice inwardly. Susan had never supported her son, especially when he had most needed her, and here she was entering his life again at the worst possible moment. Damn the wretched woman! The house had been sullied by her presence.

Small wonder Ian looked angry, but the young man's innate loyalty meant he would support friends and family, whatever the cost. Or so Maurice thought.

He opened the front door and lovingly watched Esther jump up the steps holding her father's left hand, closely followed by Yvonne. The blessed innocence of this little girl's prattle helped to lighten the air. She thought it a marvellous adventure to be surrounded by all her favourite people so early in the day. Giving Maurice a quick hug, she was then whisked into the kitchen by one of her greatest admirers. In a twinkling Christine had swathed her in a large apron, and standing on a stool the child was ready to play with pastry dough.

Megan was also in the kitchen, leaning back against the dresser drinking tea. She pulled a funny face at Esther who beamed back, happily in her element. She was a placid child, and on course for a placid life. She would never lose that knack to attract friends.

With another school term almost upon them, Maurice knew he wasn't going to have time to devote to its preparation. He had instinctively turned to John Dean for help, who said without hesitation that he would move into Maples until life settled down, secretly relishing the idea of company and the pleasant feeling of being useful.

★

The drive in the Land Rover to the local magistrate's court was undertaken in silence, everyone busy with their thoughts. Geoffrey Staples' smart suited figure was waiting for them in the corridor outside the courtroom. He extended an urbane greeting to each but his handshake lacked cordiality. A shrewd professional right out to those manicured finger-nails, he spoke in well-modulated tones.

"I've just seen Mrs Latimer." He held up a hand as Jo tried to speak. "Forgive me but we haven't much time. Mrs Latimer was fairly calm in the circumstances and understands this morning's procedure, which is simply a formality. I must get into court now. Two of you may visit her afterwards if you wish." A slight bow and he was gone.

Ian didn't mince words: "Well, I for one don't want to see her. Now I'm here I don't even want to go into court. I don't like the wretched woman – can't pretend otherwise. I don't feel sorry for her. It's her own life she's mucked up, but I'm angry how that affects ours." His face had reddened while speaking. "Strewth! Why, oh why, did she have to come back right now? It'll mean really bad publicity for the Gallery. I can just see the muck-raker that calls itself a local newspaper having a ball!"

Without looking at any of them, he swung round and walked quickly back down the corridor toward the swing doors at its end. Yvonne hurried after her husband. Maurice cursed fluently to himself. This was even more horrible than he had feared.

"Maurice, would you come with me to see Mother?" entreated a white-faced Joanna. "You know her slightly from the old days. I know you don't like her but…"

Martin started to say he would go, and Jo cut in:

"…Yes, I know that darling. I know you'd do anything for me. But I think Mother would be more comfortable with someone she knows. You do understand?"

In reply he put an arm round her shoulders and kissed her cheek. Then he held open the courtroom door and they filed in.

Never before had Maurice been in a room so deeply impregnated with human misery in all its manifestations. The room was small, oak-panelled, dark and oppressive. Even the various hospitals he had stayed in had been more cheerful, more hopeful. This room lacked hope and faith.

He felt slightly sick and wished he had eaten some breakfast.

The three sat down on a hard bench, Jo clutching Martin's hand. There was a stir among the few people present and the magistrate, a woman, entered. They all stood, she settled herself, and they sat again. Then a pathetic Susan was brought in from a side room, accompanied by a pleasant faced young policewoman. In a flat, remote voice, Susan confirmed her name and address and that she understood the charge. This was 'to unlawfully wound, with intent to kill, person or persons unknown'. Then D.I. Ford took the stand. In response to the question whether the police objected to bail being granted in this case, the policeman gave a slight, theatrical pause before answering.

"The police do object to bail, Your Worship, on the grounds of a man's body having just been found, and from the apparent injuries we have reason to believe it to be that of the missing man. I would rather not say more at this stage."

A frisson of excitement flicked round the room. Two or three journalistic notebooks were taken out of pockets, and headlines began to be written. With the sniff of a human interest story, boredom had dissolved. Jo was seated between her two menfolk, and Maurice felt her stiffen and hold her breath.

"Very well, Detective Inspector. In the circumstances the prisoner is remanded in custody for a further ten days," pronounced the magistrate.

"Thank you, Your Worship." Ford gave a slight bow and left the witness box.

Five minutes later, Maurice and Jo accompanied a court official down wooden stairs which led under the building. The man opened a door and they entered a basement room, lit by a bright centre bulb and furnished with a plastic topped table and four chairs. It was hot, airless and smelt faintly of mice. Susan was sitting on one of the chairs facing the door; a shrunken Susan with bowed shoulders. She glanced up, her lipstick the only colour in her face, but gave no sign of recognition. Then she looked down again at her hands, loosely clasped in front of her, as if absorbed in them.

Geoffrey Staples was pacing up and down the confined space, his attitude supercilious, confirming to Maurice that he had inherited none of his father's fine, gentle humanity. Jo was staring miserably at her mother, which left Maurice the sole listener to Staples. He said Susan would be taken immediately to the nearest remand centre which was about eight miles distant. He didn't want to hazard a guess at this stage what sentence Susan might suffer. There were many factors involved; not least whether Dunsett had been found dead or alive.

Back up, once more into daylight and sanity, they found D.I. Ford waiting for them.

"I don't want to ask any more questions at the moment," he said, his tone quite gentle. "Can you make sure you all stay in today? I'll call by later."

"Do we have any option?" asked Maurice wistfully.

The policeman grinned and shook his head.

A couple of hours had passed since the court drama. Maurice sat in his den, his studio on the first floor, opposite Ford who – true to his word – had returned to Maples.

The policeman's sinewy form was stretched out in an old, faded armchair, his fingertips pressed lightly together. He had knocked Maurice off balance by a discovery just imparted, akin to the earth tilting off its axis. His dark eyes watched the older man stare down to the vista of garden and copse beyond. From long experience he knew when he had initiated genuine shock – this being such a moment.

Well, he had time on his side and was prepared to wait.

He stood up to survey the room. It was pleasant, with pale blue walls reflecting good strong light that sparkled unimpeded through bare windows. The air was heavy with the smell of paint and canvas, sending him on a nostalgic trip back in time to another similar room in a grey stone house in Dunblane, Perthshire: his grandfather's home. There the windows overlooked the cathedral, whose tower dominated that small Scottish town. Grandfather had been an artist too, albeit not so well known as Maurice Caton. Chris Ford had been deeply fond of the old chap and together they had often tramped the Ochil Hills around Dunblane, he listening to woven tales of daring deeds from long ago spun in a soft Highland voice – heady stuff for an impressionable small boy!

Back in the present, his eyes travelled over canvases haphazardly stacked against the walls and then noticed a charming water colour on the easel in one of the windows. It was of a child, a little girl of maybe four or five, dressed in dungarees, absorbed in play outside an old summer-house. From the background he recognised Maples' garden, having explored it earlier with his sergeant. He stooped to examine the painting more closely. His educated eye appreciated the skill that had delicately caught the roundness of childhood. The face, with its look of intense concentration, poignantly reminded him of his daughter at the same age. He sighed. He missed her, and his son too of course. America was their home now with their mother and a new step-father. If the painting was for sale he decided to buy it – after all he had little else to spend his money on. It would be a memory of happier days.

Maurice stirred and turned round from the window to look at the detective. "Go through the details again please. I didn't take them in properly the first time. I feel so confused. Can you elaborate some more..?"

Maurice sounded completely bewildered and Ford was struck by the pale, drawn look facing him. He must choose his words with care.

"D'you mind if I smoke?" he asked on impulse.

"Go ahead," came the reply from Maurice, collecting his pipe and tobacco from a small table. Ford lit a cigarette, and after watching Maurice settle himself in the other armchair began his narrative once again.

"You heard what I said in court – about a body having been found. We're now certain that this man goes by the name of Keith Dunsett. He was discovered lying outside the casualty department of St. Hilda's Hospital at around 4 a.m. this morning. D'you know where I mean?"

Maurice nodded.

"He'd received two bullet wounds but was alive. He'd lost a lot of blood and was unconscious, but someone had tried to patch him up. He'd been lucky. One bullet had missed his heart by a whisker, and the other had simply grazed his left shoulder. Whoever had been hiding him must've thought he was going to die, panicked and dumped him at the hospital, guessing he'd be found. He's now in intensive care but the medics say his life isn't in danger. Mind you, Susan Latimer's damned fortunate not to be facing a murder charge.

"A witness has come forward who saw two people – she thinks a man and a woman – lift the body of a man from the back seat of a car and lay it by the swing doors leading to casualty. They only managed to carry the man with some difficulty. They then jumped back in the car and drove off at high speed. Our witness, a prostitute, was busy coping with a 'client' in the back of another car parked across the forecourt. She left the man to do up his trousers while she ran across to

Dunsett and then gave the alarm. It'd been too dark for her to give good descriptions of the couple or their car. Needless to say the 'client' had been otherwise engaged to see anything, and would be most unlikely to come forward anyway given the circumstances!

"It's doubtful whether Dunsett had ever allowed himself to be seen with these two associates but I think, given time, that we'll pick them up without too much difficulty. Mrs Latimer has been questioned but says she never met any of Dunsett's friends, and I for one, believe her. She's no reason to lie. His wallet was still in his jacket pocket, along with his driving licence, helping us to identify him until a matching set of fingerprints clinched matters.

"He already had form, you see. Of course, Mrs Latimer had already given us Dunsett's address before he'd been found, and we'd carried out a detailed search of his flat. No jewels or drugs were found. However… sellotaped to the bottom of a chest of drawers – not the most subtle of hiding places – was a most illuminating package. It was a large sealed envelope. Inside was a birth certificate, two letters, and two cash receipts. The birth certificate shows plainly that Dunsett's real name is Alexander Caton, aged forty-two, mother one Mary Caton, father unknown. This, together with the letters, shows beyond doubt that Alexander Caton, alias Keith Dunsett, is your half-brother, Mr Caton."

This was the revelation that had shaken Maurice to the core: it seemed unbelievable. For him the rest was routine stuff about a fairly small time crook. He was relieved that Susan wouldn't be facing a murder charge, but more for Ian and Joanna if truthful. He sat immobile, his mind feverishly ticking away. Was this the truth he had heard? He shot back over the years, trying to make sense of the facts.

He could remember one summer when he was about eight

years old, revelling in unaccustomed freedom because Mother had temporarily gone away. He'd been told she was visiting Wales, ostensibly to stay with her sister for a holiday. The reason for her absence meant nothing to him. For once there had been no one to reprimand him when his clothes became dirty and torn, and his skin had turned gypsy brown. When the day came for his return to preparatory school, Father and a housekeeper had packed the trunk, and his tuck box had been crammed with all his favourite treats. Unexpected tears pricked behind his eyes at that memory. Mother had never bothered with such caring touches.

He cleared his throat and asked sharply: "Which month was shown on the certificate for the date of birth?"

He half dreaded, half knew, the reply.

The policeman consulted his notebook.

"October. Definitely very early October."

Yes! That date fitted in with Maurice's rapid calculations. He strained for recall. There had been a gardener working at Maples for several years when he was a small boy. He'd admired him, mainly because he was adept at mending things, like a bicycle puncture. He had been a youngish, strong looking man, kindly after a fashion, named.. of course.. Alex. If his memory was correct, Alex had left by the time he'd returned that year for the Christmas holidays. He remembered feeling disappointed. But his mother, the 'oh so correct' Mary Caton, that block of stone, that unemotional woman, having an affair? Upon reflection perhaps not so unlikely, she had a handsome face, and often a passionate nature was subjugated by repression. And somehow he doubted his father's ability in the conjugal bed. Shaking free of these thoughts, he glanced up to see Christopher Ford once more standing in front of Esther's portrait. The man had a quite exceptional quality of stillness which soothed Maurice's over-strained nerves.

Reluctant to break the policeman's reverie, nevertheless another matter needed explanation.

"You mentioned that two letters were also in the package. What were they? Love letters?"

"Huh! Far from it. One was the copy of an unpleasant blackmail letter from Dunsett to your mother, and the other was her reply."

Maurice felt queasy and his voice sounded remote to his own ears.

"I see. Can you tell me about the letters? Or would that be breaking some police code or other? And you also mentioned two cash receipts. I don't follow…"

Ford broke in quickly: "I'll come to those in due course. The letters are of far more interest." He paused almost imperceptibly, and then continued briskly. "I think you've a right to know – being closely involved. It's why I've been telling you all this. It's my guess these letters were the only interaction between the two of them. Should Dunsett ever come to trial, then the letters would be produced in court I'm afraid. There'd be some washing of dirty linen in public."

Maurice shrugged, unmoved by this prospect.

Ford settled more comfortably in his chair and continued his tale.

"Dunsett's letter provides a clear insight into his complex, devious nature, revealing a Walter Mitty character. Brought up by foster parents who in time officially adopted him, it's obvious he considered himself several notches above them on the social scale. Obvious too from his bitter tone that he had made this clear to his parents. He'd apparently left home at sixteen. I doubt if he ever went back again.

"Under the terms of the Adoption Act 1976 he had the right to know his real name, i.e. his birth mother's name. Armed with this information, coupled to a sharp mind, it wouldn't have been too difficult tracking down the whereabouts of Mary Caton – especially as she had not changed her address. He probably had a look at the outside of the house and decided to try for a slice of the cake. He's a clever devil and could have charmed one or two of the villagers into chatting indiscreetly about the owner of the 'big house'. From the date on the letter he was then nearly eighteen, and already had a police record. Only minor offences – shop lifting, driving uninsured, driving while under the influence etc. – but he had begun a life of crime. In the letter he told your mother that he thought blackmail the most profitable revenge for what he saw as years out in the wilderness. He knew of your existence by the way."

Ford let this sink in, then went on:

"It must have been a great shock to her, suddenly receiving a letter from someone she'd probably almost forgotten. Was she the sort of woman to have many friends? Was she sensitive about her position in the village? We understand she was a widow by this time."

With fumbling fingers Maurice made an effort to scrape out his pipe, tapping the dead ash into the fireplace. At last, visibly relaxing, he looked over at Ford.

"Let me fill you in on my mother, Inspector. She didn't have any friends, or even acquaintances for that matter. No one ever came to the house to my knowledge, except the daily staff. She was a remote, cold person. But the villagers gave her respect and she would have been horrified to have tittle-tattle spread about her, especially the fact that she'd had an illegitimate son. And I would have heard about it! God forbid! Our solicitor, Hartley Staples, visited about every three months or so but I think it was simply to discuss her investments. I certainly didn't like her and also left home at sixteen."

This last remark merely caused Ford to raise his eyebrows, light another cigarette, and speak slowly:

"Ah... I see... I get the picture. You've filled in the gaps. I understand now why she didn't stand up to Dunsett, didn't call his bluff. She was frightened. From her reply – which was short, terse and to the point – she agreed to his demands although it went against the grain."

"And these were...?" asked Maurice.

"Well, given the circumstances, he was shrewd enough to keep the demand fairly modest; he wanted £12,000, payable in cash drafts of £2,000 each over a period of six months – the drafts to be sent to different box numbers. That method would make it damned near impossible to trace him. However, in a few pithy words, she did make it plain that it was all he was getting. But we'll never know if he would have tried again as Mary Caton apparently died a month after the second draft was paid. The greedy little fool only got his hands on £4,000 – which tallied with the two receipts I mentioned. We wondered why the money seemed to have stopped, and checked the date of her death. Not difficult to do. We've had our eye on Dunsett for some time and will be glad to build a case against him."

"Of course!" A note of grim satisfaction crept into Maurice's voice. "Mother had a weak heart, the result of rheumatic fever suffered when a child apparently. But the villagers didn't know that fact, therefore dear brother wouldn't have either. She died when I was about twenty-five, hastened on her way by Dunsett no doubt. But why the hell did he hang on to the letters and receipts? Without those no one would have known about the blackmail attempt; something he can perhaps be charged with eh?"

"In a word – vanity. I'm no psychologist, but have known enough criminals to be able to state that unequivocally. Vanity has been the downfall of more cunning minds than Dunsett's. They must have something to gloat over, to feed the emotion.

It's like a drug. Common sense urges them to destroy the evidence but they can't bring themselves to when it comes to the crunch. Even though Dunsett's scheme had gone down the pan, he'd had the satisfaction of making your mother squirm and wanted to re-live those moments. He appeared to really hate her."

"In a funny sort of way I can almost sympathise with him," said Maurice quietly. "I often wanted to hurt her, to get my own back. For different reasons she had the same effect on both of us."

Silence ensued, broken by a soft knock on the door. Joanna put her head round.

"Sorry to butt in. Sergeant Anderson's here, Inspector, and wants a word with you."

"Right. Thanks Miss Latimer. No, don't get up Mr Caton. I'll be back in a day or two, or I'll ring if there's more urgent news."

Following the trim figure of Joanna down the stairs, Ford knew he had strayed outside correct police procedure with his frank disclosures to Maurice. Assessing human nature was a well-tried element of his job however, and he liked and trusted the man. Anyway, Ford's methods of working were often unorthodox and Maurice was not under suspicion. Using trust and truth as a fertiliser, the policeman had gained a worthwhile yield. Significant pieces of the jigsaw concerning Dunsett had been slotted into place. He had taken a gamble to gain valuable insight, a gamble which had paid off.

CHAPTER EIGHT

Ian opened the door leading from their private flat into the Gallery, and stood for a moment engrossed in the overall atmosphere of the room. It exuded graciousness and charm – not two epithets he would readily apply to himself after his exhibition that morning. But he knew it was not uncommon for him to behave in a silly or childish fashion: he was aware of these traits in his character. This time, however, he felt justified because he had stated the simple truth when he admitted to dislike of his mother – no filial affection existed. Susan Latimer was a stranger to him; a stranger who had carried him for nine months in her womb, who had given him birth, but who now neither knew or cared how he lived his life. What did cause him concern was the inescapable fact that he had let down Jo and Maurice. Both these people were dear to him, he cared what they thought of him, and he could at least have been supportive. In his eyes he practically owed them his life, for God's sake!

Behind him he heard Yvonne come into the room but felt ashamed to look. She moved over to him and cuddled his waist round with her soft arms, pressing her head against his back.

"You alright Ian?" she probed gently. "Shall we run over again to Maples and collect Esther? I'd imagine poor Christine could do with a break from her incessant questions. And it'd give you a chance to have a word with Maurice."

Ian turned then and gave her a warm kiss on the lips.

"You, m'darling, are a witch. You always know exactly how I'm feeling."

She smiled. "Not so difficult when you love someone," she said complacently.

Standing back, she looked across at one of Maurice's larger paintings and went on: "D'you know, I really think that's my favourite out of all his work. The great panorama of windswept sky and clouds and fields of golden corn is breath-taking. It brings a lump to my throat."

"Yes.. he's caught the movement that's ever present in nature – nature is never still. And then he excites and lifts the senses with the clever use of colour." There was genuine admiration in Ian's voice. "At least that's my humble opinion." He gave a half embarrassed laugh. "No. I must be honest and admit I had a superb teacher in such matters."

Yvonne squeezed his arm in agreement and they stood in companionable silence admiring their Gallery, which each had an equal share in creating. Yvonne glanced at her watch.

"Give me a minute or two to put my face on and I'll be with you."

Ian watched her disappear through the door, bemused as ever by the phrase 'put my face on'. To him she looked beautiful whatever her physical state might be, but if it made her happy… Then with the knowledge that he had about ten minutes' wait he walked over to one of the bow windows and sat on the cretonned window seat, facing the room. Sunbeams danced through the curved panes, dust particles shimmering within them, the rays producing a warm, golden sheen to the parquet floor. He leaned back, pushed his left hand into his pocket, and viewed the scene with pleasure. The Gallery set an excellent background for Maurice's wizardry with the artist's palette; it was difficult to envisage improvement. Eyes half closed, he allowed the peace to lull his consciousness.

Drowsiness overtook him. Intermittent traffic sounds grew fainter, footsteps on the pavement below the window became padded, and his head flopped forward.

A light tap on the shoulder startled him awake and he looked up sleepily into Yvonne's smiling blue eyes, now emphasised with eye-shadow.

"Sorry, my love, to disturb your slumbers but the car's waiting outside the front entrance. And you know what the wretched traffic wardens are like. I couldn't see one, but still…"

"Quite. I'm right with you. I was only thinking."

"But of course – I never thought otherwise."

Laughing, they went out to the street hand in hand, first setting the burglar alarm and carefully locking the heavy front door behind them. After all, one man's creativity – a decade of work – had been entrusted to their care. It was quite a responsibility. Soon Yvonne's adroit steering had out-manoeuvred the busy traffic flow and they were on their way to Maples.

"You should find Maurice somewhere in the garden," Joanna had said, and sure enough Ian saw him sitting outside the summer-house. The infamous deck-chairs had been revamped many times, but they were still serviceable and Ian fetched the second one. After Maurice had helped assemble it, the two men sat in silence surrounded by a thick carpet of pink and white rose petals. Finally Ian cleared his throat:

"Look Maurice, about this morning, I'm really ashamed of my behaviour. I know I behaved badly. I let you down."

Maurice tapped his friend on the knee.

"If you feel you let someone down, old chap, it would only be yourself. But, if it's any comfort, I would have reacted in exactly the same way. Given the circumstances that outcome was inevitable. It's been a day for mothers one way and another. Try to think no more about it."

Ian twisted round and gave his companion a straight look for the first time since arriving. The man was lying back in the chair, his arms dangling loosely over the sides almost touching the grass, one hand holding the inevitable pipe, his face relaxed and unstrained. This last fact puzzled Ian. Considering the rapid pace of events over the past twenty-four hours, he had expected Maurice to be exhausted. He decided a bit of mental fishing was in order.

"Joanna said the Inspector had been here this afternoon. Did he bring more tidings about my dear mother? But you said mothers. I know you too well for that to be a mere slip of the tongue – hmm?"

Quickly and concisely Maurice recited the day's surprising revelations. Ian had evolved into a good listener, not interrupting, merely emitting a low whistle at the finish.

"Strewth! I see what you meant about mothers." He faltered for a moment while the full implication sank in, then went on: "Let me get this straight. You're saying that this half-brother of yours, Alexander, was a friend – if one can call him that – of my father, and it was through this association that he eventually met my mother. Gives me a creepy feeling in the gut."

"Ian, d'you remember a Keith Dunsett ever coming to see Derek, or arriving at Maples with Derek perhaps?"

"Sorry, no. Name doesn't ring a bell. But I'd only have been a spotty kid at that time. I didn't mix with Derek and Susan's gin 'n' tonic cronies. Hang on a sec' though. I couldn't have met him when you think about it. Mum – no, from now on I draw the line at calling her that – Susan said, correct me if I'm wrong, that Dunsett was her business partner, that he used to be a friend of Derek's, and that yesterday evening he seemed to know his way round the lanes, which apparently surprised her. I think that's what you just said."

Maurice groaned and tapped his head.

"My brain's going addled. You're quite right. Sorry to interrupt but, of course, it's obvious he'd never been to the house or Susan wouldn't have said what she did. I was projecting. I just know that if I'd been him, curiosity alone would have made me wangle a visit somehow or other. For Pete's sake, this was the house where Mary Caton, his victim, had lived, and for that matter died. You'd think he'd want to gloat. In fact when Barkers had it on their books to let, that would have been an ideal opportunity…"

His voice faded away and he squinted into the distance.

"… I've a strong feeling he did look round then. I'm sure in my bones I'm right. He's been all round the house and gardens. I think he wanted to look on his own. He only had to say he was a prospective client, perhaps checking on behalf of his parents, and the agent would have given him a key. After all, the house was empty."

"Yes, but…," came a naive protest from Ian, "my family had already agreed to take on the lease."

"Whenever has a little matter like that stopped estate agents still showing a house to other customers? Their motto is:- 'many a slip twixt.. etc. etc.' In their eyes they'd be securing a back-up."

"Yes, that's true," acknowledged Ian.

"D'you remember I told you I slept in the summer-house for a while after Mrs Pope disturbed me?" went on Maurice.

Ian nodded.

"Well, one night I woke suddenly with the vivid impression of someone looking in the window. I could make out a shape in the moonlight." Maurice sat up straight at his own recall. "I thought it was one of my bad dreams. Now I'm not so sure. It gives me the creeps to think Dunsett was out there staring in at me. And he would have been moving round inside the house in the dark. He never made any attempt to contact me. Probably decided I was some sort of wandering, artistic nutter and best left to my own devices. But I'd like to fathom out what little game he was playing."

"Well," responded Ian, "go over the facts again and we'll see what sort of picture emerges. Where did he meet Derek I wonder?"

Maurice paused to light his pipe, and when it was well under way, spoke slowly:

"Now that's a good idea. Okay. Chip in with anything you think I've forgotten."

He leant forward in the chair.

"Our tale begins with this young, intelligent lad who knows he's illegitimate, brought up by a couple who were alien to him. He was the proverbial fish out of water. At sixteen he finds his real mother's name. Leaves home, wherever that might be, and tracks down Mary Caton. Starts on a spot of blackmail. Mary Caton dies. End of money. Ten years pass. Dunsett is now twenty-eight or thereabouts. By all accounts he can be charming, especially to women. Is certainly amoral. Somehow I get a picture of him being drawn back, again and again, to this village. Here he almost pulled off his first big crooked deal. Then, one day, he happens to learn that Maples is about to be let. Takes the opportunity to have a good look around. Your family move in. Perhaps on the off chance he makes enquiries from the gossips, and learns that Derek had been a naval officer but took early retirement. His suspicious mind is aroused. A bit of digging throws up the fact that your father was none too scrupulous a character. Just up Dunsett's street or so it would appear."

While the pipe was re-lit, Ian interposed.

"He more than likely first struck up conversation with Derek in the local. That's where Derek spent most of his spare time. But I don't understand why he didn't invite Dunsett to the house. All sorts of odd bods used to arrive. Aah…I think I know why. Susan was a terrible flirt."

Maurice registered mild surprise but let Ian continue.

"Oh she was. Most definitely. I realise that, looking back. Anything in trousers was fair game. Probably Derek had Dunsett marked down as a womaniser and wanted to keep the two apart, not wishing to lose his useful hostess.

"Derek still belonged to a couple of naval clubs in London. Often disappeared up there for several days. Recognising they were birds of a feather, perhaps he suggested they meet there. Maybe they cooked up some shady wheeler-dealing together which made both of them a tidy bob or two. Then Derek started drinking heavily and eventually died."

"What did Susan do then?" queried Maurice. "I've forgotten. I know she left Maples. You were at Art College and spent your holidays with me at Mrs Denning's."

"She went up to London and stayed for a time with friends. Possibly Dunsett was drawn to discover the previously unseen Mrs Latimer. I should imagine he would have found it easy to wangle a meeting. It's certainly not difficult to come by all kinds of information if you have a mind to. Anyway they met. Something must have clicked enough for them to open their jewellery business on the continent. Once that was up and running, they opened the second shop in this country."

Maurice took the pipe from his mouth and almost shouted:

"Yes! And Dunsett seemed to make damned sure it was close to Maples for some devious reason I can't fathom. Susan apparently never knew he'd met Derek in the village. He simply introduced himself as an old friend of her husband's, I expect. The rest we know about."

Ian frowned: "What a bloody awful pair to have for parents."

Maurice was silent a few moments, lost in a brown study. He glanced at Ian as if making up his mind on something, then said quietly:

"Ian, listen to me for a minute. Susan and Derek are just two people who joined together and gave you physical life. They could have been anybody, though they must have had certain qualities, certain characteristics that you needed for purposes of your own. But, from what I know of them, they weren't a real father and mother to you. A father is someone who fathers, who cares about your well-being: you could say I was such a person. A mother is someone who mothers: Mrs Denning was such a person. I know I'm considered an outsider in these matters but I really do think a great deal of tribal claptrap is talked about families. I do wonder how many folk actually *like* their families? Or do they spend time with them because they feel it's their clannish duty? One thing I'm quite sure of is that Susan and Derek Latimer have nothing to do with the Ian Latimer sitting here. For one thing it's psychologically known that the ego is renewed every seven years. You're not the same ego they knew, or professed to know! And before you ask me, you and Yvonne *are* a *real* father and mother to Esther because you care about her happiness. I know because I've often watched the three of you together."

Ian had listened keenly while Maurice was talking. He replied in a subdued voice.

"Thank you, Maurice. Thank you very much. You've given me a lot to mull over. I won't forget what you've said."

"Try to remember, Ian, that your past does not have to affect the 'you' here and now unless you allow it. You control your reality – no one else does. And by altering your thinking about the present, you alter your attitude to the past and future. I know it's a lot to take in all at once but changing attitude *can* have a dramatic effect on your life."

★

Two weeks later Maurice walked down the village street with the joyous sensation washing over him of a man reprieved. What a difference imbibing a few words can make to our life, he reflected. He felt like the 'before and after' in an old advert. Half-an-hour ago he had approached Alec Wendell's surgery with a heavy heart. He was there to learn the results of a blood test taken five days previously. At that time the doctor had looked at him with some scepticism.

"Hm! Don't know how you've managed it, Maurice, but you look a damn sight better than you did. I thought you'd be flat on your back by now considering what you've been through lately. What magic elixir have you been drinking? If I didn't know you for a teetotaller I'd have said you'd been taking that 'wee dram' I often prescribe as far and away the best medicine."

Maurice tapped his nose knowingly with his free hand. The other arm was having a large needle inserted and he quickly looked elsewhere. Should he make a feeble attempt at the old Hancock joke? He decided that one had been quoted ad infinitum.

Now, today, he didn't feel one bit like joking. The results had literally just arrived and with a thumping heart he watched Alec Wendell tear open the buff envelope and scan its contents. The doctor's face broke into a broad grin.

"According to this, Maurice, your blood count's almost back to normal. I'm absolutely delighted, old chap."

He jumped up, came round to Maurice and pumped his hand. Then, sitting on a corner of the desk, legs swinging, he benevolently regarded this patient as if personally responsible for the change.

"You know what this means don't you Maurice? It's what we were hoping for – much better in fact. It would appear that the leukaemia has gone into remission – which sometimes happens. I'm the first to admit there's a hell of a lot us quacks don't know," he stated with magnanimity.

Maurice looked at him. He'd always liked this bluff, well-meaning man: today he positively loved him. His artist's eye noted the Celtic colouring of black hair liberally frosted with white strands, dark blue eyes set off by a swarthy skin. It wasn't difficult to picture his stocky build wrapped in bright tartan.

"Any questions you want to ask me?" Alec continued.

"Does this result mean it's unlikely to come back?"

"You know me better than that. I'm not going to commit myself. Let me simply say that in my experience there's an 80-20% chance in your favour."

"I see. Well, I think it's gone for good."

"The more you believe that the better. Carry on with the prescriptions I gave you. You know where to find me if you need anything. By the by, how's Mrs Latimer?"

"I understand she's alright physically," explained Maurice. "But Joanna said she found her extremely withdrawn and depressed on the couple of visits she has made to the remand centre."

"Only to be expected," came the laconic reply. "Sensible girl that Joanna," he went on, "you're lucky to have her at Maples."

Maurice nodded silent agreement, got up to take his leave, then hesitated.

"Alec, I can't remember because I wasn't around much at the time, but did you treat my mother during her last illness?"

Wendell showed no surprise at the question and offered an immediate reply.

"No. She was my father's patient. I wasn't long qualified and naturally the older patients preferred to stay with him, but I knew your mother. Any particular reason for asking?"

"Just curious. I'm trying to fit a puzzle together. Anyway, I won't keep you any longer."

They shook hands, Alec clapped him on the back, and Maurice went down the old fashioned, slightly dusty hall toward the front door. Alec's wife, Helen, was on the phone at a small table that served for the reception area. She smiled and waved a hand to him as he passed. He noticed a large hole in the elbow of her somewhat shapeless cardigan. He hoped the Wendells never changed.

★

On entering his own hall, from upstairs came the sounds of bustle and activity. The students had arrived for the autumn term. Anticipation tingled through his veins at the thought of his art class next morning. He felt fit and able to cope.

Such feelings were a far cry from his trepidation on that day, just over a year ago, when those same students had first arrived at the school. Butterflies had fluttered in his stomach while he had stood on the top step watching the mini-bus draw up. What would these young men and women be like? The little he had read and heard about inner city youngsters had done nothing to assuage his fears. However, within minutes of meeting the teenagers any misgivings had dissolved. Enthusiasm had spilt out of the five boys and three girls – six would-be artists and two musicians. Rough and ready they might be in speech and appearance but this was not reflected in their attitude to their studies. They had known this to be their opportunity of a lifetime.

Joanna had a 'told you so' look about her which he had found faintly irritating. Why couldn't she be a doubting Thomas like anyone else? But the unenviable task of choosing the eight young people had fallen to Martin and Joanna: a task he would have hated. He would have been unable to look into the eyes of those left behind; their disappointment would have been heart-rending. He had grown more emotional with age. Once he wouldn't have cared. Common sense had told him that the house could not accommodate more than eight, but his secret ideal was to keep open house for all waifs and strays.

The attention of educationalists and therapists had been caught by what they regarded as a pilot scheme and the phone crackled with their desire to see for themselves. Martin had wisely restricted the visits to an absolute minimum.

"Little and not very often is the wisest maxim in this case," he suggested to Maurice, "but still you never know who you might need in your corner one day."

The media had proved more of a problem. The team had all agreed the press should be kept well away. Therefore, when Maurice had almost stumbled over a photographer hiding in the shrubbery one morning, he had difficulty keeping his hands from the fellow's throat. Instead he had vented his anger with the aid of a few choice Anglo-Saxon words. A decision was made to accept the offer of an interview with the local paper. It could then sell a sober version of the story to the national dailies, which would soon hopefully switch away to yet another so-called human interest anecdote without further ado.

After arranging this, Maurice had expected either a gangly youth in an ill-fitting suit or a female in short skirt to appear – but he had been proved wrong. The editor, a sensible, articulate, elderly man, had arrived in person. He had admitted sympathy with their aims and the published article was a faithful facsimile of their conversation, which had prompted a warm note of thanks from Maurice. After that, the presses ceased to roll on the Maples story.

★

And today, one year later, the students still sounded satisfied with their mode of life: no obvious protest was discernible from the voices vibrating round the landing. The powers that be were also delighted with the outcome of the experiment.

Maurice moved briskly down the hall toward the office, which in its former life had functioned as a cloakroom for the storage of coats and boots. What had then appeared a good-sized room shrank quickly following its conversion. Packed and chaotic, an overflowing jumble of forms, plus screwed-up bits of paper together with biros that never wrote, added to the air of tight confusion in which all remaining space was filled by a knee-hole desk and swivel chair. Sitting in the midst of muddle, Maurice and Joanna attempted to answer letters from various bodies, fill in grant applications for the local council and so forth. In a flush of optimism Joanna had labelled two office trays In and Out, while Maurice acquired an old manual typewriter.

He now came to an abrupt halt outside the office door and listened, hand poised over the knob. From within came the familiar tap of the typewriter but sounding pleasantly rhythmical, almost musical – the keys caressed instead of hit. He opened the door on a room transformed to apple-pie order. John Dean beamed over the top of the machine at Maurice's surprise.

"John! You old marvel. It all looks – well – different. I had no idea you could type. A man of many parts it would seem. But I don't…?"

"Understand why I did it? You know me – the mad, obsessive musician. No.. it's simply that I hate anywhere in a mess, indoors at least!"

A picture of John's ultra tidy sitting room flashed into Maurice's mind. He understood.

John seemed embarrassed. "To be honest with you, Maurice,

I've been itching to organise this room for ages. I've been slipping in here each day after you'd gone out and doing it bit by bit. The letters and forms are quite straightforward. I don't think I've made any gaffes. I was relieved to find you don't have a computer. I realise they serve a useful purpose, especially where boring, repetitive jobs are concerned, but I've never felt an urge to operate one. The complicated instruction manuals put me off for starters. On glancing through a friend's, I thought a special course would be needed just to understand it."

Maurice grinned in sympathy.

"My sentiments entirely. I can easily do all I need with a typewriter, and I'm in control with no extra machinery to mess with. And those flashing screens are a damned bad strain on the eyes. Everyone needs to work creatively, but in this day and age speed seems to have become more important than craftsmanship. I suppose we'll have to put up with being called old fuddy-duddies."

John drew in his breath. "Amen to that," he nodded ruefully.

"Well anyway, thanks a lot old chap," continued Maurice. "This is an enormous help. The paper-work was starting to pile up."

His friend looked down at his hands with a self-deprecating smile, his face quite pink. He carefully placed the cover on the typewriter and asked:

"How'd it go at the doc's? I must say you're looking more relaxed than I remember for many a long day."

"Let's say for the moment that I've had excellent news. I'll tell you about it later. We'd better go and see how the youngsters are settling in."

"Before we disappear Maurice, d'you mind if I return home to sleep from now on? I don't think I'm needed full-time anymore, and I must have a blitz in the garden before it gets completely out of control."

"Strewth. What have I been thinking of?" Maurice felt guilty. "I've been selfish. The trouble is you're too kind, John, and folk take advantage of your good nature. Of course it's okay. You don't have to ask me for heaven's sake! You're such a good friend to us all."

"Thank you kind sir for those flattering words. I'll be back tomorrow to see my two students. I've worked out an exciting programme – at least I think it's exciting. They're both ready to advance, especially Megan. She shows real promise. Oh – I nearly forgot. That policeman rang. What's his name..? Ford. A sensitive fellow if I'm not mistaken."

"You're not mistaken," murmured Maurice.

"Said to tell you," went on John, "that he'd be calling by sometime tomorrow morning."

CHAPTER NINE

Absorbing this information, Maurice knew it would be difficult to meet Chris Ford again until one or two puzzles and conundrums were straight in his own mind. He decided that some time alone was in order.

A good-natured, boisterous lunch had been hungrily eaten by all the young people tightly squashed together around the large patio table. Christine Pope had surpassed herself producing lamb risotto, mixed green salad and hot crusty bread, followed by a lemon meringue pie, with the meringue piled so high and fluffy that a puff of wind would have blown it away. Chatter ceased while full attention was paid to this delight. Then, with coffee served and cigarettes lit, more noisy banter broke out. Within reason anything was allowed on the first day of term and, to give the students their due, they never overstepped the mark. There were no hard and fast rules; they were a self-regulating body. One law however was sacrosanct: respect for privacy. The summerhouse was never encroached upon, this being Maurice's domain. Leaving the group to clear the dishes, he slipped away unnoticed.

The September sun still had strength, enough to make the summerhouse unbearably stuffy. He phewed for breath in struggling to undo a rusty window. Why did no one ever remember to leave it open? He grumbled, conveniently overlooking the fact that only he visited the den. A slight breeze rustled the fading roses, their scent sweetening the air.

He glanced round the small wooden room. His mother used to sit alone here in the dusk, a book lying unopened on her lap. As a small boy he would crouch behind a bush, watching, not daring to interrupt her solitude. Any affinity existing between them was superficial. They were strangers. But now, a quarter of a century after her death, he felt an understanding. His age at this moment almost equalled hers when she died.

Tears filled his eyes at the thought of the two lovers, Mary Caton and Alex the taciturn gardener, meeting here. He was certain they had kept their tryst in this place. He tried to see Alex waiting for that lover each evening, the den being hidden from the house. Had his father suspected? Maybe he had, but preferred to turn a blind eye. Often a woman in love is a soft, gentle creature, and Father could bask in some reflected warmth. The lovers' relationship would have been doomed from the start. The social mores of the village were strictly class structured at that time. Possibly today it would have stood a slim chance, who knows? And of course, down through history unusual liaisons had survived. Perhaps Mary hadn't been brave enough to defy convention: a question to languish unanswered?

Now, with a suddenness which surprised him, an incident from boyhood, subliminally long buried, rose to the surface. He must have been about seven years old at the time but its events were still crystal clear, like a series of moving pictures. His prize possession then was a two wheeler bicycle, a Christmas present from his father. He loved it. One morning, pedalling furiously along an outer path of the gardens, he had hit a tree root and been tipped off. He was unhurt but the treasured cycle had a buckled mudguard. Close to tears, he limped it back to where he knew Alec was working in the vegetable plot.

"Come on boy, don't take on. We can soon put that straight," was the man's only comment. Bending down, he swung the bike up in his arms with ease, and carried it round to the garage.

The young Maurice had trailed miserably behind, convinced the end of the world had come. Alex collected his tool kit and, true to his word, soon repaired the damage. The man was wheeling the cycle round the cobbled courtyard to test it when Maurice had noticed his mother approaching. His heart had dropped. She would be infuriated by his carelessness, but she had seemed unaware of him. Her eyes were on Alex.

Looking up at both their faces, Maurice had been aware of a softness flowing between them. His mother seemed to shine. She had put a hand over Alex's, still holding the bicycle, and stroked his fingers. Alex's other hand moved to cover hers. His mother had leant closer until their shoulders were touching. Maurice remembered feeling puzzled because she had never looked at, or touched, either his father or himself with such gentleness. Over forty-five years later he recognised the emotion to be love. Mary and Alex had loved each other: of that he was convinced. Theirs had been a true love affair. Not lust springing from boredom and curiosity, but the love that can flower between a man and a woman. Somehow it seemed inevitable that a child should be conceived from this union.

He had never loved any woman with intensity. Faint memories stirred of the girl he had almost married, acknowledging how pallid had been his feelings. He liked women, liked their company, felt affection for two or three, but preferred to keep it that way. Nevertheless, he twinged with envy that he had never been in love.

He caught too a glimpse of the grief Mary must have endured in deciding to relinquish her baby. Her lover's child would have mattered to her – it was all she had left of him. Such insight into his mother's complex character unravelled much that had bewildered and hurt him when a boy. It explained her increasing distaste for him – her husband's offspring – a distaste she finally made no attempt to conceal. How she must have ached for Alexander to replace him.

After her death the solicitor, Hartley Staples, had handed over all Mary's private papers. Legal matters bored Maurice, and caught up in his own concerns he had initially put them away in his desk. But one rainy afternoon he had become inquisitive and idly flicked through the bundle. The discovery of two large cash withdrawals from her account not long before her death had intrigued him because his mother was a niggard with money. Using this recall now, with the reason for her behaviour already known, he was able to enter her lonely, friendless world with compassion. The revelation of Alexander's vicious, greedy character alias 'Keith Dunsett' must have acted like a crushing blow to her. She would have turned from him in disgust, vaunting high morality. Her death warrant had been signed by that young man about whom she had doubtless woven fragile day dreams.

A sharp, cool breeze caused him to shiver. For a moment he thought he saw her staring at him, almost pleadingly. She seemed tiny. He inclined himself toward her in the birth of forgiveness from understanding. All doubts gone, he knew what he would say to Christopher Ford next morning. In buoyant mood Maurice returned to the house.

★

"I'll have to credit you Maurice," allowed D.I.Ford, "with knowing full well that what you're suggesting I would consider foolhardy. I know you're not stupid and I don't really want to stop you. However, I do think it's unwise."

Ford sounded oddly agitated, his normal cool professionalism appearing to have deserted him. His lanky frame paced the sitting room carpet, one hand in his pocket while the other continually rubbed across his moustache.

Sergeant Anderson's small, pale blue eyes followed those movements implacably meanwhile. He was seated beside a round lamp table, pen held over his notebook. Ford gave a slight impatient shake of the head in his direction, so the sergeant shut the book, crossed his feet at the ankles, and watched and waited. 'The guv's getting involved in this one,' thought he. 'Wonder why?' He glanced round at the comfortable surroundings. 'Nice house – untidy but tasteful. Unusual people. Very artistic.'

Since Maurice was seated beside Joanna on the sofa, eyes on Ford, it gave the sergeant an opportunity to discreetly observe him, with enough perception to recognise that here was someone out of the ordinary. There was a self-containment about him, his face wearing an atypically stubborn expression, a face deeply lined round the mouth and eyes, slim hands with long fingers, thick curly hair turning grey, lived-in clothes worn with unconscious style. Withal he saw that this man bore a similarity to the 'guv'nor' which he couldn't quite identify. Physically the two were different types, but a certain quality in both made them appear alike. Of course the guv' was interested in art and this chap Caton was an artist – well known by all accounts, although he hadn't heard of him. He also knew Ford had been lonely since his divorce, with nothing much in his life outside work. Caton and the boss would be compatible, could be friends, and Ford was always loyally concerned towards the few people he counted as friends. That would explain the guv's disquiet – he didn't want Maurice Caton to get his fingers burnt.

Satisfied with this conclusion, Anderson folded his hands across his ample stomach, settled more comfortably on the hard back chair and listened, knowing his opinion would be sought and considered afterwards.

"Look," Maurice was protesting, "I know what I'm doing. Dunsett is out of intensive care and in a side ward, which doubtless you'll have learnt from your constable at his bedside. What I'm simply asking of you, Inspector, is to find out if Dunsett will see me. Don't you understand?" His voice grew louder. "I must confront him face to face. I'm pretty damned sure he's curious about me too. I know enough of human nature to say that."

Ford turned his attention to Joanna.

"Miss Latimer.. Joanna. What d'you think of this idea?"

Joanna uncrossed her legs, smoothing her skirt, and looked up at him.

"Personally, Inspector, I think it's a good one. You could say I've a vested interest with my mother closely involved, but I can understand Maurice's reasons. And who knows? Dunsett might open up to him."

"Not that one, Miss Latimer," interrupted Harry Anderson. "He's crafty. We've been after him for quite some time."

Three pairs of eyes looked at the new entrant. Always unobtrusive, it was easy to overlook his presence in a room; but he was now fixed upon, so he qualified his remark:

"Dunsett will play Mr Caton like a fish on the end of a line."

At this, the "fish" sounded irritable.

"I realise that, Sergeant. I do have some intelligence and can work out a few things for myself."

Maurice was tired. He'd had another restless night and was in no mood to brook interference. He knew the police could veto his suggestion, but after that lone sojourn in the summerhouse yesterday he had made up his mind to talk to Dunsett. It had become important: he needed it as much for his own peace of mind as anything else. He squeezed sore eyes tightly together, trying to rid them of the unpleasant sensation that tiredness caused. He must hold his temper if he was to achieve his objective. He began again:

"What harm can it do? He might well be abusive – probably will. But I can handle that."

He felt the opposition weakening and pressed on:

"Look.. put yourself in my shoes. And in Jo and Ian's shoes come to that. This chap Dunsett has suddenly become involved in all our lives. Right out of the blue I find I've a half-brother who's a petty crook, and if that's not enough, this half-brother is shot by the twins' mother. As a result she will probably be standing trial for attempted manslaughter. Jo and Ian are my best friends. I want to do all I can to help them. Surely anyone would feel the same in my position? I merely want to talk to Dunsett. In a funny way I feel I owe him something. After all, he was the son my mother put to one side. He might have turned out very differently if our roles had been reversed. I've never experienced this clannish family feeling that most people claim to have in their lives. I just want to accept him, if I can, as a fellow human being."

He stopped, feeling exhausted. He knew he had some way to go before the leukaemia finally left his body, and had been trying to pace himself. These efforts were not helping matters.

Chris Ford sat down in one of the fireside armchairs.

Hands on knees, he leaned forward and grinned.

"You win. We'll have a word with Dunsett on your behalf."

"Thank you," acknowledged Maurice. He liked this man; there was an innate honesty about him. However, the reason for his visit today was still obscure.

"I'm sorry, Inspector," he said. "I've been rattling on when you obviously wanted to see us about something else."

"Yes," agreed Ford. "We had a call yesterday from our colleagues in the next county to inform us that they've picked up Dunsett's two accomplices. I gather they're more than ready to squeal, which is why we're on our way over there. And also, since we were almost passing your door on the way, I wanted to let Miss Latimer know personally that Dunsett, true to form, pointed the finger at her mother, who will be charged in the near future with attempted manslaughter."

Joanna grasped Maurice's arm so hard he almost cried out.

"If she's found guilty," asked the girl in an ominous voice, "what sentence is she likely to get? Can you tell me?"

"Your solicitor is the person to advise you on that one," responded Ford. "It depends on many factors – provocation, her state of mind, remorse, her age, etc. It would be quite wrong of me to say anything at this stage. You understand, don't you?"

Joanna nodded forlornly. Ford stood up to take his leave, followed by Anderson. Maurice quickly asked:

"Just before you both disappear, are you *allowed* to tell us anything about Dunsett's partners in crime? Were they a man and woman as first thought?"

Ford glanced across at his sergeant.

"Harry knows more about them than I do. Simply give the bare details please Sergeant."

Anderson flicked through his notebook until he found the appropriate page, then reported:

"You were quite right, Mr Caton. They were a husband and wife team apparently. It was the woman, most likely, who tried to do a patch job on Dunsett."

"Thanks very much, Sergeant." Maurice sounded subdued.

Joanna was seeing the policemen to the door when Ford hesitated, turned, and said:

"Try not to worry. I'll keep in touch."

Maurice recognised this small courtesy with a slow nod, and Jo's return found him staring out of the window. She went over to him, slipping a hand through his arm. "What do you think's going to happen Maurice? I feel all at sixes and sevens. Can't seem to concentrate. Life seems unreal."

Maurice looked down affectionately at her worried face.

"I don't have any easy answers, my dear. I feel as confused as you. We must try to take a day at a time – not leap ahead in our minds. Just get on with what's under our noses, otherwise we'll go slightly potty."

Joanna's expression brightened. "Meanwhile," she determined, "we've a school to run with a hundred and one things to do – like sorting the laundry which I was in the middle of when interrupted. Underwear doesn't wash itself."

"Really! You do surprise me. I always thought it did," quipped Maurice.

Jo giggled at this small release of tension.

"And," went on Maurice. "I'll soon have an art class waiting, full of would-be Picassos and Monets, plus the odd stray Lowry."

The older that one grew, the more complicated life seemed to become. What created this, Maurice pondered? Was it that an acuity of vision developed with age, providing a wider, more bewildering perspective? At times one was presented with such a dazzling array of choices, it was difficult to steer a steady course. And relationships between human beings continually wreaked havoc in the world; in fact, probably had done since homo sapiens first arrived on this planet. He sighed. The world's problems would have to take care of themselves – he had enough of his own to be going on with. But the people in his life were ineffably dear to him. To be without Ian, Joanna, little Esther, Yvonne, John or even Christine Pope would rob him of a blessedness, a richness he couldn't bear to contemplate. And now here he was, journeying by car to meet another person whose life had become entwined with his own. What would Keith Dunsett look like? What attitudes would he hold?

Maurice's thoughts were halted by Jo's pulling up sharply. Applying the hand brake, she looked sideways at his discomfort.

"Sorry to jolt you Maurice. I didn't expect the lights to change so fast."

"That's okay. Must give the foot soldiers a sporting chance."

She smiled. "This takes me back to those days when I used to run you about to visit Ian. D'you remember?"

"I'm not completely gaga."

Ignoring this remark for the green light, she geared the car and trailed off in the wake of an elderly, erratic driver while saying:

"That's when we first really got to know each other. I suspect that before then you'd dismissed me for a flighty teenager with nothing much between the ears."

"Something like that," agreed her companion.

"I remember I was intensely jealous of Ian's friendship with you."

Maurice looked at her in some surprise. "I didn't know that. I thought you were content with your friends, with your mother."

"Well, I wasn't. Everything bored me in those days. My friends were silly little girls always talking about boys, about make-up, things like that. And Mother wasn't much better. She was obsessed with meeting those she described as the 'right people'.. Ugh. I really envied Ian. He'd managed to distance himself from such fripperies and had his serious work. And then I hated myself for being jealous.

"After all, I was the favoured twin. Neither parent cared much for Ian, and I scarcely bothered to look at his paintings. I fully understand his feelings toward Susan at the moment. I'd be the same in his place. Then when he was so badly injured it was a relief to be able to do something useful at long last. It's funny in a way, because if he hadn't been hurt then I would never have got to know you, and through you discover what I really wanted to do with my life. I consider myself very fortunate."

"I rather suspect you would have found out sooner or later," replied Maurice. "Your natural compassion for your fellow man is so strong it would have forced itself up to the surface. It would have found an outlet somehow or the other."

"Well, yes," conceded Jo, "but the marvellous thing for me is that it happened the way it did. I know many folk feel they've wasted a chunk of their life by finding themselves slotted into a wrong situation. I'm jolly thankful for my good fortune. Life has been kind to me. Oh I know Susan is a problem at the moment but I've got things in proportion where she's concerned. She made her bed and must lie on it. It might help her to grow up. I'll do all I can to help but ultimately it's up to her."

Maurice listened to these resolute words with a deepening sense of pride and respect for the speaker. Without fuss or flap she had made the difficult transition from child to woman, and would doubtless meet all life's problems head-on until she had found a solution. But he'd had no inkling of her jealousy of Ian. She had never mentioned it before. Not for the first time he was struck by how little we know about each other – even those closest to us. We only ever see the tip of the iceberg. Had Ian been aware of his sister's angst? Probably not, since Ian liked to seek counsel from him on major issues. This made him a rare man, because most folk tried to hide their emotions under wraps – even from themselves, he mused. We prefer to keep the voyage from birth to death a private one, despite surface camaraderie.

The car slowed. Leaning forward he rubbed at the misted, rain spattered windscreen to produce a blurred view of the hospital car park. They had arrived. Despite all good intentions to the contrary, his heart felt heavy like the rain. He was not looking forward to this visit, which could be an awkward and painful one, draining his meagre physical reserves.

Small hospitals were an improvement on big ones, but they still didn't rate highly on Maurice's list of favourite places. Joanna had offered to accompany him, but he knew this was one meeting he had to face alone – much to her barely disguised relief.

"Ah well, shopping calls," she breezed, and made good her escape.

The ward had a few dressing-gowned men shuffling up and down exchanging somewhat dubious jokes. The young nurse on duty looked at him with incurious eyes, pointing out the door of a side room. He knocked and entered.

At a glance his artist's eye perceived the carefully contrived scene inside, and his lips twitched in amusement. The man lying on top of the regulation hospital blanket, propped against snowy white pillows, was attired in a Noel Coward style dressing gown, complete with matching silk cravat casually knotted at the neck. It was a facile attempt at sartorial elegance – designed to impress.

Drawing closer to the bed he saw the sharp, uncanny resemblance that Dunsett bore to their mother. It was apparent in the slight build, the narrow face with angular, pointed chin, the mousey brown hair worn unfashionably long in his case, the pale skin, small hands and feet. Maurice drew a deep breath.

Fiddling with his necktie, Dunsett spoke first:

"Didn't think you'd be able to stay away for long, old chap. Guessed you'd want to gawp at the black sheep of the family." The voice had flat London vowels which he was making a conscious effort to improve. "Pull up a chair and sit down, there's a good fellow."

An awkwardly hovering policeman offered his seat, retreating with obvious relief to a corner of the room, and there drew a newspaper from his pocket. Maurice made himself comfortable, pushing out his legs. He began to relax, for a reason only he knew. Dunsett's eyes watched him warily.

Those eyes were his most remarkable feature – dark brown, holding a brilliant, almost mesmeric quality in their depths. Undoubtedly he felt disadvantaged in bed. Well, that was understandable: he wasn't used to being in a situation he couldn't dominate. Maurice still said nothing – just looked at his fellow protagonist, who began to fidget in the stretched silence. With a wintry smile, his tone was acerbic:

"Cat got your tongue, Maurice? Nothing to say for yourself?"

Maurice was abruptly jolted from his poise. His mother had used those identical phrases when he had been extra tongue-tied in her company.

Something moved on the blanket. Dunsett's hand was creeping toward him, fingers open like a claw. Instinctively he drew back and Dunsett gave an unpleasant snigger. Maurice felt annoyed. The man had sensed his discomfort and was making childish capital from it, playing at spiders on the bed – the behaviour of an overgrown schoolboy. From that moment Maurice's attitude hardened, reflected in his voice.

"Merely having a good look at you Alexander. After all, you know what I look like don't you? It was you skulking round the summerhouse, flattening your nose against the window one night when I was sleeping in there. Your usual modus operandi I suppose. Your way of taking a little exercise when not writing nasty letters to elderly widows."

Dunsett stared at him with pure venom. This time Maurice was prepared and regarded him coolly. Dunsett's eyes slid away. He attempted a light reply;

"Who's this Alexander? The name's Dunsett, old chap. Keith Dunsett."

"Among many others I've no doubt," fired the retort. "Don't

play silly buggers with me. And let's drop the 'old chap' routine. Both of us know that Alexander was the name given you by our mother. So, if we're to have some sort of sensible dialogue let's cut the cackle, because I don't intend to repeat this visit. You are Alexander Caton, son of Mary Caton and Alex Marks. Your father was a fine man, and from enquiries I've made I'd say it was certain he knew nothing of your existence. He died five years ago. Mother was a difficult woman, but didn't deserve the kind of treatment you dished out. She had a weak heart and getting your letter was most probably the final straw that killed her. On second thoughts I can't think of you as Alexander. Keith Dunsett suits you better. I'll stick with that."

Dunsett's expression never changed. There was no flicker of emotion. He gazed straight ahead.

Maurice cleared his throat.

"However, I can understand you felt cheated…"

This provoked a rude interruption; "You bet your sweet life I felt cheated. You've had it easy all the way, haven't you Maurice? Parents, big house, money, good schools… very cushy. Me? – I was just pushed to one side in case I was a nuisance.. an embarrassment. My presence might have caused tongues to wag in the village. And she didn't want *that* did she now? Well, she was going to pay for her mistake. I had to take any job going whereas you became a well-known artist, owning Maples – which should by rights have been half mine. And now you've even got your fancy piece living with you. She's a damn sight peachier than her scrawny mother."

Dunsett began to thump the bed in frustration. The policeman looked up startled, and then went back to the sport's page. Maurice felt knotted up with anger at the injustice of Dunsett's words. Remembering Sergeant Anderson's warning however, he was determined not to be "played with like a fish on the end of a line". He refused to give Dunsett that satisfaction.

Yet, with sympathy, he fully understood how an emotional woman like Susan Latimer had lost her head when goaded.

Dunsett began to whine: "*Now* look at me. Nearly lost my life because of that stupid bitch. I wasn't really going to hurt her. Just have her frightened a bit. Women will only do as they're told if you frighten them."

Interesting, thought Maurice. Martin had been right in his assessment. After pondering why there had been two cars in the lane on that eventful night, he had concluded that Dunsett hadn't wanted Susan killed, simply intimidated enough to provide a cast iron alibi for the police against those jewel thefts.

So a partner in crime had been hired for the dirty work. Dunsett had no intention of doing the deed himself. Far from it! He was too much of a coward. A rendezvous had been arranged at the remote farm track, but plans had gone awry with Susan's use of her gun. The sight of Dunsett's blood-soaked figure slumped over the steering wheel must have panicked the accomplice. Dunsett's weakened state would have offered an excellent opportunity, however, to extract information. Somehow the man had hauled the inert body into his own car and driven away. Luckily for Dunsett the wife must have seen the extent of his injuries, and the rest was history.

While these thoughts had been racing forward, Dunsett had provided a peevish background. Maurice had caught snatches of such phrases as: "always was badly treated"; "never had any money to call my own"; "didn't have your advantages"; "cheated out of my rights"; etc. Maurice's gorge rose in disgust. This man, who society chose to call his half-brother, was a nasty piece of work and – praise be – nothing to do with him. He didn't adhere to the ridiculous nonsense of 'blood ties'. Suddenly he longed to be gone from the hot, stuffy room. He glanced across at the square window. It had stopped raining and a small patch of eggshell-blue sky could be glimpsed. It looked clean and fresh.

He bent over to pick up a brown leather briefcase from beside his chair. Clicking it open, he took out two items – an A4 sheet of paper and a soft, green suede pouch closed with a drawstring. His companion's eyes darkened when he spied that pouch. He made a lunge, but it was out of reach. He watched in fascination as Maurice slowly loosened its drawstring and poured a trickle of the contents into his cupped palm. The over bright hospital lights caught the glitter of uncut rubies, emeralds and diamonds.

"How the hell did you find them?" Dunsett demanded furiously, dropping the 'man about town' facade.

"It wasn't altogether difficult," enlightened Maurice, replacing the jewels. He rubbed his nose with the back of his hand, beginning to enjoy the situation. "In fact, you disappointed me. I didn't think you'd be quite so overt. It was almost as though you wanted me to find them. I guessed you'd have a twisted satisfaction in hiding them somewhere at Maples. It's fairly easy to come and go without being spotted. They've probably been there for quite some time. But in the summerhouse! Tut-tut! I would have expected somewhere a little more imaginative. What about all those outhouses eh?"

Dunsett pressed his lips together and half closed his eyes as if resigned to fate. He appeared to be barely listening.

"Mind you," Maurice blithely continued. "Must give credit where it's due. You did cover your tracks quite well. It took me all of five minutes to find the disturbed floorboard behind the deck chairs. I liked the imported dust. Nice touch I thought. Bought from a joke shop was it?"

He turned to speak to the policeman.

"Officer, would you come over here a moment please?"

The young man reluctantly folded his newspaper, looked at the two men, then stood up.

"Yes sir. How can I help you?"

"Well, you can begin by taking this into safe keeping."

The briefcase was held out, and the policeman grasped its handle.

"What has this to do with me, sir?" His curiosity began to stir: maybe something was afoot to break the yawning boredom.

"Open it and take a look."

The case was laid on the bed, opened, and the suede pouch removed. Catching the sparkle of its contents, the constable let out a low whistle. He scattered some of the jewels over the blanket in amazement. His glance flicked from Maurice to Dunsett, who turned his head away.

"As soon as you are able, please give the case, with its booty, to D.I.Ford," Maurice requested with a grin.

"Yes, but..?"

"No buts. I'll be able to tell your inspector exactly how they were found and anything else he may want to know."

"Still sir, I have to give you a receipt."

"Okay. Receipt away all you want."

A heavy silence crept into the room, broken only by the policeman's under breath muttering while he struggled to recall correct phrases. Finished at length, he handed the receipt to Maurice who pushed it into his jacket pocket. The gems were gathered up and replaced in the case. Now keenly watching every move, Dunsett began to cross and uncross his ankles with impatience. The officer looked uneasy.

"I won't be much longer," Maurice reassured him.

Heedful, the man returned to his corner of the room and placed the case carefully on the carpet. This time he didn't read his paper but instead watched the tableau at the bedside.

Half a minute passed however, in which both averted their

eyes in silence. At last Maurice picked up the typewritten paper off the bed, glanced swiftly at the words, and put it down again. He felt at an impasse, uncertain how to proceed. From the corner of his eye he noted that Dunsett's demeanour was oddly composed, hands at rest on his bent knees. Maurice sensed a change taking place in the other; a calm, subtle change which he felt was genuine. It was a fragile moment – a crossroads for this unhappy man.

They looked at each other and, for the first time, Dunsett held his gaze. The hint of a smile lessened the hard network of lines around his mouth. While the pregnant pause lengthened, an air of acceptance settled over Dunsett. He gave a brief shrug.

"Okay, Maurice. You win. I admit that."

"No one is a winner here," replied Maurice gently. "Not me. Not you. And certainly not Mother. But I've done what I sensed she wanted, and come to see you."

"And I know that's more than I'd have done, had the roles been reversed."

Dunsett spoke quietly. Maurice had to strain to catch the words. Something intangible hovered delicately in the air between the duo. He responded on impulse:

"Look Dunsett.. Keith.. I'm sorry. I never thought to hear myself saying that, but I am. I know it's your own fault you're in this mess but that doesn't stop me wishing events could have worked out differently.. that perhaps – who knows? – Perhaps we could have got to know each other. I felt I must say that."

Again silence. The muffled sound of a tea trolley being pushed round the outside ward could be heard, with the accompanying clink-clatter of cups and spoons. Small beads of sweat were visible on Dunsett's upper lip. He gave a slight sigh and began to talk:

"I.. I thank you for those words, Maurice. I'm not such a complete bastard" – he gave a small grin at the use of the phrase – "that I can't recognise sincerity when I hear it. Yes – you were right when you said I wanted you to find the gems. I didn't realise it at the time, but I do now. Of course I could have found a safer hiding place if I'd really wanted to. Truth is, I wanted to finish the whole sordid business – my awful way of life I mean – but still couldn't stop myself from arranging that business with Susan Latimer. It was blind panic – I was terrified at the thought of prison again. In the same way that I couldn't stop myself behaving to you the way I did when you came in the room. Pathetic isn't it? A devil drives me on, mocking me, saying do this – do that. In a way I wish Susan had finished me off. I've often thought of killing myself but never had the bottle. I'm only too aware of my many shortcomings. I've a filthy, resentful temper. I'm a shit but not all bad. It sounds corny but I've had a lot of time to think, lying here in bed. I'll go to prison for two, maybe three years – I've a bad record. Perhaps I'll be able to get some help. Then I can start again with a clean slate. This time I'm really going to have a try. I've promised myself that much."

Fatigue overtook him, shaking his body. To prevent tears spilling he bit hard into his lower lip.

Maurice could also recognise sincerity when spoken. He had no idea whether Keith's resolve would be strong enough to keep his promise but knew he wanted to help. Cautious by nature however, he didn't answer immediately. He had no wish to rush headlong into something he might later come to regret. On the other hand, those students at Maples could well have ended up like Keith if they had not been given their chance. He rubbed his chin thoughtfully. A decision reached, he picked up the typewritten sheet again, folded it with care and put it in his breast pocket.

Tapping the pocket, there was a smile in his voice when he spoke:

"I'd gone all professional and had my solicitor draw up an agreement for you to sign. But that's not my usual way of doing things. Never has been."

Keith raised his eyebrows in enquiry, naturally curious about the document.

Maurice told him: "It was merely getting you to promise to keep away from Maples. I'd some idea that the court would have been more lenient with you if you'd signed. But I no longer feel such things are necessary between us. I must be completely honest and say that I don't want to visit you in prison. The emotional turnabout is too soon for that. However, I would like you to come to Maples and see me, see us, when you get out. Then we can figure out where to go from there – all right?"

Keith opened his mouth but no words came. He simply nodded.

"Meanwhile," carried on Maurice, "I'm going to make you an allowance of one thousand pounds a year. I think Mother would have wished me to do that. It's not much I know but it'll give you a little money of your own."

He looked at his watch.

"Time I was off. You must be tired. I know I am. Remember what I said. I meant every word."

Touching Keith's arm briefly, he turned away without looking at him.

On the way out he asked the constable how soon he should give a statement about the stolen gems.

"No later than tomorrow morning, please sir. They'll be expecting you at the station by then."

"I'll be there, officer."

In the corridor, waiting for the lift to arrive, Maurice sat on a chair thoughtfully provided. His head felt hollow, with every noise magnified; if he closed his eyes he would float off into space. At last he regained himself enough to step outside the main doors of the hospital, blinking in the strong sunlight. He wended his way in search of Joanna and found her leaning back against their car, hands in her trouser pockets, face tipped up to the sun. She straightened up on his approach, took one look at her friend and said:

"Home?"

"Please," he affirmed.

Keith Dunsett lay back against the soft pillows. He was tired, truly tired. He closed his eyes. Behind the lids he could still see Maurice's face and welcomed the burgeoning seed of hope it gave.

A pain killing injection the nurse had given was having the desired effect and his limbs became heavy and relaxed. His mind felt muzzy and his thoughts began to wander. He remembered once again a time, many years ago, when he had found himself in a strange town on Christmas Eve, and how he had stood at the back of a church and listened in awe to a boy's clear treble voice reaching the roof with the words of a well-known carol. Despite himself its beauty had touched him. Of course, ten minutes later had found him laughing and drinking in a nearby pub, but the memory remained with him thereafter. He would wake some nights, arm thrown across a frowsy girl, and moving away from her in distaste, would turn on his side recapturing the nostalgia.

Now he found himself thinking about his foster parents – a kindly, well-meaning couple, their terraced house too small to contain the difficult, ambitious boy. He looked down the years at Dad setting off in the early morning to begin his postman's round. Local folk had liked his father, had warmed to his caring nature, laughed at his trite jokes. And Mum, pride shining out of her plain face that her Keith had won a scholarship to the local grammar school, anxiously trying to get him there on time. He shuddered when he recalled how he had thrown their love back at them. He had despised their smallness, left home, and never saw them again.

Exhausted by emotion and drugs he fell asleep.

CHAPTER TEN

'Christmas at Maples symbolises all I love best about the house,' thought Esther. And this year, to add to the magic, it had even snowed. She trudged up the drive, Wellington boots crunching on a crisp white covering. How snow transformed the landscape, bare branches looking thick and puffy under their unaccustomed weight. In places the bark showed through, creating a chequered effect, and everywhere bird tracks ran in all directions.

Making a mental note to scatter extra breadcrumbs, she rounded the corner close to the house. Here the wind tugged her, whipping the fine snow into drifts. She hurried up the steps, wriggled out of her boots, and opened the front door.

Familiar though the house was, she still drew comfort from it every time she entered. Today it was particularly warm and welcoming. She quickly hung her duffle coat, shook her fair hair into place, and looked around with pleasure. Wall lights were switched on, and the glow from their deep pink shades was reflected in a highly polished brass jug which stood on the hall table, over-spilling with dark green holly sprigs, red berries abundant among their stems. The grandfather clock was decorated with an ivy head-dress, long trails hanging down on either side of its face. The banisters of the curving staircase were entwined with gold and silver garlands. The air was filled with spicy, aromatic scents which wafted from the kitchen. Beyond its partly closed door, Christine Pope's country voice rose and fell merrily.

Then the door opened wide, and a man came into the hall, carrying a sagging wicker basket loaded with logs. Puffing slightly under the weight, he gave the girl a shy glance.

"Oh.. hello Esther. Has it stopped snowing yet?"

"No. If anything it's increasing."

"Er.. did you see anybody on your way up here? Anyone at all?"

"Good Lord, no. There was absolutely no one about. Oh, but doesn't everywhere look pretty?"

The man seemed at a loss to know how to respond to the cheery question, his eyes refusing to meet hers. To fill the clumsy silence she chattered:

"Well, I'm off to pinch one of Christine's mince pies. See you later, Keith."

He nodded and humped the logs into the sitting room.

Christine's round, apple-dumpling of a face creased in a warm smile when she saw Esther. While watching her favourite girl grow up, Christine had long woven a fantasy that she was her own daughter – the one she had ached for but never had. Each time she had shopped in the local market town she had glanced at little girls' fancy clothes, imagining dressing the child in frills and flounces. Such adornments would not have suited Esther. Her placid, down-to-earth personality was better emphasised in the simple clothes Yvonne wisely chose. This afternoon she wore faded jeans, with a blue polo neck sweater exactly matching her eyes, her only jewellery being a gold cross and chain. At that difficult age of fifteen she still possessed a biddable nature, only displaying on occasion the stubborn streak reminiscent of her father.

"Hi Christine. I'm on the scrounge for one of your mince pies – or perhaps even two if you can spare them?"

"Why yes, m'dear. You 'ave as many as yer want. D'yer want a cup o'tay wiv 'em? You mus' keep warm this weather," fussed Christine, ignoring the fact that the Aga was almost red hot.

"No thanks. I'd much rather have a coke. Snow's jolly thick. You won't be able to get your bike through to get home."

"Ah no, me son's coming ter fetch me, dear, 'e brought me this marning. Mind you, 'e drives like some blinking fancy racing driver. I'd be safer on foot. Since he passed that test there's no bloomin' 'oldin' 'im."

Having suffered a recent hair-raising drive beside the young man in question, Esther shared a laugh with her friend. This open countrywoman had figured large in the girl's life and she knew it was mutual. Esther was that rare human being who attracted love and friendship with consummate ease: 'To know her is to love her,' paraphrased one of her friends without envy.

"That Keith's bin in 'ere trying to get me to talk," sniffed Christine. "It's no use. I jus' can't warm to 'im. I can't forget all that's 'appened. I jus' can't. It's more than flesh and blood culd stan'. And tha's a fact!"

Esther withheld mention that she had overheard Christine chattering earlier with the man in question. She knew that Christine had a conveniently short memory when it suited.

"I know.. I know, Chris," she soothed. "But my guess is that he's lonely. And after all he's paid his debt to society. Three years in prison is a long time. Gosh! I couldn't bear to be shut up like that." She shivered. "Not to be able to go for walks in the countryside. Never to see green fields and woods and spring flowers. All the lovely things."

"Ah there m'dear. Oi'm that sorry to 'ave upset you. One week to Christmas and oi'm going on like some moaning minny. 'Ow's your present-buying getting on?"

"Really well," mumbled Esther through a mouthful of her second mince pie, trying to surreptitiously brush away the crumbs. She had a sweet tooth. "I managed to find that clip-on bow tie for Dad I told you about – the pale green one. You remember?"

"'Course I do," came the stout rejoinder. "You always 'ave such wunnerful ideas. Oi can never think of anythin' different."

Esther's reputation in the present-giving stakes had risen from when, at the age of eight, she had bought her mother a pineapple.

"A pineapple! Fancy that," an admiring Christine had told her husband, whose long experience of his wife's prattle enabled him to nod and rustle his newspaper in the appropriate places. Christine lacked imagination and only thought in terms of soap, diaries and socks. 'Useful', she called them, while his secret hankering was for a box of the best Cuban cigars. Closeted in his greenhouse, smoking a cheap cigarillo, he would fancy he caught a whiff of fine Havana tobacco. It stayed a dream.

Above the sound of the kettle whistling in Maples' kitchen, scratches could be heard from outside the back door. Esther jumped up.

"That's Sophie! I thought she was with Maurice."

As the door was flung wide, in bounded a medium size brown and white dog, shaking her fur vigorously over the quarry tiles. With whimpers of delight she jumped up at the girl who hugged her warmly.

"Look at you. You're soaked through. You've been rolling in the snow, you cheeky monkey. Stand still a minute and let's get you dry."

The dog's soft eyes shone with appeal at the beloved voice. Esther found an old towel and began to rub her dry, the dog meanwhile trying to lick her face and causing her to dissolve in laughter.

"Oh dear," fretted a guilty Christine, "she went out when

Keith fetched them logs. Then what wiv one thing and another 'oi forgot she was still in the garden. Is she all right?"

"Yes, don't worry," Esther reassured. "She's been having a good time. She'd have soon been back if she wasn't. Dogs aren't daft."

For Esther, Sophie was the icing on the cake at Maples. It was impossible to keep any pets in the small flat above the Latimer Gallery – either a cat or a dog. Much as she had longed for both she understood. Then, one day, Joanna had rung and told of a surprise waiting at the house. Hardly daring to hope, Esther had hurried over on the bus and run up the drive – to be greeted by a Heinz 57 tornado, barking with mad excitement, rushing through the house slipping rugs in every direction and eating voraciously.

Jo had read an article in the local paper about an animal rescue centre which had opened in a nearby village. For some while she had been thinking that Maples had the ideal house and garden to give an unwanted dog a loving home. After making sure that everyone in the house was in total agreement, she drove over to investigate.

"I won't necessarily be choosing a dog today," a grinning Martin was airily informed. "I'm simply having a look."

"Oh quite," he assented, not believing her for a moment. He was leaning in the open window of the car and gave her a warm kiss.

Sure enough – one look at Sophie's eager, trusting face and Jo's heart was lost. The dog in return couldn't believe she had so many new friends. She blossomed: her sparse, thin coat growing thick and fluffy.

Now she was snoring in her bed which was pulled close to the Aga, fur gently steaming in the warmth, paw over a biscuit bone. Esther put her feet up on the range, helped herself to a couple of chocolate biscuits, and settled down to hear Christine's gossip.

★

Upstairs in his room Keith lay on the bed, arms clenched tight at his side, trying to calm his shaking nerves. A staccato gust of wind, blowing the ever thickening snow against the window, made him jump. Wearily he swung his legs over to the floor and stumbled across to close the heavy blue velvet curtains. Switching on two table lamps he looked around, appreciating all he saw. Solid comfort was apparent in the good oak furniture, the slightly faded but quality Wilton carpet, the easy chair, and the two silver backed hairbrushes lying on the dressing table; a couple of Maurice's own water colours completed the scene. It was all a far cry from his dingy bed-sit in a rundown area of Pimlico.

He sighed, reached for a cigarette, and fiddled with the dial of his radio until he found a jazz programme. Pacing the floor, he thought long and hard about his current position. If only he could feel more at ease during these sporadic visits to Maples: heaven knew he wanted to enjoy himself. Many days of his wasted youth had been spent prowling outside the house and grounds, simmering with impotent rage at the considered denial of his birth right, resenting Maurice, hating Mary Caton. The anger had long ago dissolved and he was finally here, so why did he continue to feel a fish out of water? Most of the fault probably lay at his door, but part of the trouble was in not having a niche within the household. In trying to create one by cutting the grass, lighting the fire, walking the dog etc., he only ended up feeling demeaned.

To be fair, from the day of his first visit nearly everyone had been pretty decent to him. He recalled how nervous he had been, afraid of putting a foot wrong. True, Ian and Joanna had been cold and distant, but considering his past treatment of their mother who could blame them? Oddly enough, Susan's sudden death from a heart attack a couple of years ago had improved matters. Her health, already poor, had never recovered from the shock of spending eighteen months in prison, albeit an open one with a fairly relaxed regime.

But her death meant that her shadow no longer hung over Maples. In particular, Ian's attitude had noticeably softened toward him. Keith had long suspected that this younger man had disliked Susan, and was now freed from many years of smouldering bitterness. Christine Pope climbed 'on her high horse' occasionally and tried to put him in his place, but a touch of earthy humour would usually win her round. The child, Esther, was a good kid; John Dean was a kind old boy; Martin Hurst treated him fairly; Christopher Ford was straight with him. Therefore, the responsibility to fit in remained in his court. He must make more effort if only for Maurice's sake.

Maurice: for a while he had endowed that man with almost saint-like qualities. Then closer acquaintance revealed a good man but a very human one, battling to cope with his highs and lows just like everyone else. During each successive visit Keith had learned more about the character of his benefactor. Gradually the story unfolded of Maurice's struggles with lack of self-worth, with poor health, but most of all with Mary Caton and her cold, harsh treatment of the sensitive boy who had tried to understand her. Keith was jolted when he realised how much happier his own childhood had been; indeed, it would have been even better if he had accepted his parents as the kindly couple they undoubtedly were. They had showered him with love which he now acknowledged was more important than material goods: talking to John Dean had opened his eyes to this fact. Since his release from prison seven years ago he had renewed contact with his foster mother. Now a widow, she still lived in the small, terraced house he had once considered beneath him. Shy, awkward, tentative advances were made at first, but then came increasing warmth from both sides. They met two or three times a year.

The background music suddenly changed tempo and began to irritate. He flicked off the switch, and sat down heavily in the chair, hands clasped between his knees. The plain truth, staring him in the face, was boredom. He was bored with country life. At heart a town person, a Londoner, he felt perfect relief when the time came for his departure home. He loved city life. Despite its shabbiness he relished the hustle and bustle, the crowded streets, the noise, the pubs, the traffic, and above all the shops. His forte did not lie in the realms of long walks, reading, or listening to classical music. He enjoyed recording old westerns, but Maples did not possess gadgets; in fact television was rarely watched, except maybe the odd documentary or wild life programme. He now knew with certainty that this visit would be his final one to the house. There was no blame attached to either side. The two different modes of living simply did not mix.

This Christmas then was to be his only one at Maples. Maybe, in retrospect, it had been unwise to accept Maurice's well-meant invitation; but he did have his own urgent reasons. Left to his own devices he would not have bothered to celebrate: Christmas dinner would have been an instant meal on a tray, eaten while watching television, followed by an alcoholic doze. He could have accepted his mother's offer, but this was also extended to include her sour-faced elderly neighbour with whom his only common ground was mutual dislike. Therefore, private reasons apart, the lure of a country Christmas with all the trimmings was irresistible, although the prospect of bon viveur and bonhomie was unnerving.

Late last night, with the household asleep, he had slipped downstairs and added his few paltry presents to the growing pile under the decorated tree, convinced he had chosen the wrong gifts. The holiday stretched endlessly before him, the advent of snow making it impossible to reach the pub. And he did need to get there: it was vitally important. But the house, situated in a dip in the valley, would soon be cut off from the village and no snow plough would bother to clear such an isolated spot.

It had been during his last visit to Maples in late summer that he had fallen into the habit of wandering up to the Globe Inn some evenings, glad of its welcoming atmosphere. He deliberately never went near the village during the day in case he should be recognised from his sleazy past with Derek Latimer. He knew this to be highly unlikely since age had altered him, yet he was anxious not to run any risk. He felt it would let Maurice down. Although Keith was far from a completely reformed character, he was nevertheless learning the rudiments of decent behaviour. However, the Globe had changed hands in recent times and he felt safe there. Careful to restrict his drinking to a couple of pints of beer, he never stayed long; sitting apart from the regulars on a bar stool held little appeal. Once a gregarious fellow, ever eager to buy a round often for complete strangers, he had now become a loner.

But the hot, sultry weather of that August had made him a more frequent customer. After taking Sophie for a shady evening stroll it had been pleasant to sit outside the inn sipping an iced lager, the dog content to share a packet of crisps. Then one warm night came the man. Keith had been seated at his usual table, idly watching a pretty girl teasing her boy-friend, Sophie flopped at his feet, when his attention had been caught by a man pulling out a chair at a nearby table. His profile was horribly familiar. He turned his head slightly toward Keith, lit a cigarette, and lifted his glass. Those three simple movements flicked open a window of memory for Keith. He had been in prison with this man. They had not shared a cell, but enforced close proximity acquainted you with everybody's small habits and gestures. Painfully aware of the other's reputation, Keith realised that no mere chance had brought this unpleasant character to the quiet village. But what did he want? What was going on in that devious mind? There would have to be a reason; an amoral reason. Despite the heat, Keith shivered.

The man drained his glass, banged it down on the table, stubbed out his cigarette under his foot, stretched, yawned and stood up. For one tantalising moment Keith thought he was coming over, but without a glance in his direction he sauntered off to the car park; even his walk had remained the same. Seconds later he was backing a new Jaguar out on the road, revved noisily and was gone.

Sheer curiosity returned Keith to the pub the next evening, but of the other there was no sign; nor on the following day. The episode, small enough in itself, tensed his nerves. It represented menace, accompanied by a heavy sense of foreboding. It reminded him of a way of life he was struggling to leave behind. Eventually, after his homecoming to London, the incident slowly faded until it was finally gone.

Then one cold November morning the letter arrived. He had a paucity of mail except for bills, so letters aroused a small-boy excitement. Hearing post drop on the mat, he came out from his tiny kitchen, tea mug in hand, a shabby old fawn dressing gown hanging loose over his pyjamas, and stooped to pick up three envelopes. The two obvious final demands he stuffed in his pocket, but the third, being hand written, intrigued. He slowly turned it over trying to decipher the postmark, then roughly tore it open. Pulling out a single sheet of cheap, lined notepaper, he skimmed the contents. His heart started to thump. He felt giddy. Moving back to the comparative warmth of the kitchen, he sank abruptly on the kitchen stool and read it again. There was no address or signature, being brief and to the point. It stated baldly: "I shall know when you are next staying at the big house. Make sure you visit that pub. By the way, that young girl's still pretty for the moment."

The message was crude but effective, more frightening in what it did not say, than in what it did. He stared at the cracked lino, a maze of unanswered questions running through his mind. What the hell did this man want? Whatever the outcome he was determined to handle it alone. This time Maurice was not going to be involved in his troubles. Still, there was nothing he could do about it now; nothing until contact was made again. One lesson Keith had learnt in prison was patience. Everything came to an end eventually.

Christmas Day was peacefully unfolding at Maples, each person there enjoying it in their own peculiar way. Maurice quietly relished the warmth generated within the old house. It was a home, tailor-made for gatherings built round the spirit of friendship. He regarded with pleasure the group relaxed close to the sparky fire, replete from the rich Yuletide lunch. Although it was only mid-afternoon, dusk was already pressing against the windows, but by silent consent no one wished the lamps switched on or the curtains drawn. The spiralling flames and Christmas tree lights worked a special magic, hinting at the promise of dreams soon to be fulfilled.

Ian was seated on a sofa, legs stretched out to the fire, his arm casually lying across Yvonne's shoulders, his restless energy stilled for once. His wife, features serene as ever, curled a stray lock of blonde hair behind one ear while bending forward to look at her daughter, her rope necklace of glass beads reflecting the firelight. Esther herself was seated on the floor, her head leant back in contentment against her father's knees. Mother and daughter exchanged a smile.

Joanna was in her favourite armchair, from whose depths many years before she had first outlined her 'great project' for Maples. She looked elegant as ever, despite a rounded shape announcing pregnancy, wearing a dark green, loose-fitting dress, its white lace collar a sharp contrast with her brown hair. Not for her the modern maternity trend of slouching in a pair of striped dungarees. Comfortingly perched on the wide arm of her chair was the familiar calm presence of Martin, cheerfully turning over in his mind names to fit this longed for baby. After two disappointments both of them were only too aware that time was slipping by, and they could not believe their good fortune that this pregnancy was advancing, to use Alec Wendell's colloquial expression – 'bloomingly!' Neither wished to be told the sex of the infant before the event – that would spoil anticipation, so favourite names were being short listed. Although Jo was a twin, she had been reliably informed that only one baby would emerge. According to Alec, twins often skipped a generation; both parents-to-be at heart thus secretly relieved.

Quiescent in another comfortable chair stretched the lanky frame of Christopher Ford, the fingertips of his bony hands pressed together in familiar pose. Reflective in mood, he considered his decision to take early retirement from the force a year ago, on a chief inspector's pension, the wisest choice of his life.

Two factors had strongly influenced his judgement. When Harry Anderson's well deserved, and in Ford's eyes, long overdue promotion to Inspector finally arrived, the rotund former sergeant was offered that post in a small Lake District town, close to the beautiful Derwent Water. This prospect delighted Harry and his wife: to be given the chance to live and work in countryside already explored on caravanning holidays had a golden touch. Ford and Anderson had been a team for a long time, and Ford knew he did not want to start 'breaking-in' a new man.

It was an emotional moment when the two men parted. The usual trite phrases were uttered: "Give us a tinkle sometime…" "Keep in touch, old chap…" "Don't forget to look us up if you're ever in the area…" But when they finally shook hands and looked hard at one another, each knew they would not meet again. Both were sensitive enough to know that a relationship could not be resurrected once the thread was broken, for whatever reason. By way of compensation, fond memories would remain with them, and any new friends would benefit from a stored bank of experience, kindness, and understanding of human frailty.

The second factor in Ford's persuasion was his growing desire to write. Not the mundane detective story that retired policemen imagined would become a best seller, but the romance of his Perthshire boyhood, growing up walking the hills in the company of his artist grandfather: the best companion a boy could wish for, and a magic weaver of tales. Of primary importance to Christopher was the need to preserve for future generations many of the stirring Scottish stories and ballads told him by the old man; stories to fire the blood and quicken the senses.

But his home did not lend itself readily to writing and thinking. After his divorce he had bought the lease of a somewhat cramped flat which had the dubious merit of being close to headquarters. Still numbed at that time, unable to think clearly, he had chosen a purpose built block, not because he was drawn to modern architecture, but simply because it was impersonal. Scarred by the tirade of his ex-wife's reproaches, he decided that never again would he indulge in the luxury of attachment to anybody or anything. This new block boasted the advantages of a cleaner, no gardening, and he never had to meet the neighbours – although he heard them often enough through the thin walls. It suited him. It suited his odd working hours. It afforded him precious time to adjust to living alone after many years of being a husband and father.

Once retired, however, the walls seemed to press in on him. The rooms felt claustrophobic, making his tall frame appear even more awkward than usual. Inconveniences, such as hitting his head on the edge of the kitchen cupboard and having to bend double over the tiny wash basin, which had once been mildly amusing, now irritated. He soundly cursed the vagaries of designers who decided everyone to be of standard height, and a short standard at that! He wasn't so unusual, for Pete's sake! He had met plenty of men as tall, or taller, than himself. But, more to the point, there was nowhere to accommodate a desk or filing cabinet.

Anyone at Maples who had a problem to solve, or an idea to mull over, invariably turned to Maurice for advice. In spite of grumbling that he was being turned into a "wise old man of the woods", he always provided a sympathetic ear, with his head wreathed in pipe smoke. Christopher strongly suspected that the grumbler was secretly chuffed at being consulted in this manner, and therefore felt no compunction in sharing his own problem with Maurice. But the no-nonsense solution took him by surprise.

"The answer seems straightforward enough to me, Chris. Move in here – lock, stock and barrel."

"What!... permanently you mean? Give up my flat? Sell it? I can't do that... "Christopher stuttered.

"Why not? What's to stop you?"

"Well..."

"Yes?" Maurice had a sardonic grin.

"I simply can't impose on you in that way. You've enough on your plate as it is."

"Nonsense," snapped the reply. "You've never seemed

comfortable in that flat of yours to my way of thinking. In all the years we've been friends, I've only known you to treat it like a hotel room. It has nothing of you in it. And you know we'd love to have you here. One thing we're never short of is space, and I hate seeing empty rooms going to waste. I'll tell you something in confidence, Chris. I've been wanting to make a similar offer to John, but I needed to find a tactful way of broaching the subject. I can be much more direct with you. Between you and me, I know he's damned lonely. He keeps finding excuses to spend more and more time here, bless his old heart. And on top of that I'm pretty sure he's having a difficult job making ends meet. After all, it's many years since he was a top notch performer, and although he's not extravagant – far from it! – his savings must be running low. Most of his roof urgently needs re-tiling, which by my reckoning would make a big hole in his bank account.

"But this is where you can do a good turn. If he knew you had decided to take up my offer, I'm almost certain he would jump at *his* chance. You could both have two rooms apiece on the top floor. It's quieter up there – all the racket goes on downstairs. Maybe you would like to use one room as a bedroom and the other as a sitting room/study. And there are lovely views from the top windows."

Christopher began to open his mouth but Maurice was there before him.

"I rather think I can guess what's coming next. What about money? Well, what about it? We can come to some arrangement over rent if that's what you'd like. Still, take your time to think it through. I realise it's a rather radical step and I don't want you to feel hustled in any way."

Without feeling the slightest bit hustled Chris had already made up his mind. To his pleasant surprise the flat sold quickly to a short couple who seemed to think it would make an ideal nest in which to bill and coo. He didn't argue, simply wished them well, and they and the flat passed out of his life for ever.

He moved happily into his new quarters, and three months later John Dean became his contented neighbour on the top floor.

All things considered, Christopher Ford felt a lucky man this particular Christmas. He sighed, opened one eye, and turned his head lazily to the right. Sitting close to the Christmas tree, totally absorbed in a game of chess, were John Dean and Megan Smart, the lights from the tree giving the board an almost surreal appearance. He regarded the players.

John had shed ten years since living at Maples; he looked spruce in a fawn cardigan and well-cut dark blue shirt. His companion still dressed in the Bohemian fashion of long skirts and swirling scarves but now her clothes had colour and design that fascinated him. Her face had a becoming glow of health. This person had matured beyond all recognition from the pale ghost encountered on his first visit to the house. The development of her serene, gentle sensitivity was appreciated by the children and staff of the local school where she taught piano and singing. This still left her time to quietly take over the role of Man Friday for Maurice as Joanna bowed out. Megan was a valued member of the ever-growing household.

Then, in leisured manner, Christopher shifted position slightly until he could better observe the thin figure sitting apart from the rest of the group. He mentally saluted Keith Dunsett, who today had made a gallant attempt to mingle, his small gifts displaying remarkably good taste. Chris grinned. Surely not many ex-coppers would be opening a box of initialled handkerchiefs from a man they had once helped to put behind bars? Esther had whooped with pleasure after unwrapping a framed photo of Sophie; a photo taken by Keith, revealing skill and patience to exactly capture the dog's soppy grin. When, on impulse, she kissed his cheek, the man looked ready to cry.

CHAPTER ELEVEN

From the hearth the logs' sputtering embers gave out a faint, eerie light, sufficient to outline Keith hunched on the edge of an upright chair, shoulders bowed. Chris's policeman's nose sensed trouble. He wished he knew what ailed the fellow. However, if his hunch was correct about Maurice, then that worthy would be only too aware of Keith's wretchedness, and wisely wait for the other to make the first approach. As ever, Chris marvelled at his friend's breadth of understanding and compassion that embraced full acceptance of Keith.

He glanced across at Maurice, but in the rapidly darkening room it was difficult to see clearly. He appeared to be dozing, chin sunk on his chest. Maurice's friendship was important to Chris. He recalled once checking a dictionary definition of friendship: 'one joined to another in intimacy and mutual benevolence...' The words perfectly described his feelings towards Maurice. 'Mutual benevolence...' – it was a heart phrase. Real friends had been scarce in Chris's life – to be counted on the fingers of one hand. Harry Anderson was one, and his grandfather had been another. His marriage had lacked either friendship or companionship. Once strong physical attraction had burnt itself out, nothing had remained to fill the ever widening cracks.

Maurice was not dozing. Instead, he used the cloak of half shut eyes to puzzle over Keith's obvious agitation. But that enigma had to be left unsolved, for when darkness finally enveloped the room the same mutual consent that had sought relaxation in its dusky shadows, now craved bright action.

Esther was first to scramble to her feet, switching on table lamps and drawing curtains. Her companions blinked, stretched, yawned, and sat more upright in their chairs, smiling at each other, for all the world like a tableau coming to life.

"I'll make a pot of tea, and cut the cake," tempted the girl, already on her way to the kitchen followed by Megan, blithely ignoring mock groans that greeted this announcement.

Joanna too disappeared, saying she simply must "spend a penny". Maurice banked up the fire while the other men moved restlessly round the room. The fresh logs caught hold, enticing Martin and Ian to warm their backs. Yvonne smiled. It was such a typically male stance.

The iced cake duly admired and nibbled, the younger members voted for a game of Monopoly. Maurice seized this opportunity to escape up to his den. Sophie pattered close to his heels until, once inside the room, she jumped in her basket and lay watching him. He bent down and absentmindedly fondled her ears, his thoughts centred on Keith. He had felt a certain pride in that chap's demeanour today, aware that the occasion would have been a strain. But, however strong the temptation, he must refrain from interfering. Nevertheless, he was half expecting the knock when it came.

"Come on in. It's not locked," he called.

Keith put his head in and asked half apologetically:

"Am I disturbing you Maurice?"

"Good heavens, no. Pull that chair over here. Sorry if it's on the cool side in here, but my canvasses can't stand too much heat. Come to that, neither can I."

Keith flicked his usual embarrassed glance around, never knowing quite how to respond. He stood in awe of Maurice's artistry.

"Oh.. that's okay. The sitting room was getting rather warm anyway."

He took a deep breath and plunged on.

"Maurice.. um.. I.."

"Yes, Keith," encouraged Maurice, wondering what was coming.

Silence: broken only by small snuffles coming from the dog basket. Keith stared down at his hands. What a different fellow this was, reflected Maurice, from the cocky man he had first met. Life, and the passage of the years, had not been kind to Keith. His hair was coarse and straggly, his mouth pulled down at the corners, and he was painfully thin. It seemed like the waste of a life. He was intelligent, but did not bother to exploit any natural talents, such as the photographic skill exhibited that afternoon, animals being notoriously fickle subjects to capture. But then many people seemed to drift aimlessly through life.

Keith's voice cut through his musings:

"It's no use, Maurice. I've tried. I really have. Please believe that much. And I don't want you to think I'm ungrateful because I'm not. Far from it. I appreciate all you've done for me."

His face screwed up with tension, he leaned forward, the palm of his left hand rubbing back and forth on his knee.

Maurice was nonplussed.

"What on earth are you trying to tell me, Keith? I've no idea what you're on about. Do be a bit clearer. Take your time."

Keith hesitated again, and for a moment Maurice felt he was going to clam up. Then words rushed forth:

"It's the countryside. The open spaces. The lack of people. The lack of noise. There's nothing to do. Nowhere to go."

He looked pleadingly at Maurice, who was stumped by the unexpected answer, and could only repeat blankly:

"The countryside! But. .but I simply don't understand you.

What's wrong with it? Do for pity sake spit out what's bugging you. You won't hurt my feelings, I assure you."

Keith visibly relaxed, settling back in his chair.

"Well.. to be absolutely honest.. it bores me. Bores me silly. You see, Maurice, I'm a 'townie' through and through. Born and bred, so to speak, to live out my days in a busy town. Oh, I know folk talk about getting away for a break to the peace and quiet of the countryside – have a rest, or go walking – all that kind of thing. And to be fair I can see its attractions; I'm not a complete Philistine. But the quiet unnerves me. If I wander off the path I panic that I'm going to get lost and then feel a right fool. I only come to life and feel safe when there's plenty of noise and bustle around me. Even prison made me seem in the thick of things! And I love all those things I know you detest – shops for example."

He grinned and Maurice chuckled. It was a long standing joke within the household that Maurice hated shopping. His clothes had to be falling apart before he would consider replacing them.

"You're right there, Keith, and I appreciate your frankness. It just never occurred to me how much you'd miss a busy atmosphere. I feel guilty to admit it. We're all in the habit of projecting our own likes and dislikes onto others, fondly imagining they'll share in them equally. But why should you like what I do, for goodness sake?"

He held up a hand as Keith started to interrupt.

"No.. hang on.. let me finish. I understand. I really do. I'd hate to be cooped up in a town – even for a day or two – as much as you hate living out here in the sticks. And, of course, we're particularly off the beaten track, especially at times like these after a heavy snowfall. We could be on the moon, we seem so cut off from the rest of mankind."

To his surprise, this last innocent remark triggered Keith's previous agitation. He began firing questions.

"But we could get out if we really wanted to, couldn't we? Not by car, I realise that, but on foot surely? After all the snow can't be that deep. It would be safe if you were wearing a thick anorak and wellies, wouldn't it?"

Unclear as to where this line of questioning was leading, Maurice replied:

"Certainly, so long as you knew where you were going. But there's no need for any of us to venture out. There's an ample supply of food and logs in store."

Keith's face wore a mulish expression and he bit hard on his lower lip. Now what was troubling the fellow, wondered Maurice? There was no doubt he was referring to himself. What was pressing enough for him even to consider floundering through the snow? With one breath he professed to a genuine fear and dislike of the countryside, frightened of becoming lost; and in the next clumsily finding out if he could travel through quite deep snow on foot. And where was he planning on going? None of it made any sense. He sighed and waited for a response.

"I was just curious that's all," mumbled Keith. "I didn't know how deep snow had to be before it was unsafe."

A patently transparent lie, regretted Maurice. Keith used to be capable of far cleverer cover-ups than this, but he let it pass. He sensed there was more to confide.

"Look, Maurice, I won't be coming to Maples again. I meant it when I said I'm grateful to you. I know only too well that precious few would have treated me the way you have, but I'm better off staying in London. It was a mistake to start coming here in the first place. I see that now. I should never have accepted the invitations but I simply couldn't resist them. You can always visit me in my flat..."

His voice tapered off lamely. That was a stupid remark. Maurice had never been to his run-down flat, and, in the light of his earlier comments, he was hardly likely to do so now.

Maurice gave him a sceptical look.

"I think you know how unlikely that will be, Keith. Since I don't wish to come to London and you don't like the countryside, it is doubtful we'll see much of each other once you leave here. No use pretending otherwise. But no hard feelings, I promise you. I respect your decision. And you know you can always turn to me if you need help in any way."

"I knew you'd understand Maurice. I've tried hard to fit in but…" Keith opened his hands expressively. "I'll stay on if I may until the snow clears."

He paused, turning his head away, and then spoke quickly.

"D'you know, I may have a go at getting through to the 'Globe' in the next day or two. I'd like to say my farewells to the regulars. They've been a decent bunch on the whole. Well.. anyway I'll leave you to it for now."

He stood up, hovered awkwardly for a moment, and then slipped from the room.

The air was tainted with stale sweat. Maurice moved stiffly over to one of the sash windows and opened it at the bottom, letting in a draught of icy air together with a flurry of snow. He savoured the cold purity. A large snowflake settled on the inside sill and he marvelled at its unique design. He touched it gently but the warmth of his finger altered its shape and it was soon just a small pool of water.

He returned to his chair, thinking hard. What really lay behind that exchange with Keith? He did not doubt the sincerity of the man's remarks about boredom. Those rang true. In hindsight, Keith's presence in the house always created tension, albeit slight. Therefore, his decision not to visit again meant there would be no real regrets on either side. What was a tissue of lies, however, was his weak excuse for reaching the 'Globe', ignoring considerable discomfort. It was totally out of character, and highly suspicious as a result.

★

"Where the dickens is Keith off to?" queried Martin.

He beckoned to his wife who was putting away the cutlery after lunch.

"Come and look, do! He's dressed for a polar expedition."

Joanna joined him at the dining room window, linking her arm snugly though his. She giggled at the sight of the figure struggling up the drive. His back was to them, but she could see that he was dressed in one of Maurice's old anoraks which was too big for him, a pair of wellies, one of Esther's long woollen scarves, and a red bobble hat. He grasped a stout stick in his right hand, and with head bent against another snow shower was making slow progress.

"I did wonder why he was asking Esther if he could borrow her boots. Of course, his feet are smaller than any of you other men, so yours would have been too large for him. But where the heck can he be going?"

Her back ached from the weight of the baby and she rubbed it with a balled fist. Although tired and looking forward to an afternoon nap, she was intrigued by this mystery presented by Keith. She went in search of Maurice.

Four days on from Christmas Day, with the snow thicker than ever, no one could leave Maples. Much as he loved all the occupants of the house, nevertheless Maurice was beginning to find their constant company something of a strain. Joanna guessed this, but her curiosity overcame any reluctance to disturb him.

Heavily mounting the stairs, she tapped on his door.

"Come in, Jo," came the response from within.

"How did you know it was me?" she asked.

"Well," quipped Maurice, "none of the rest of us sound like an elephant climbing the stairs!"

Poking her tongue out at him, she lowered herself carefully in a comfortable chair. Maurice picked up his paint brush, and after raising his eyebrows at her in enquiry, stood looking at his canvas.

"Maurice.."

He grinned, guessing what was coming next.

"Yes, Jo."

"D'you know where Keith is off to? Have you any idea? Martin and I have just seen this extraordinary spectacle of him doing a Scott of the Antarctic double act. I've never even known him go out in the rain before."

"He's most probably off to the 'Globe' to.. how did he put it?.. to say his farewells to the regulars."

Maurice paused to let this tit-bit of information sink in. Joanna pounced on it immediately.

"Is he leaving us for good, and if so why? Tell me all."

Trust a woman to spot the connection straight away, admired Maurice. He filled her in on the details of his conversation with Keith.

"I would have told you before this, Jo, but I've not had a chance to see anyone alone these past days," he grumbled benignly.

"Probably the best thing that could happen all round – Keith leaving I mean," said Joanna complacently. "After all, he never quite fitted in with the rest of us. He always seemed.." She paused, about to say 'an intruder', but changed her mind and inserted "an outsider".

★

The man under scrutiny had never experienced prolonged severe weather in his life. Snow in London quickly turned to slush, the wheels of cars and buses splashing it over one's shoes and trouser legs while melting. Therefore, in contrast, on first leaving the shelter of the house he enjoyed the sensation of soft powdery snow under foot. The silvery spattered trees and shrubs lining the driveway made him feel secure. He kicked the snow around, tentatively at first, and then with more gusto, the action taking him back to childhood. Whistling tunelessly he scuffed open one of the wrought iron gates and turned into the lane.

The wind clawed at him, tearing at his clothing. Now there was no breath left to whistle. The icy air stung his cheeks. He stopped and gazed around in bewilderment. All familiar features had disappeared under a dazzling white quilt. With difficulty he could just see the tops of hedges sticking twigs up here and there.

Anxiety nagged him. He would never make it to the village. He would have to return to the house. But he would feel humiliated. It had now become a personal challenge to reach the pub. He steadied himself, leaning on the stick. Then he noticed that the snow hardly came to the tops of his boots. The wind was sweeping between the hedgerows, blowing the snow up against them, creating a more shallow path to walk on. He pushed the stick down through the snow and met the ground about four to six inches beneath. Surely, he reckoned, if he kept a hedge on either side of him all the time, then within about twenty minutes he should reach the main A road leading to the village. Here a snow plough should have cleared a way for traffic and walking would be easier. Wrapping the scarf across his mouth, he set off moving cautiously, boots scrunching on ice crystals.

His watch told that he had been slipping and sliding for nearly half an hour. However, the hedges were still either side of him and he could feel the ground. It could not be far now. He rubbed his eyes, staring at the featureless landscape. Then, taking another step forward, he found himself sinking into wet, dirty snow nearly up to his waist. He had reached the road at last, only to be thwarted by the snow plough's work. The deep, mushy snow sucked at his already damp clothes and held him fast, as if in quicksand. He panicked, twisting round furiously in an attempt to pull himself free. Pressing forward with all the weight of his body, he at last stumbled onto firmer surface. He was almost crazy with relief. A car swooshed past, spraying water. He could not have cared less. He had made it.

Ten minutes later he was approaching the 'Globe' forecourt, where a dirt encrusted Land Rover stood alone in the car park. On unlatching the pub door, the rush of warm air that greeted him felt like a furnace against his frozen face.

Four pairs of eyes stared in amazement at the dishevelled figure stamping on the mat: only after Keith had pulled off his woollen hat did recognition dawn for the landlord. Letting out a low 'whew', he hurried round from behind the bar, to help the man shuffle off his sodden anorak and trailing scarf.

"Good God, Mr Dunsett, whatever has brought you out in this awful weather? What a day to choose! Come over to the bar, man, and get a warm drink inside you."

He called to his wife who had vanished into a room behind the bar.

"Jean!…Jean! Are you there? Where've you gone? A hot toddy straight away for this gentleman. He's frozen."

"Kettle's on already. Won't take a jiffy to boil," came the woman's calm reply, jangling aside a beaded curtain which hung over an open doorway, and returning to the bar.

Dressed in wine red crimplene trousers, she was short and stout, somewhat older than her husband, with an unflustered air about her as she walked over to the wide fireplace to throw a couple of logs into the flames. She only spared the traveller one curious glance. Her husband, in contrast, fussed over Keith like a mother hen, pulling off his boots and hanging up his outer garments. If truth be known, this sudden arrival created a welcome diversion in an otherwise slack, boring period, and he delighted in the small drama.

Cautiously sipping the hot whisky, Keith winced as the blood began to flow again through his thawed limbs, but he felt more human. He sneaked a covert glance at the other two occupants of the pub. One looked like a young farmer, and was the probable owner of the Land Rover. The other was a regular who bored all and sundry with tales of his advanced age, and how he had lived in the same cottage all his life, in the forlorn hope that someone would buy him a drink for 'old time's sake'.

The young man appeared to have troubles of his own. He leant heavily on the bar, one of his fists clenched, muttering under his breath. After drinking two beers in quick succession, he fell silent. The old chap opened his mouth, started to say something and then changed his mind, shrinking back in his corner, his rheumy eyes flicking from one to the other.

The publican was washing glasses beneath the counter, watching Keith.

"Feeling a bit warmer, Mr Dunsett? You had a tidy walk. I'm surprised you wanted to leave the comfort of Maples."

"Much warmer, thanks Gordon," acknowledged Keith with a smile. "I didn't realise that the snow was quite so deep. But you know how it is – Christmas with all the family around. Gets a bit much." He couldn't prevent a boastful tone creeping into his voice. "Everyone on top of each other. Needed a break. Wanted to get out of the house for a bit."

"Ah yes. I know exactly what you mean," replied Gordon, who didn't at all. Like most landlords, to him Christmas meant work, and since he and his wife were childless, family Christmases were a blurred memory. However, he made it a policy to always agree with the customer. In his experience this often relaxed them, made them confidential, and he had long sensed that there was a mystery surrounding Keith's spasmodic visits to the big house and would dearly love to hear the whole story. Keith would have been amazed if he had heard some of the gossip that buzzed round the village concerning him.

"Been busy? Many people in?" Keith made the enquiries casual.

"Hardly a soul with this dratted weather. Takings are right down the pan."

"Mostly men on their own, I suppose? Trying to escape from the washing-up."

"Well, no. Funnily enough it's been mainly couples – young couples with nowhere to go. It's a long, cold drive to town and the cinema. If they can get there at all that is: it's even too cold to stop for a bit of canoodling on the back seat."

Keith smiled automatically.

"Then today," went on Gordon, "we've only seen old Jack, young Simon," a nod went in their direction – "and yourself."

As if waiting for a signal the young man slammed down his tankard, and without a word hurried from the scene. A minute later came the grating sound of the Land Rover's engine being revved, then pushed roughly into gear, until gradually the noises faded off in the distance.

"Money troubles I believe. Farm's rocky financially. Simon's looking for a way to get the bank off his back. He's becoming rather desperate." Gordon seemed to think an explanation was necessary.

Keith merely nodded.

★

Hunched miserably in front of a too hot fire, Keith felt at a low ebb. Half an hour had gone by and he was uncertain of his next move. Nobody had entered the pub since the farmer had left. He looked over his shoulder at the bar. The old man was asleep, Gordon was polishing glasses, while his wife was seated on a high stool idly flicking the pages of a magazine, but Keith received the uneasy impression of being watched. He stared at the curtain over the open door behind the bar. Did it twitch or was that his over-wrought imagination? He groaned: he had struggled all this way, the fear of that man's threat driving him on, and now nothing. But Jensen was not someone to ignore; observation of his influence inside prison was evidence enough. Keith shuddered on recalling the last sentence in that all too brief but chilling note received in London:… 'By the way, that young girl's still pretty for the moment.'

The thought of harm befalling Esther made him recklessly angry. He was genuinely fond of the kid. But if no contact was made today, what could he do except return to London and wait for the next move? And he had no doubt there would be one. He caught a sudden glimpse, which made him squirm, of how his own cat-and-mouse behaviour in the past must have affected his victims – Mary Caton, his mother, for instance. Perhaps he was being given a chance to set the record straight.

He stood up, bracing himself for the cold journey ahead. The movement caught the attention of the woman, who slowly lowered her short body off the stool and came toward him. Assuming she wanted to collect his empty glass, he held it out. Taking it in one hand, with the other she pulled an envelope from her trouser pocket and placed it on the table. She turned her back, walked over to the bar, put the glass down in front of Gordon, and, still without a word, climbed a staircase which evidently led to living quarters above, and disappeared.

Keith stared down at the cheap, crumpled envelope. It looked identical to the one received through the post. His heart was beating a tattoo and he felt he would choke. He took a deep breath to steady himself, giving another quick glance round the room. Old Jack was still asleep, Gordon was now reading a newspaper, and no sound came from upstairs. What was this woman's involvement with the letter? Unable to answer his own question, he impatiently rubbed sweaty palms on his trousers, and, with his back to the bar, tore open the envelope. The contents were terse: 'Return to London. You will be contacted there. Remember the girl. It was as well for her that you followed instructions today.'

Quickly stuffing the letter in his pocket, he began to pull on his anorak, which was damp and clammy. Gordon moved over to him.

"You off already, Mr Dunsett?"

"Yes. I'd better make a move before it starts to get dark."

He finished winding the scarf, Esther's scarf, round his neck, and went on:

"By the way Gordon, I won't be down this way for some while, so I'll say 'cheerio' for the present. Thanks for your help today."

On that note he left the pub, and began the trudge back to Maples, leaving the landlord feeling somewhat deflated.

CHAPTER TWELVE

Ten days later found Keith feeling a different man. He was warm; replete from lunch in his favourite cafe; there was not a sign of snow; and he was surrounded by shops and bright lights. On passing a teenage boutique his ears were assailed by a blast of pop music but he welcomed it. In his opinion it had more life and verve than the classical recordings Maurice favoured.

For a short time, wrapped in noise and bustle, he could almost believe that the nightmare surrounding him was a figment of his imagination. Of course it was not, for a man like Jensen did not make idle threats. Yet, for the present, Keith believed he had done all that was humanly possible, deciding to relax and enjoy life. He had money in his wallet – Maurice had seen to that – and the idea of going to the cinema appealed. He discovered the film was familiar, so he toyed with visiting a cheap club but found that the notion palled at once. Never mind, he would walk his beloved London streets instead. He belonged in them. He had tried to behave and fit in at Maples in order to please Maurice, but in the end he could only be himself. He could not become a clone of Maurice. To be fair, that man had never assumed it, but Keith had made him a role model. Therefore, in his own eyes and in private moments, he felt he lacked the integrity of his mentor. He would have been pleasantly surprised if he could have seen himself through Maurice's window on the world.

When he had finally reached Maples on that desolate, icy afternoon, he went in search of Christopher Ford. He had to share this burden with someone and, as he was adamant not to involve Maurice, Ford was the only other candidate. Naturally, the ex-detective urged immediate contact with the local police. Keith refused. He knew he was being watched and was anxious that no harm should overtake Esther. Besides, he pointed out, Jensen was clever. There was nothing to connect him with Keith, who had only caught one brief glimpse of his adversary. The woman's involvement remained a complete mystery: if questioned she would only clam up. No: all he could do was return to London and wait. Once he knew what was required, he would try to ring Chris from a call box. Chris would keep his eyes and ears open, but was by this time an extremely worried man, who decided to make discreet enquiries of his own.

Dusk was falling, with more than a hint of frost in the air, when Keith came home to his flat. He turned the key and went inside.

"Damn it", he muttered under his breath, "must've left the lights on when I went out."

The brightness of the living room temporarily dazzled him after the dark streets, and his eyes took a few seconds to adjust. What he saw made his heart lurch.

On his rickety, frayed sofa sat three people – Jensen, Simon the young farmer, and wedged between them – Esther.

"What the hell! Esther!.. my dear, come over to me. Come here."

He held out his arms in desperation, scarcely knowing what he was saying. Hearing the words, Esther tried to stand up but was roughly pulled down by Jensen.

"Why you!.. let her go!..leave her alone!" Keith moved toward her.

"Shut up. Sit down. Over there on that chair. Now!"

Jensen did not raise his voice. The tone was flat and nasal. Keith knew that type of voice; you did not argue with it, you did what it said. He sat on one of his two sagging chairs and waited, surveying the bizarre scene before him.

Antony Jensen was leaning forward, hands on his knees, the glint of a knife showing between the fingers of his right hand. He was not a big man, but was muscular and fit looking. His head was small with dark, lank hair hanging in a fringe over a low forehead. His eyes reminded Keith of a snake he had once seen – they glittered. Dressed in well-cut jeans and expensive leather jacket, he was aged about forty.

Esther, pale but calm, had her fair hair tousled and there were streaks of dirt on her face. She was wearing the long woollen scarf he had borrowed, and the laces of one of her trainers was undone.

Simon, while sporting the apparel of a young modern farmer, was having a struggle to control his trembling hands.

Keith's mind was moving quickly, somewhat to his surprise. What Simon was doing here could only be guessed – 'a soft boy if ever I saw one', he thought. Jensen must have some kind of hold over him. But it was more important to recall everything he knew about Jensen. One slightly comforting fact was that he had never been associated with a sex offence; Esther should be safe there. But he was known to be a violent and intimidating man who had bullied the weaker prisoners. Keith had kept out of his orbit and, since his own reputation in those days was that of a 'hard man', he was left alone. He remembered with a certain chill that Jensen had been in prison for taking part in a raid on a post office, during which an employee had been badly hurt.

Esther's voice broke the brief silence, making Keith jump.

"I simply must go to the loo. I really must. You wouldn't stop before. Please." Her face turned pink with embarrassment at the request.

Jensen turned his head sideways and looked at her. He pulled a lock of her hair and she winced, but held her ground.

"Please," she reiterated.

Jensen made up his mind.

"Okay. Okay. Don't whine. Where is it, Dunsett?" He glanced round the tiny room.

"Across the outside hall. I have to share with another flat."

Jensen let out a breath through his teeth.

"Come on, girl. You're a bloody nuisance. Christ, what a dump this place is." He impatiently hauled Esther to her feet.

"Stay put, d'you hear?" he harshly snapped at Simon, who did not look at him.

He hustled Keith and Esther in front of him. Keith opened the flat door and they quickly crossed the narrow hall. Jensen made a cursory inspection of the dingy toilet to satisfy himself there were no means of escape and Esther shut the door. Jensen pressed Keith hard against the hall wall, the point of the knife held to his throat. Keith could see beads of sweat on the other's upper lip, and hear his unsteady breathing. He knew he was in no real danger since Jensen needed him for an undisclosed purpose. At least, he thought grimly, the man does recognise a basic human need. Maurice had taught by example that there was good in everyone. Perhaps if I can find and appeal to the good in Jensen..?

Introspection was halted by the sound of the flush, and Esther emerged. She gasped at the sight of the knife but Keith managed to give a small wink. Jensen laughed, flicked the knife shut, and slid it in his jacket pocket.

Once back inside the flat, he started shouting.

"No more time wasting. I've some talking to do. Come on. Sit down."

Esther took the opportunity to sit on the other chair which she pulled close to Keith's. Jensen leant back on the sofa and lit a thin cigar. Simon gazed at a spot on the wallpaper.

"Now listen hard, Dunsett, because we've not much time before we leave here. You're going to help me on a job."

"I'm not going to be helping you on any job, so think again."

"Oh but you will, you know. After all, you don't want anything to happen to our pretty girl here, do you? You'd like her to stay pretty, eh?"

The crude threat made Keith seethe, but he remained silent. There was nothing to be gained from a childish exchange of words. Besides, he did not want Esther to grow even more frightened.

Jensen carried on:

"We – that's you, me and the young ponce here – are going to break into a large, very classy jewellers; break in tonight and make ourselves a small fortune." His eyes gleamed at the thought. "The place I've lined up has my girlfriend working on the inside. She's going to arrange to have the alarm turned off, and I won't have any problems opening the safe. I'm the expert there. You're an expert on jewels, and I need someone who can spot the best ones quickly. And let it be clearly understood that I want nothing but the best, the very best. It's not going to be like some stupid old film where they grab handfuls. No! I want the cream, only the cream, and you're the cat who's going to spot it."

Keith decided to stall.

"You know damn well that it's years since I'd anything to do with the jewellery trade. What makes you sure I could pick out the cream as you call it, even if I wanted to, which I don't? I haven't kept my eye in."

"Because it's one of those things you never lose the knack for, that's why," retorted Jensen. "And you had a reputation of being one of the best in your field. If anyone can sniff out a classy stone, it's you. Mind you," he sneered, "you certainly haven't been paid for any jobs lately that's for sure, or you wouldn't be living in a doss-house like this. What's the matter? Wouldn't that arty brother of yours give you a hand-out? He must be a tight fisted bugger."

"No! He's not! He's not!" exploded Esther.

"Shut up, d'you hear? I'm not interested in what you think. Speak when you're spoken to, girl."

"NO! I won't shut up. I'm not staying here. You've no right…"

Jumping suddenly from her chair, she made a wild dash for the door. Quick as a panther, Jensen was there before her. Swinging back his left arm, he slapped her hard across the face. Whimpering, she stumbled back to her chair, and huddled down on it. Keith put out a hand and stroked her shoulder.

"Stop that. Don't touch her. She asked for it," snarled Jensen. "And that, Dunsett, is only a small sample of what the kid will suffer if you don't co-operate every inch of the way with me. Now do you understand?"

Anger gripped Keith, but he knew he was no match physically for the man. He would have to hear him out, and try to keep one step ahead mentally.

Forcing himself to sound relaxed, he said:

"Well, I suppose there might be something in it for me. I could do with some extra cash – this place is a dump, I grant you." He waved a none too steady hand around the room. "I certainly wouldn't shed any tears over kissing it good-bye. You've got me over a barrel anyway -" indicating Esther "- so tell me the rest."

He pointed to Simon.

"For starters, what the hell is *he* doing here? He looks an amateur. I've never worked with amateurs, and I don't intend to begin now. He makes me uneasy." Keith was highly superstitious. "He'll bring bad luck."

His puzzlement about Simon was genuine, which lent force to the words. It gave him an edge in the encounter causing Jensen to bluster.

"He's the driver. We need a good driver, and that's what he is, take my word for it. I've seen him in action on a racing track. Don't worry about him. He'll be a good boy and do as he's told, won't you?"

He poked Simon in the arm, and the young man pulled away in sharp distaste. Jensen laughed. Good, thought Keith, Simon is only here under sufferance which means I may get a chance to win him over. He decided to adopt a softly-softly approach with Jensen.

"Well okay," he conceded. "I'll accept for the moment that he is all you claim, but where's this job going to take place? And you said we're leaving soon. Where to?"

"You've heard all you need. It's a high class jewellers, the alarm will be switched off, the safe shouldn't present too many problems, and we've a driver. Your job is to pick out the gems."

"But why," protested Keith, "do you need to open the safe? From what I know of jewellers, the goods are left under padlocked grilles. Easier, surely, to cut through the metal?"

"Because there will be a wad of notes in the safe tonight, plus the fact that the combination to all the grilles is kept in there as well. Satisfied?"

"But what about Esther? You're surely not planning on taking her along?"

"No, course not," retorted Jensen. "Jean'll be here in a few minutes and then we'll be off."

"Jean? Who's Jean?"

"Doesn't matter."

"Doesn't matter?" spluttered Keith. "Doesn't matter?" Of course it bloody matters. The whole thing is a cobbled together affair – a non-starter. For someone who was considered a tough professional, you're scraping the barrel, Jensen. No plan to speak of; two men who want no part of it; a young girl as a hostage; and now some unknown woman about to arrive. The police will pick us up straight away. They must already be looking for Esther."

"Shut up. It'll work I tell you." Jensen's right hand was clenched in a tight ball and Keith backed away. The other man made a conscious effort to relax, looking at his watch. Keith heard the outer door to the building squeak open and footsteps approached his own door, the tread sounding hollow on the uncarpeted floor. There was a soft knock. Jensen swiftly responded, letting in a short, stout, middle-aged woman – Jean, the landlord's wife from the 'Globe Inn'. She struck an ordinary figure muffled in a drab woollen coat and cheap scarf, the kind of woman who would never receive a second glance in a crowd. No one spoke. She moved into the centre of the room.

"Well?" she demanded of Jensen, not even glancing at the other three.

"Fine. No problems. Everything's set up. There won't be any trouble. They'll both do as they're told. Dunsett doesn't want to see the girl get hurt."

"Most touching. I said it would work." Her voice crackled like rough sand-paper. "We must get out of here straight away. Did you dump the Land Rover?"

"Yup."

"Good. I've a car outside."

She signalled for the others to stand up. Like automatons they obeyed, Simon unable to take his eyes off Jean. Keith just felt in a dream. They were hurried down the steps that led to the street, where a two door saloon car was parked at the kerb. The street appeared to be totally deserted. They were pressed in the car, Esther seated in the back between Jensen and Keith, the woman in the front, with Simon as driver.

Jean gave directions, and after they crossed Lambeth Bridge Keith realised they were headed for South London. Ending monotonous twists and turns the car finally drove into a narrow side road and halted. They all sat in silence. Keith rubbed a hole in the condensation running down his nearside window, and peered out.

They were in front of a small terraced Edwardian house in a mean street which had seen better days. The kind of street where nobody knows their neighbour and no awkward questions are asked. His heart sank. What would happen next?

Maurice, thankful for the ever deepening dusk which shielded his distress, tramped the grounds of Maples, Sophie at his heels, her kind eyes watching him. "What can I do? What can I say to them? I love Esther too – more than I knew."

He repeated this refrain to himself, like a kind of mantra. It seemed to help keep the lid on his emotions which threatened to overwhelm him, frightening in their intensity.

Ever since Chris Ford had broken the news, the extraordinary news, that Esther looked certain to have been abducted by some villain called Jensen, and that Keith of all people had been trying to protect her, Maurice had watched Ian and Yvonne's anguish with a sense of helplessness. Without any hesitation they had turned to him, leaving the Gallery and driving over to Maples, their ever ready source of comfort in time of trouble. And he had failed them. In his bewilderment he simply could not find the right words; everything he said sounded banal to his ears.

Truth be told he was afraid of exposing his own feelings, of letting down his guard: stirred too by his friends' acute anxiety. Joanna and Martin had been of far more use. Yet Maurice was the one who was always advocating honest expression of emotion. Why, he could recall urging the young Ian in a field only a few hundred yards from where he was standing now: "…Cry as much as you want. There's nothing sissy about it. It's good for you. Tears are a healthy safety valve…" And here he was, running away from their drawn faces, to retreat to the garden. What a hypocrite! But it was the only place where he could breathe freely. Ian's quite natural anger had affected him, adding fuel to his own. He had never in his life before felt so.. outraged.. yes, that was the word.. outraged. Anyway, dusk had become starlit night and he must return to the house where he could at least glean precious titbits of news.

Ian's raised voice could be clearly heard through the closed sitting room door. Maurice's heart sank. This was not the time for recriminations, and somehow there was something covertly false about the emphasis in the speaker's voice. He seemed to be protesting too much, even allowing for the circumstances.

"You know damned well you should've told us this might be on the cards. We are her parents for God's sake!…"

Maurice reluctantly entered the room. Ian rudely ignored him and continued with his dressing down of Chris: "…and we had every right to know what was brewing. We could have protected her. Taken her away somewhere. And now look what's happened!"

"How could you possibly have protected her?" flustered Chris. "In all fairness you couldn't keep her wrapped in cotton wool. It would only have served to frighten her. Keith had no firm facts or details remember – only a few vague threats."

"Keith! Keith!" spat Ian, flashing Maurice an angry glance. "That wretched man! He's been trouble with a capital 'T' ever since you first invited him here, Maurice. You knew full well what he was like – the kind of people he would attract. It was unforgivable of you." A nerve twitched in his left cheek as he swallowed back more harsh words.

"Oh no," groaned Maurice softly. "Don't let this awful event drive a wedge between us. Not after all these years, and all we've meant to each other. I couldn't bear that."

Yvonne obviously shared his concern because she wrapped an arm tightly across her husband's tense shoulders and soothed:

"Hush, darling, this is Maurice you're talking to – our friend, your best friend. And it's Esther we must be thinking about now."

Ian stared at the floor, and Yvonne turned beseechingly to Maurice. He stated quietly:

"No, Yvonne. Ian has been clamping down hard on this particular issue for a long time, I realise that now. It's better all round for resentments to come to the surface and there be dealt with quickly and cleanly. If this terrible thing is the catalyst, then so be it. Let him have his say."

But Ian said nothing. The heavy silence lengthened until Maurice felt an inexpressible sadness pervade the once happy room. Suddenly Ian roughly shook off Yvonne's arm and stumbled out. They heard the cloakroom door open and bang shut.

His departure effectively lightened the atmosphere, with the friends exchanging glances. Maurice sat down in the vacant seat beside a distressed Yvonne, taking her hand.

"My dear, best to leave him alone for the moment. He's always reacted this way in the past if placed under any kind of pressure. He'll have a talk with me in his own good time. Try not to worry about him."

Joanna added her weight behind this, saying that Maurice was correct about her twin, and did Yvonne want anything – a cup of tea or a drink perhaps? Yvonne shook her head. In her heart she only wanted one thing – her beloved Esther. She felt an ache in her breast, as if the girl had been torn from it. Would it ever heal? For once in her unselfish life she did not spare a thought for Ian. She thought only of herself.

Maurice quickly noted the wan faces of the other loyal friends gathered in the familiar room – Martin, Megan and John, and then sought news from Chris. Yet that ex-professional, now alerted to sound optimistic as in similar situations, could hear the strain filtering through his own voice. "Nothing else to report since we last spoke," he assured. "It's clichéd I know, but everything that can be done is being done."

He paused, rubbing a finger across his moustache, debating how much to divulge. Yvonne appeared remarkably self-possessed but one could never be sure with mothers, and that wretched Ian hadn't been any help. He never had liked the fellow. However, he felt he knew her well enough to take a chance. Besides, all of them deserved to be told the truth, and the truth need never be feared. He carried on:

"I'll fill in some of the gaps for you."

There was a palpable quickening of interest among his audience while he hastened on:

"Keith came to me about ten days ago with an incredible tale of how he was positive that an ex-convict named Antony Jensen had sent him a couple of threatening letters hinting, albeit not too subtly, that Esther would be harmed if Keith did not follow instructions."

Chris gave Yvonne a quizzical look – so far so good. With a sense of relief he continued:

"Keith seemed to know enough about Jensen, from the time spent in prison with him, to take the threats seriously. He was genuinely concerned for Esther, and displaying considerable courage – although misguided in my opinion – had made up his mind to do as bid. He absolutely pooh-poohed any idea of contacting the police, and didn't want you bothered Maurice. Muttered that he'd already been enough of a nuisance to you through the years." Maurice moved impatiently in his chair but kept quiet. "I was reluctant to press him, worried that if I did he might keep any further briefings close to his chest. He'd made up his mind to go it alone and I couldn't budge him. Anyway he hurried back to London to await developments, promising to keep in touch, which he did. Four or five days later he gave me a buzz on my private line simply to say there was nothing to report. However, we both knew that Jensen was biding his time."

Now it was Maurice's turn to feel annoyed with Chris, echoing Ian's words from a short time before.

"But you could have told me, Chris, or at the very least given some sort of warning."

The hapless Chris defended himself.

"Please believe me when I say that in these circumstances the fewer folk that are in the know the better. Believe me too when I say that I had to bite my tongue to stop blurting out all I had been told. And I wasn't idle, wasn't standing by doing nothing. Doubtless you can well believe that I've plenty of contacts, good contacts, left in the force. I knew that two reliable ex-sergeants had started a detective agency in a town not far from here – private eyes in other words. Knowing their reputation for getting excellent results I drove across to put them confidentially in the picture.

"Well, within forty-eight hours they had come up with a lot of useful information. To begin with, Jensen has kept a clean slate since coming out of prison about four years ago. He set up in business as a money lender – a loan shark to you and me – but kept squeaky clean. No shady dealings – was even VAT registered! But it still gave him a handy way of finding out a lot of private gen about people. Next my two colleagues discovered that the landlord's wife of our village pub, 'The Globe', a woman by the name of Jean, was Jensen's older sister. I should imagine you all know her by sight. She had brought Jensen up, you could say not very well since he's been in and out of trouble from a young kid, but by all accounts the two are very close. Being local, obviously it would be a mere doddle for her to find out a good deal about Keith, and also be aware of Esther's comings and goings.

"In addition it came to light that Simon Marsden, a local young farmer…"

Maurice's head jerked up at the mention of that name.

"…owes a considerable sum of money to Jensen – money borrowed to finance his gambling habits – and that the young fool had even handed over the deeds of his late parents' farm, which he had inherited, as collateral…"

John Dean tut-tutted at this point.

"…and that also, as a side line, he fancies himself as a racing driver."

Chris paused here to collect his thoughts. Stunned by the unfolding tale, his listeners were fascinated to learn more.

"One of the chaps tells me that Marsden hasn't been at the farm today – which is unprecedented according to his head stockman. Add to this the fact that her worried husband has reported Jean missing from the pub, plus Esther hasn't been seen since leaving Maples straight after breakfast to return to the Gallery, and the mystery deepens. So we are presented with the scenario of Marsden, Jean and Esther all reported missing on the same day. In addition there is this tenuous connection between Keith and Jensen.

"Anyway, Yvonne, as soon as you rang here to find out why Esther hadn't come home for lunch when expected, one of my private eyes drove like a bat out of hell to London. Keith's not being on the phone made any contact well-nigh impossible, and we didn't want to involve the police at this stage." Chris flicked back his cuff and consulted his watch. "He should just about be there by now. He'll ring me from his car to report."

On cue the phone started to ring in the hall. Everyone jumped. Chris moved swiftly to answer it. His listeners sat like statues straining their ears. They caught phrases like: "I see, yes"; "Good, good"; "Well done". Yvonne clutched Maurice's hand until her rings bit into his flesh. The receiver pinged and Chris returned. Without preamble he said:

"Bob was parking his car a little way down the street from Keith's flat, when five people matching the sketchy descriptions I'd managed to provide came out and drove off in a dark coloured saloon. He managed to tail them for a while before losing them in the labyrinth of roads that make up the approaches to South London, roads already congested at this time of day with rush hour traffic."

At the word 'losing' Yvonne had gasped. Chris gave encouragement.

"Yvonne dear, the Metropolitan police are in on the search now. Bob's partner has put them in the picture. They've a good description of the car including part of the number plate. Nothing can be rushed at this stage because Esther's – and for that matter Keith's – safety is of paramount importance."

Martin broke in: "You tell us that Esther, the woman Jean, and this chap Marsden have been reported missing and have now been spotted in the company of Keith and Jensen. But why? There has been no ransom demand for Esther, and Marsden seems an unlikely candidate to get involved. Can you give an educated guess just what the plan might be? And what was Jensen serving time for?"

These were the kind of questions Chris relished. He felt on safe ground. He had not realised quite how much he had missed case conferences. Stretching out his long legs and pushing his hands deep in his pockets, he gave his considered opinion.

"To answer your last query first, Martin. Jensen served time for his part in an armed raid on a post office. He was a professional safe breaker. Could crack open almost any make of safe. I've been giving a lot of thought as to what his plan might be. On the face of it, you could say it's more than amateurish in its make-up but I reckon he must be planning a raid on a warehouse or a quality jewellers; more likely the latter. Keith's undoubted expertise in the field of precious stones make him the reluctant kingpin of the whole job. You see, these days it's far easier for a clever fence to dispose of a few extremely fine jewels rather than a job lot of inferior gems, therefore Keith is needed to pick out the crème de la crème. Via his sister, Jean, Jensen had winkled out Keith's Achilles' heel – his genuine fondness for Esther. Jensen abducted Esther to ensure Keith's full co-operation.

"The woman, Jean, has probably gone along to hold onto Esther until the job is over. Jensen has most likely promised to wipe out Simon's debts, and return the deeds of the farm, if Simon would agree to be the driver. Fat chance of Jensen being so accommodating. That lad really must be a sucker."

"Can I interrupt, Chris?" asked Megan, pushing her hair back from her eyes.

"Yes, of course. Go ahead."

"My question is this. With all the contacts Jensen must have in the underworld why hasn't he picked a much more professional team? He seems to have complicated matters by deciding to take Esther along for instance."

"A fair question, Megan. The simple answer is that he couldn't get anyone to work with him – and he did try apparently – but he was considered unlucky, to have a jinx on him. Prisoners are a superstitious bunch and after Keith had been released from the prison something happened involving Jensen. I don't have any details but from then on he was shunned; something of the kind crops up from time to time. After he got out it would seem he decided to keep his head below the parapet, go legit. and wait. It must have been like Christmas when *both* Keith and Marsden dropped in his lap."

★

Nobody had anything worthwhile to contribute after that, and one by one drifted off to their various parts of the house.

Another half an hour dragged miserably past with Ian pointedly avoiding contact with Maurice. Following his outburst the young man was left to his own devices, moodily stirring the dying embers of the dining room fire, barely able to speak to Yvonne, to offer needed comfort and support to the bereft mother. He knew he was behaving badly, selfishly. Why, oh why, whenever the crunch came in his life did he have to act the heel? His friends' opinion of him had dropped to an all-time low, while his view of himself was rock bottom. He loved Yvonne dearly and knew her to be a great blessing, and of course Esther mattered, of course she did. However, the unpalatable truth had to be faced that Ian Latimer was the most important person in Ian Latimer's scheme of things.

He had always keenly resented anything that disturbed the even tenor of his life. If life did not follow his carefully laid plans, he panicked. Everything had to go his way and today's drama had muddied the waters. Many had considered his attitude to the loss of his right arm amazingly brave.

What they did not know, not even Yvonne or Maurice, was that he had contemplated suicide while in hospital- he had stock piled strong pain killers by holding them in his mouth. Then he had hidden the tablets in a box of soft crayons provided by a therapist who had stupidly imagined he would attempt drawing with his left hand: such insensitivity still rankled.

But his moment of decision came and went. Youth was on his side and a natural healing of body and mind had begun. He wanted to live. The tablets were flushed away; he met Yvonne; Esther was born; and the Gallery was created. Life was organised again.

His attention was caught by a car engine revving. A furtive glance through the window showed Yvonne, outlined by the porch light, strapping herself in the driver's seat. Well, he didn't blame her for leaving without him; he seemed intent on building a high wall around himself. Still, conscious of a sharp pang that she was left to face their cosy home empty of Esther's chatter, he wanted to run after her, to join her. Too late! – the car was moving away, the tail lights becoming blurred dots.

★

Maurice was angry, his stomach churning with emotion. He bolted the door of his studio retreat and paced the floor, struggling in vain to gain command over errant thoughts. Ian's shabby treatment of Yvonne, his failure to be rocklike when she needed it most, had horrified and saddened him. Her faithful friends had gathered round, but naturally she wanted her husband. How dare Ian treat this gentle, loyal woman in such cavalier fashion? This was a side of Ian he really did not like. It had shown itself before, but never so unwrapped. Moreover he was no longer a mewling boy but a man… Maurice halted in his tracks and clapped a hand to his forehead. How could he have failed to spot the obvious, not to notice what was right under his nose? For emotionally Ian was not a man – he was still the thirteen year old boy he had met all those years ago. Yes, he had an adult veneer but that was all, and because he had had the good fortune to marry a more balanced and mature person, many of his defects lay hidden.

Perhaps, with the aid of some expert help, he could get Ian out of short trousers! This prospect encouraged him, providing an essential diversion from the numbness which had descended on him since Esther's disappearance, giving him a project to concentrate on. First, though, he needed to enlist Yvonne's help in the scheme. It might relieve her to keep occupied.

With that warm glow in his heart, experienced by charitable human beings when they have a chance to be of service, he hurried downstairs, almost missing his footing with haste. Thrusting wide the kitchen door he checked from the threshold. Quickly tired of their own company everyone was seated round the table; everyone, that was, except for Yvonne and Ian. Dejected faces brightened as they turned to him – his speed must mean good news. Guilty for a moment at raising their hopes, he shook his head, and they turned away to stare down into congealing cups of coffee. Sophie's pleasure at his entrance brimmed over with a frenzy of barking, accompanied by playful assaults at his trouser legs; in her world something must be about to happen. His fingers automatically scratched her neck.

"Ssh.. quiet Sophie please. Not quite so much noise." scolded Joanna.

Peace restored, Maurice was able to make his voice heard. Pulling up a spare stool he enquired: "Where's Yvonne?"

"She's gone home, Maurice," informed Martin. "She felt she'd be closer to Esther there."

"Gone home," repeated Maurice. "But I need to talk to her. It's important. I'll ring her. She must come back."

They all looked at him as if he had gone mad. However, they knew him well enough to know that once he had a bee in his bonnet he was completely single minded. John Dean became spokesman. His courteous voice pointed out that it *was* eight o'clock p.m. The fraught woman couldn't be expected to turn around and drive back to Maples. Maybe a chat on the phone would be sufficient, and would Maurice share with them the reason for this sudden urgency? Did it concern Esther?

Hearing John's words, Maurice flushed with shame. His behaviour equalled in selfishness the person he was trying to help. What was he thinking of – expecting Yvonne to return simply because he'd had an idea? Shaking his head in dismay, he said Esther wasn't directly concerned and then went on to take the group into his confidence. Did they agree with his assessment of Ian? Heads nodded in unison, John adding that positive thinking was badly needed at this time.

"By the way," queried Maurice, "where *is* Ian?"

In the dining room as far as they knew, or appeared to care. The man's behaviour had already placed him outside their charmed circle. What they did not know, however, was that Maurice had failed to close the kitchen door, and in the hall Ian stood listening to their conversation, too embarrassed and ashamed to enter. He felt a lonely stranger in their midst.

In the kitchen Megan was curious. Why had Maurice wanted to contact Yvonne then and there?

"To be honest, Megan, I really don't know. Fifteen minutes ago it seemed imperative. Now I feel rather silly. I suppose I wanted to sound her out, to check if her opinion of Ian tallied with mine. After all, she does know him better than any of us."

"Well, Maurice," cut in Jo, "it certainly tallies with mine." She leaned back in her chair to make herself comfortable, folding her hands above her thickening waistline. "I know full well that, as his twin, I've never been particularly close to Ian. To be blunt I've thought him an oddball in many ways – terribly childish. I've often felt to blame because I know I didn't treat him at all kindly when we were children – in fact, not to mince words, I was a bitch! And then came that awful business with his arm which somehow only added to my guilt. A good deal of nonsense is talked and written about the closeness of twins, that special relationship etc. etc. Well, maybe it's true with some twins but certainly not us. He's got much to be thankful for – Yvonne, Esther, the Gallery, good friends here at Maples, but still he behaves like a selfish child if life does not go his way. I almost get the impression that Esther's disappearance is a nuisance, an unwelcome interruption…"

"No, Jo, no, surely not!" broke in John Dean. "Don't say that. Don't even think it."

"Why not, if it's true?" retorted Jo, swinging round toward him. "Don't stick your head in the sand, John. I tell you it bloody well is true. You can't deny he left Yvonne in the lurch today, just when she needed him most. Poor fellow, he simply couldn't cope."

John sighed and placed his hand on her arm, a gesture which brought unexpected tears to her eyes. Swallowing hard, she continued:

"Life can be a bugger at times but we have to buckle down and get on the best way we can. However, I do think it's terribly important for Ian to know that we want to help him and, moreover, how we feel about him. Call it the silly fancy of an expectant mum if you like, but I truly believe that it will bring Esther safely back to us if Ian can be jolted out of his self-absorption and begin to consider others."

She started to cry in earnest, fumbling for a handkerchief which Chris supplied. Martin knelt beside her, rocking her gently in his arms, while the others waited patiently for the storm to subside.

The listener at the door stole quietly back to the dining room, tears running down his face.

CHAPTER THIRTEEN

The insistent telephone ringing in the Gallery's flat made Yvonne jump. Pulse leaping in anticipation, she hastened to answer it. Before she could speak, Maurice's voice cut in to reassure that he was no bearer of bad tidings, merely eager to consult about a somewhat different matter – one that nevertheless was closely linked with their present problems.

The relief that washed over her when it dawned that his call wasn't terrible news about Esther made her grip the receiver as if it were Maurice's arm. She was incapable of speech. Anxiously the voice at the other end enquired if she was still there? On stammering assurance that she was, he briefly outlined her friends' thoughts and concerns about Ian: no instant reply expected but perhaps she could mull over their flow of ideas? Her face crumpled while she listened to that dear, familiar voice. Again she felt a stab of anger that Ian could treat this kind man so peremptorily. She knew without hesitation that the group were right in their summing-up of Ian's behaviour.

She made up her mind on the spot. She had only been back in the Gallery for a mere fifteen minutes but already was wondering how she was going to face a night alone there; every sound she made echoed round the empty rooms, emphasising her loneliness.

"Hold everything," she almost shouted down the line. "I'm

coming back to Maples. I thought I'd be closer to Esther if I returned here, but I feel shut out, cut off on my own."

With that she slammed the receiver, grabbed her coat, ran out to the car, turned it and accelerated away.

★

Maurice put down the silent phone and stared thoughtfully across the hall. The shut door opposite seemed to be wearing an invisible notice stating 'Keep Out'. An essentially private person himself, he was reluctant to intrude upon another's space. About to turn away he heard the sound of crying coming from the room – much more than crying, harsh sobs which seemed to be tearing the man apart. He couldn't ignore such distress and opening the door quietly, went in.

Ian was standing at the window, hands pressed down hard on the sill. The fire was almost out and it was cold in the room. With an involuntary shiver he went over to Ian putting a hand on his shoulder, waiting until the sobs lessened. The two men stood side by side, staring out of the bare window into the inky darkness beyond.

Ian spoke in an unsteady voice:

"I thought I didn't care but I do – about Esther I mean. I thought I had become such an unfeeling so-and-so that I was incapable of any normal human emotion. But I *do* care. I do! And I've failed Yvonne today, let her down badly yet again. Left her to face our flat on her own. I'm worthless. A one armed cripple. And I heard what you all had to say about me in the kitchen." Maurice twisted his head round in surprise.

"Oh yes," droned the weary voice, "I've even stooped to eavesdropping. But every word spoken about me was the truth. I must be some sort of freak."

He shook his head, and turned away to slump in an armchair.

"I just wish Esther were back," he grumbled. "It cuts me up to think what might be happening to her. I've pushed Yvonne away. I shouldn't imagine she'll want anything further to do with me after this. I don't blame her. I want life to get back to normal. I can't face myself. I wish I'd killed myself when I had the opportunity back in the hospital. I would have been better off out of the way. I couldn't bring myself to tell you or Yvonne about that little episode either."

Leaning back in the chair, he covered his face with his hand.

Maurice wisely kept silent. Moving away from the draughty window he hunkered before the fire, carefully splintering the logs' remnants with the poker until sparks flew up the chimney. Then he laid two small logs on top, and stood with one elbow supported on the mantelpiece listening to them begin to crackle. Satisfied they were well alight he closed the curtains and switched on a couple of table lamps; already the room felt cosier but Ian did not stir.

Maurice gave his friend a long, compassionate look. Of all people, he knew from first-hand painful experience how it felt to wallow in self-pity; to see life only in shades of grey with no meaning, and therefore to be ended. Ian's last sentences had all begun with the pronoun 'I' – a sure indication he was wrapped up in himself; the only encouraging sign being his genuine concern for Esther.

And the other obvious evidence was that he needed far more help than all his friends could provide. They would support him but he needed professional therapy. Today's trauma had unplugged something from deep inside his psyche, something he had desperately tried to suppress; but the effort needed to do so was more than he could cope with, as strong emotions rose to the surface. Layers of himself were beginning to peel away.

However, for the moment, he was best left on his own, decided Maurice. He pulled one of the ever present travelling rugs off the back of the other armchair and tucked it round his friend's knees; at least he was warm and comfortable. Putting the fireguard in place, the faithful man cast a swift look round. No more could be done for the present. Ian's breathing sounded rhythmic: he was asleep.

★

On re-entering the hall Maurice jumped, as with a flurry of cold air the front door opened without warning and in rushed Yvonne, discarding her coat across the bannisters, and scattering raindrops over the carpet. Seeing Maurice she burst in tears.

"I'm just.. so.. glad.. to be back here," she gulped. "Is there any..?"

He shook his head, holding her tenderly to him. He could smell her damp hair and feel her shaking. Poor girl: she was under enormous strain.

"Where's Ian? I must talk to him, comfort him. I know how depressed he can get," came her immediate concern. "I'm no longer angry with him, you know."

Maurice pointed at the dining room, then putting a finger to his lips he led her toward the kitchen. Like a child she followed. Luckily the room was empty and he sat her at the table. Ever a practical man he asked:

"A cup of soup, Yvonne? I think we've all drunk enough coffee for today." He rummaged in one of the cupboards. "Well, we aren't exactly spoilt for choice. It would appear we can only boast tomato or vegetable."

"Vegetable, please."

To allow this sweet-natured woman time to recover her equilibrium, Maurice busied himself mixing the soup in a couple of chunky mugs, pouring on boiling water. He arranged cream crackers on a plate together with a generous wedge of

Cheddar cheese. Pleased to notice that she was healthily hungry, he sipped his soup and waited for her questions.

"Oh, that feels a lot better. I didn't realise how much I needed to eat. Thank you, Maurice."

A little colour had returned to her face, and she looked round the kitchen, managing a smile, smoothing her hair and winding a stray curl behind her ear. Maurice cleared the empty mugs and plates into the sink and sat down opposite her. "It was silly of me to think I could manage on my own," she admitted ruefully. "One needs to be with friends at a time like this. True friends, I mean. Ian and I are lucky to have you, and everyone else, to support us."

"You know you'll always have that. We'll always be here."

She leant across and squeezed his hand.

"I know. That's what makes me feel safe somehow, in spite of the world tumbling down around my ears. But listen, Maurice, you were quite right in your assessment of Ian. I've known for a long time that he can't face up to certain things. But why did you point to the dining room and…? Ah! – He's asleep, isn't he? He's always napping these days. I think it's an escape route for him. But how can we, can I, help him? He simply won't discuss the problem." She sighed. "And we used to be so close with no mysteries in our life. What can I do, Maurice? I don't know which way to turn."

Maurice's first impulse was to comfort, to soothe her agitation, but he held back. Yvonne had also suppressed emotion far too long. She needed this outlet. She began talking again:

"And what are the police doing about Esther and Keith?" Anxiety sharpened her voice. "We've heard nothing. Nothing at all. Oh, Maurice, I should have talked over my worries with you – about Ian I mean – but I felt it would be disloyal to him." She paused and then went on:

"Oh dear, my mind keeps jumping about this evening.

It's gone back to Esther again. I know we'll hear just as soon as there's any news. I do trust Christopher, but I don't feel I can bear this. It's too much at once. Why doesn't something happen?"

Her hands stretched out to Maurice, to be firmly held between his own. They sat in silence for a minute or two and then Maurice said slowly:

"Listen, Yvonne, I was equally slow off the mark about Ian, ignoring warning signs which were plain to see. Because I met him when he was a boy I thought I knew him, but of course I don't – not really. None of us really know one another. But let me fill you in."

He recounted how he had heard Ian sobbing and all that the distraught man had blurted out. She felt hurt, convinced that she had kept the pact for truth made when they married. Maurice probed gently:

"Are you sure? We all keep painful things locked away in corners of our minds; locked away from ourselves, from our loved ones, from the world at large – but most of all from ourselves. If you and I could muster enough honesty and realism to face the truth, doubtless we'd uncover some harsh facts. After all, we're far from perfect human beings, which is why we're on earth to learn lessons. And we've all done and said things we regret. Ian is trying to admit his mistakes and I feel the time is not far away when he will seek help. But he does need professional guidance, with us, his friends, supporting him in the background.

"However, enough of Ian for the moment, all our energies need to be concentrated on Esther. We'll go…"

He broke off. The phone was ringing in the hall. Feet clattered down the stairs. Someone answered it and began to speak excitedly. Yvonne jumped up, hands locked together. A brief pause, then another voice took over, crisp and professional.

The receiver pinged as Martin burst into the kitchen shouting "Good news!" Yvonne's knees trembled and she sat down. Close on Martin's heels followed an upbeat Chris, words tumbling in haste.

"The car's been spotted by my eagle-eyed detective on the very point of being driven away from outside a house somewhere in south London. Don't ask me how he found it again but he did! Apparently there were three men inside and the driver fitted the description of Marsden. He's discreetly tailing the car, and since there's not much traffic around so late in the day he won't lose it. The Met. are on standby and they will be alerted wherever the car ends up.

"And more encouraging news! My other chap had managed to reach his partner and stayed behind in the street to make seemingly innocent enquiries from a few of its residents. By luck he knocked up an elderly chap who was extremely chatty. The old boy described a woman living three doors away from him who sounds like Jean; that house is where we *think* Esther is being held."

Looking at Yvonne, he emphasised: "I must stress *think*, my dear."

She nodded, never taking her eyes off his face.

Chris continued: "Also the woman doesn't live there on a permanent basis, which ties in since she spends much of her time at 'The Globe'."

Maurice chimed in: "How are the police going to discover if Esther is definitely there, and if she is, more to the point how are they proposing to get her out? What happens next in cases like this?"

By this time everyone in the house had gathered around the kitchen table, all that is except for Ian. Emotions were running high and Chris's gaze went from face to face while he sought to reassure and explain:

"To make a charge stick on Jensen he has to be caught red-handed, caught with his hand in the till so to speak. So, once he has entered the premises he is heading for, the police will swoop. When the signal comes through that he's been arrested, together with Marsden, then the police will enter the house in Larkhill Road, Kennington, South London where a search will be made for Esther. A search warrant has already been applied for…"

'Don't start being long winded and policeman-like now;' thought Joanna. 'For God's sake, get a move on. You can be pompous at times. Yvonne doesn't want to hear all this.'

But Yvonne wasn't listening any more. She had heard the most significant words. She thought she would faint, the relief was overwhelming. Esther would be home tonight – she would be back with them tonight. Then suddenly, horribly, doubts crept in, swirling round her mind like strands of fog. Supposing, just supposing, these clever detectives of Chris' were wrong. Maybe they had the wrong house, the wrong road, the wrong woman? Would Jensen really have parked his car outside the very house where Esther was being held? Would he have been that cocky? Surely not. But still there was a slim chance and she held it fast to her. She must tell Ian. It was wrong for him to be ignored. He had always loved Esther. She must go to him. Immediately.

Scraping back her chair she ran from the room, banging back the door. Her voice could be heard crying out:

"Oh my darling, my darling…"

Maurice silently clicked shut the kitchen door.

★

The three men had left the house in Larkhill Road; the two women were alone. For one, youth was but a distant memory, while the other was struggling to loosen the bonds of adolescence. Jean gave her companion a curious glance. She had certainly not relished this job of warder when Antony had outlined his plan. The thought of coping with a hysterical teenager was anathema. But this girl was not hysterical – if anything she was almost too calm. Jean gave her a closer look. She wasn't pretty, instead the word 'comely' came to mind. A funny old-fashioned expression but it suited this girl in her sitting room. Although she was hardly a guest, nevertheless it gave Jean immense pleasure to have someone in the house who appreciated all she saw. She had been quick to observe the delighted reaction which had lit the girl's face when they had first entered.

Jean loved her home. 'The Globe' was a place of work, to be endured while its usefulness lasted. But this was a real home, bought ten years ago with money left her by an elderly uncle. Gordon knew nothing about either the money or the house. They lived totally separate lives, husband and wife in name only. No, this was her secret. Even Antony thought she had persuaded a bank manager to give her a mortgage. But she had paid cash for the property, not keen to have other people stick their noses in her affairs. She had taken time to find the right house, choosing the district with great care. She did not want a middle class environment, nor did she want to live in an overcrowded area, having endured deprivation when a child. The selected house was deliberately left in its original condition on the outside; that way it would not attract attention from the neighbours or casual callers. She had not the slightest interest in gardening, only in interior design. On long weekends free from 'The Globe', and on vacations, she came to the house. It was her precious refuge. With an almost religious fervour, she set about turning it into a palace.

To begin with she had pored over glossy 'house beautiful'

magazines, but quickly came to realise that she possessed natural good taste and started to trust her own judgement. Her confidence grew. She wasn't in any hurry, sensuously taking time to find the right piece of china or furniture. It was sweet pleasure to discover that objects did not have to be antique or expensive to give delight. Even her taste in clothes changed as the house flowered, the wardrobe filled with feminine, silky dresses. Gordon's somewhat frumpy wife had become a lady of fashion.

Always on her arrival at the house the first priority was to soak in a hot, scented bath in her glamorous bathroom. Then she would carefully select a dress, its well-cut, flowing lines disguising her plump figure. Downstairs she would pour fine wine into a cut glass goblet, watching the firelight reflected in its crystal facets, the only regret being that there was no one to share all she had come to treasure.

But tonight she was not alone. This girl, Esther, had been brought up to recognise beauty and graciousness, having lived all her life in the shadow of an art gallery. Jean had often walked past the Latimer Gallery, too shy to go in. And she watched Mr Caton when he strolled through the village. He was undeniably a man of quality; there was an air about him which was natural and genuine, an air she knew she could never achieve.

Once more she wondered why she had agreed to Antony's plan when first suggested. He had assured her that any risks would be minimal and, of course, the money was a lure. Her savings were dwindling and there were still one or two more alterations she wanted to do in the house. Besides, since the day of his birth, she could deny him nothing. She loved him. She knew he took full advantage of her softness but didn't care. After all, the girl would not be hurt, only held hostage for a few hours. She knew Antony had a violent temper and conveniently tried to forget the reason for his last prison sentence. But he had never been violent toward her and she was sure she could control him where the girl was concerned. She was also sure that neither Dunsett nor the girl would be able to identify her house as she had deliberately brought Marsden to it by a roundabout route. In this area of South London every street looked identical, with rows of terraced houses each a twin of the one next door. Her neighbours didn't know her and she would never again return to 'The Globe'. She felt safe from detection.

Esther was puzzled by this woman. Since they had entered the extraordinary house, her attitude had altered. She seemed a much softer person. In Keith's flat, and in the car, she had sounded rough, abrasive, somewhat frightening in fact. The outside of the house, seen dimly by the light of a street lamp, had given that impression too. When she was pushed into the narrow hall she had dreaded to find dirt and decay with peeling wallpaper and bare floorboards, but the exact opposite was revealed, causing her to gasp. The hall and sitting room were gracious and lovely, indeed stylish. Keith's bewilderment was obvious too as he quickly glanced round, raising his eyebrows.

Now the men had gone and there was only Jean.

"Sit down, girl," came the demand. "I'm not going to hurt you if you do as you're told."

Esther felt the truth had been spoken and perched uneasily on the edge of an armchair quite unable to prevent herself from staring round the room in amazement.

"Quite a surprise for you then?" Jean sounded smug.

Esther cleared her throat: "Yes…yes.. it is."

"You like it, do you? Like my house, my home?"

"Oh, I do! I do! It's really lovely."

Esther spoke with sincerity. It resembled the interior of a room featured in a Sunday paper magazine, but there was more to it than that because it wasn't simply a showcase – it had heart and warmth. Nothing jarred, colours blended. There were thick carpets and rugs in soft weaves, attractive fabrics had been chosen for the matching curtains and chair covers, delicate pieces of fine china were dotted here and there, while gentle lighting enhanced the whole scene.

"Tell me," asked Jean wistfully, "is it really tasteful? I haven't overdone it, have I? You would know because you have been brought up surrounded by lovely things – all those wonderful paintings. Is it the sort of room your mum and dad would approve of?"

"Oh yes, they would, very much indeed."

"Good. Good. Tell me, your dad's only got one arm. I often wondered how he lost it?"

"It was a hit and run driver," recounted Esther, wondering at the same time about this dumpy little Jean-figure seated opposite. "He was knocked down and badly injured. The doctors couldn't save his arm. He was about twenty or twenty-one, I'm not quite sure which. Anyway he couldn't continue with his art course so eventually he and Mum opened the Gallery."

"You don't know how lucky you are to have decent parents and to live somewhere proper and nice. Tony and I didn't."

Jean began to talk at length about their awful home life and how she had struggled to look after Antony. Esther's eyelids drooped. The room was warm, she was emotionally drained, besides being hungry. She simply wanted to sleep. Languor was overtaking her when Jean shook her arm none too gently, jerking her awake. The woman did not want her captive audience to sleep; she craved someone to talk to.

"You need a drink to buck you up. Wine or sherry?"

"Oh.. no, no thank you. I don't drink alcohol. A cup of tea…?"

"Tea!" Jean laughed, a hoarse sound as though she was out

of practice. "Of course, I was forgetting. How old are you, girl?"

"Fifteen – fifteen and a half strictly."

"Well, Miss 15 ½, are you hungry?"

"Oh gosh yes, I am," came the heartfelt reply.

"I remember I was always hungry when I was fifteen. I ate a lot of fish and chips in those days. Can't produce fish and chips for you but I should be able to rustle up something in the kitchen. Come with me."

Esther stood up feeling slightly queasy, and followed the woman up the hall and into a small, square kitchen which was clean and functional.

"Beans on toast with a pot of tea okay?"

Esther nodded and sat down, suddenly afraid she might faint. Everything was so unreal. This woman sounded like one of her friends' mother asking what she wanted to eat. But she wasn't anybody's mother; she was her captor and her awful brother had dragged poor Keith off on a burglary job. The thought occurred to her that perhaps she could make a dash for the front door while the woman was preparing the snack.

It seemed Jean had read her thoughts because she calmly walked over to the kitchen door and locked it, dropping the key in the pocket of her trousers. She looked again at the girl.

"Here! – you need a glass of water and to put your head down between your legs. You look ghastly."

But, once Esther had eaten, and drunk two cups of hot, sweet tea, she felt much stronger. Jean washed up neatly and then turned round to Esther asking half shyly:

"Would you like to see the rest of the house?"

"Yes, yes I would very much. But first could I *please* telephone my parents to let them know I'm okay? I can't possibly tell them where I am because I've no idea. But I know they'll be so worried about me."

For a split second Jean hesitated and then her face hardened.

"No. Tony said no contact and that's that. It's no good trying to butter me up, girl. You must wait 'til Tony gets back, then we'll take you home. You'll have to make do with that."

Esther nodded, resigned to her fate. The door was unlocked and Jean led the way upstairs. There were only two bedrooms, one in use as a lumber-room while the other was delightfully feminine. Jean proudly opened the wardrobe to show off the quality clothes hanging neatly inside. The bathroom, being the exact opposite to the somewhat austere one at the Gallery, brought a smile to Esther's drawn face. Mum and Dad didn't go in for frills and fancies.

Downstairs again, the last room unseen was the dining room. In here the only furniture was a round mahogany table and four matching chairs, the table laid with four elegant place settings. For her age Esther was blessed with a sensitive imagination and, looking at the place settings which she guessed would never be used, the pathos of Jean's life suddenly revealed itself to her, the loneliness and the vulnerability. She was a head taller than this woman and could look down at her. She noted the grey hairs springing through the tinted parting and the sagging skin under the small eyes. Unexpected tears filled her own.

As though on cue the woman looked up, saw the tears glistening, and was aware of sympathy. She was amazed. The tall girl was so calm, so placid that Jean unconsciously leant towards her. It was a strange sensation but she felt relaxed just standing beside her.

At that precise moment the doorbell rang long and loud while a fist hammered on the front door. They both jumped, the spell broken.

"Quick," shouted Jean, "get in the kitchen. Hurry! Hurry!"

She hustled Esther down the hall, pushing her roughly into the room, where she fell on her knees.

With the door locked, Jean smoothed her hair, and walked

swiftly toward the noise resounding through the house. Perched awkwardly on the narrow top step were two men, unmistakably policemen. Her heart missed a beat. Her dreams were over.

"Yes, what do you want?" she enquired, trying to sound unconcerned.

One of the duo produced a warrant card and in a flat monotone recited:

"We have reason to believe you are holding Esther Latimer here against her will and we have a search warrant…"

"Well, I'm not, and you will do no.."

By this time, Esther had crawled to the kitchen door and started to thump it shouting "Help me! Please help me!" with all the strength of her lungs.

One of the men pushed Jean aside and ran down the hall.

"Out of the way, Miss," he yelled, putting his shoulder to the door. After two emphatic attempts the panel splintered and he was inside.

Esther was free. Yvonne's dearest wish would come true. Her daughter would be home that night.

CHAPTER FOURTEEN

The season was spring, poignantly warm and scented, leaving the cold winter to memory. The place was Maples, in bloom with daffodils, pink and white hyacinths and young bluebells, the plump silky buds of pussy willows eager to break open, giving release to the catkins inside. The time was mid-afternoon, a tea tray laid on the patio table where Maurice sat alone. Tea ignored, he was deep in thought.

He knew he had done all that was humanly possible but a part of his life was now over, never to return. He stood up and strolled across the lawn, pausing to look back at the house; he could clearly see the window of the room in which, over sixty years ago, he had been born. For six decades the old house had wound itself in and out of his life. Memories crowded in.

There was early childhood with the shadowy figure of his father in the background. A new bicycle, the mudguard buckled, and Alex the gardener mending it, watched by the diminutive shape of his mother, her face aglow as she looked at her adored lover, their unborn child stirring in her womb. Then came the unhappy adolescence with his desire to paint being continually thwarted, which finally drove him from the house. A decade of loneliness and despair followed, trying to conquer the paralysing symptoms of low self-esteem. By compensation, the last three decades had been a colourful tapestry woven with incident – meeting Ian, finding fulfilment from his paintings, bringing

Maples to life with the infectious enthusiasm of worthy young students, the dark shadow of his illness, thankfully long faded, and through it all the love of wonderful friends, Joanna, Chris, John; suddenly there seemed so many of them after time spent in the wilderness. Sweet Esther. Kind Sophie. And, of course, Keith. No, today he should be known by his given name – Alexander Caton.

How peaceful it had been in the old village church this afternoon, he reflected. Then leaning back in the carved oak pew, overlooked by stained glass windows, he had savoured the perfume from great bunches of white narcissi, lovingly picked that morning by Megan and Esther. The priest's voice was quite soothing in its way, although the words intoned were totally meaningless to him. The organ began to play quietly and he stood to watch his brother's coffin carried past. He followed it out into the spring sunshine. The others gathered round and there he left them. He had no desire to attend the burial. He turned his face toward Maples, toward home, with a fervent wish that life would settle down after all the traumas of the last three or four months.

The day of Esther's kidnap had started the whole train of events.

It had been an ordinary peaceful morning with members of the household drifting in and out of the kitchen for breakfast. Christmas behind them, Esther had decided to return home in time for lunch at the Latimer Gallery. A lift from Martin was offered but refused because the snow was quickly melting and she felt a need for fresh air after being cooped up in the house. She dawdled down the drive, fascinated by the extraordinary shapes of icicles dripping off the trees, only to arrive at the bus stop in time to see the bus disappearing down the lane.

She muttered under her breath, aware that it would be at least an hour, if not longer, before another turned up. Retracing her steps back to Maples she halted when an old Land Rover drew up alongside her. The steamy window was wound down and she recognised Simon Marsden, the young man whose family farm bordered Maples' grounds.

He saluted her and said in friendly fashion:

"Hello, Esther, just missed your bus? Hop aboard. I can give you a lift. Where're you off to?"

"Home, Simon. But that will be right out of your way, won't it?"

"Not at all. I'm on my way to town as it happens. Something to pick up from there. Make yourself comfortable if you can. Farmers' vehicles are always rather smelly I'm afraid."

Esther grinned and clambered onto the rickety, torn passenger seat, which was liberally covered in dogs' hairs. A definite, strong, but not unpleasant, aroma of animal feed pervaded. No qualms troubled her about accepting Simon's offer; after all, he was a neighbour, indeed Maples' only one, and she'd often chatted to him over the boundary fence. And it had been Simon's father who, in Esther's romantic eyes, had performed the role of linkman in bringing Maurice and Ian together. If he hadn't allowed Maurice to put up his tent Ian might never have met him. Esther shuddered. It didn't bear thinking about.

Unravelling the twisted seat belt which looked as though it had been chewed by the dogs, she gave her companion a sideways glance, quickly assessing him in the way of all young girls when on the verge of womanhood. Privately she considered him to be somewhat affected both in speech and clothes. He was a shade too smartly dressed to be described a 'hands on' farmer, but at twenty-six, tall and well built, with a thick head of corn coloured hair, she had to admit that many of her friends would call him 'dishy'. For a fleeting moment she caught herself wondering what it would be like to be kissed by him, to feel his hands begin to unbutton…'Stop this, Esther Latimer,' she admonished herself sternly. 'Pay attention to what's happening.' But to her surprise nothing was happening. The ignition was turned off and Simon was staring straight ahead, hands clenched round the steering wheel. She gently touched his arm and he started, looking at her as if he had forgotten her existence.

' "Are you all right Simon? You seem troubled."

"Yes, yes, I'm okay. Just a bit tired, that's all." He sounded testy. He took a deep breath, appearing to have made up his mind about something.

"Excuse me a moment," he said, leaning across her to reach a mobile phone from the glove compartment. "I must make a quick call before we set off."

He pulled up the aerial, tapped out a number and waited. A few seconds elapsed and then he spoke briefly:

"The goods will be delivered in about half an hour. Make sure you're there on time. No, no problems."

He retracted the aerial, placed the receiver on the dashboard shelf, but still sat on in the same position. Esther was taken aback to see beads of sweat on his forehead despite the chill air. With an obvious conscious effort he said:

"Right then, let's get you into town."

The words sounded flat but this time he did switch on the engine and they moved off.

All through her life Esther had found it easy to talk to people regardless of age or gender. As a small child she had first chatted endlessly to her favourite doll, and then Christine Pope – no mean talker herself – had been on the receiving end, hard pressed to keep pace. And this particular situation in which she found herself today presented no problem to Esther. She was always naturally straightforward. So she conversed happily with Simon on a whole range of subjects: animals, especially dogs, Christmas past, her plans to train as a nurse. However, the nearer they came to their destination the more monosyllabic his answers, until finally they dried up. She was aware that he kept glancing at her. A vague uneasiness caught hold, thoughts began to creep in about the vulnerability of females accepting lifts. But no one had ever hurt her in her life. She had never had any reason to be frightened before.

Their journey had brought them to the outskirts of town, where Simon was halted before red traffic lights. She swivelled in her seat and met his eyes, surprised to see an expression in them, of sadness – like the sadness of an animal left on its own, unable to cope.

"Is something wrong, Simon?" she probed gently.

For a fleeting moment he seemed about to speak, but the lights changed and instead he simply shook his head. Then she recalled overhearing Joanna and Maurice discussing this young man only a few days ago. She had been absorbed in nursing pamphlets at the time, so had only paid scant attention, except to gather that he did have severe financial difficulties. There had even been gossip in the village that he might lose the farm. She had shivered inwardly, glad that nothing of a similar nature impinged into her own safe existence.

But worry would explain his somewhat strange behaviour today. Yes! That was it. Perhaps he'd had a nasty letter from the bank manager that same morning. Having reassured herself she settled back and relaxed, looking forward to seeing her parents once more. The three of them got on well – or so she naively imagined.

Two minutes later found her sitting bolt upright. Simon was jerkily negotiating a busy roundabout and he missed the turn off that would have led straight to the Gallery. Still fairly unperturbed she quickly pointed this out:

"Hang on a minute, Simon, you've missed my road. You'll have to go round again, or we'll get tangled up in the one way system."

Ignoring her remarks he mumbled:

"Believe me, Esther, I'm truly sorry about what's going to happen next. I really am. But I have no alternative. I really don't. You *must* see that! Please…*please*.. try to understand."

The Land Rover was swaying slightly from side to side, other drivers were hooting, while he drove round again, looking anxiously for a turning.

"What are you talking about Simon? I don't know what you mean. A-a-ah! Ouch! Oh, why don't you slow down?"

Simon had abruptly taken a left hand turn, accompanied by more hooting and gesticulating from further irritated drivers, jolting Esther sharply against the grubby, damp passenger window. She banged the side of her head and began to feel queasy. A white faced Simon was increasing the vehicle's tempo, speeding it up an unfamiliar road. They flashed past a Catholic church, and then Esther recognised one or two landmarks. She now knew where they were. Simon was heading for a select area of town, where, joked her father, they only ate 'posh nosh', and houses for sale were only advertised in glossy brochures. Simon slowed to normal speed, appearing calmer.

"I'm sorry about that, Esther. I'm sorry about everything."

She shook her head, saying nothing. They were driving past undoubtedly luxurious houses with wide frontages, but she ached to be at the much loved Gallery, or back at dear old Maples, both real homes with heart and warmth. Tears pricked her eyes. For all their glamour these other houses were sterile, empty of any character.

The Land Rover was slowing to a halt outside a house which perhaps was marginally smaller than its neighbours. Simon turned and spoke quickly, each point emphasised with a stab of his forefinger in the air.

"Listen, Esther. No! – Don't interrupt because there isn't much time. Whatever happens, *don't* annoy the man who's about to join us." His voice tightened. "Here he comes now."

Esther spun round and saw the front door open. A man came out and banged shut the door behind him. He walked down the path toward them. It was like watching a film in slow motion.

"Remember," hissed Simon in her ear. "Keep your mouth shut. Shut!- D'you hear?"

"But..but..what? I don't understand!" Her heart was beating so rapidly she could hardly speak.

However, Simon was no longer listening. His fascinated gaze was fixed on the man who was by then slowly rocking back and forth on his heels, balancing on the edge of the kerb, while staring in at Esther. His face was close to the glass and she instinctively drew back. It was a hard face, with a lank fringe of hair edging small, crafty eyes. She trembled and pressed her chin down into the comfort of her long woollen scarf, determined not to cry.

The man sauntered round to Simon's door and indicated to him to get out. He then climbed into the back of the vehicle and settled himself quite comfortably on a pile of empty sacks behind Esther. She could feel and smell his garlic tainted breath on her neck. He tweaked the end of the scarf and menaced:

"Marsden didn't tell me you were pretty."

She pulled away and he laughed.

Simon got back behind the wheel and they drove off.

Less than twenty-four hours had passed since Esther had first come face to face with Antony Jensen. How could one day seem that long, she marvelled sleepily? Never in her life had she felt this tired. But the drama was over.

It was now the middle of the night. At last she was on her way to Maples, travelling somewhat uncomfortably in the back of a police car, accompanied on the journey by a sour smelling policewoman and a fresh faced young constable – a 'rookie'. Reaction to the day's events overwhelmed her and she fell asleep.

The policeman regarded her weary figure with admiration, which had dawned when he saw her first in the kitchen of that extraordinary house. As she ran idle fingers through her short fair hair and tidied her pullover, she had impressed him with her calm demeanour. However, when she straightened up after tying her shoe-laces, he noticed tears glistening on her eyelashes which she quickly blinked away. Certainly not the hysterical type, unlike many females, he decided. Her main concern was to ensure that her parents had been told of her safe release; and also, oddly enough he thought, what was going to happen to Jean Preston?

She asked this question while they were squashed together in the narrow hall where Jean was being led out through the front door. She had looked beseechingly back over her shoulder at the girl who managed a small smile and a nod, stressing to her companion that she had never felt threatened in any way by Jean. The panic had only surfaced in the older woman when the police were hammering at the door; until that moment she had felt strangely like a guest.

Esther awoke suddenly. The car had halted outside Maples. The front door stood wide open, the porch light showing all her dear ones gathered in a group. She stumbled awkwardly from the car. When one figure broke away from the rest, she felt familiar arms hugging her close and caught the scent of her mother's sweet perfume. She was home.

★

Esther meant to sleep long into the next day; indeed, the rest of the household followed suit – except that is, for two people.

Maurice had only catnapped for the few remaining hours of the night. Dawn's thin light found him wrapped in a much worn plaid dressing gown, seated in an armchair pulled round to face the window. He just couldn't stop grinning from sheer relief and joy. Relief for Esther's safe return, and joy and pride in the part that Keith had played in her protection. He watched as pale streaks threaded their way through the dark sky like strands of white wool, and sent out a prayer of thankfulness. Until this moment he had not allowed himself to picture a scenario where Esther might have suffered serious harm. The thought made him shudder.

He moved quietly down to the kitchen, grinning yet again as he passed the room where Esther lay asleep, then he made a pot of coffee, found two fairly clean mugs, and set out a tray together with a packet of biscuits. He carried this up to his room, needing some time to himself since the day ahead hardly promised to be a quiet one.

Christopher would be anxious to present his latest, no doubt somewhat pedantic report, and next there was the sensitive issue of Ian to be faced. Last night he seemed to have been the only one present to have noticed Ian standing well to the back of the excited group gathered to welcome Esther. The man had looked a picture of apathy. True, his gaze had longingly followed his daughter who was being ushered upstairs by Yvonne. Esther had turned upon the staircase to blow her father a kiss, but he had already moved back towards the dining room on his own. The girl's face was puzzled.

Maurice shaved and dressed quickly and sat composing himself for what he knew might be a tricky encounter. He did

214

not have long to wait. His own door left slightly ajar, he clearly heard the dining room's click open. He moved another easy chair near his own and shook some biscuits out on a plate. He had kept the coffee piping hot on top of his gas fire.

Ian did knock but came in before Maurice could answer. He seemed to have aged several years overnight. His clothes were crumpled, the empty sleeve hanging loosely down, and there was two days' growth of beard on his chin. He didn't look at Maurice pouring coffee; he simply slumped in the vacant chair and began to eat and drink greedily. Maurice waited, thankful that at least Ian had come to him, not having been at all sure that he would. His throat ached that this old friend, of abundant courage and enthusiasm, had lost hope.

Two or three minutes ticked by – a strain even for Maurice, well used to quiet reflection. Ian's voice sounded loud when he broke the silence.

"I need help. I'm not stupid – I know I do. I can't go on like this. I seem to be hurting everyone around me. I think I'm going mad. Please help me. You've never failed me yet."

Maurice let out an almost audible sigh of relief, knowing the plea had to come from Ian first. He stood up, and pulled his chair round to face him. Sitting down again, he found himself under close scrutiny. They exchanged a long look, full of memories and affection.

"You know I'll do anything within my power, Ian. Anything. But first of all try to drop the idea that you're going mad because you *most* certainly are not. You have put yourself under great strain – unnecessarily so, I might add. But I know exactly what it's like to feel as you do."

Ian gave a brief nod of acknowledgment. Both men remembered Maurice's fragile state of mind when they first met, although Ian was too young at the time to understand the problems the other sought to overcome. Now he knew.

Maurice was thoughtful, anxious to offer wise counsel. Then he heard Sophie scratching at the door and got up to let her in before she awoke the slumberers. She padded over to his chair, jumped up and sat there looking at him. It was a favourite game she loved to play. He pretended to be cross, snapping his fingers sharply and pointing to her basket. She got down slowly, hanging her head, and curled up in her bed, her paw over her nose. Rewarded with a biscuit treat, she thumped her tail, looking up at Ian, her eyes warm with emotion. Despite his misery he laughed out loud, he couldn't help himself, she looked so funny. Maurice could have cheered, aware that Ian was not a great animal lover and that Sophie generally ignored him. But her sensitive nature had intuited his pain and tried to help. She had broken the ice.

Heartened, he began to pat his pockets, seeking pipe and tobacco. Ian handed both to him off a small table beside his own chair, thinking as he did so that Maurice, his pipe and thought provoking words were inseparable. He leaned forward in his chair.

"Maurice, d'you think I should see a psycho? I can't seem to feel anything you see; I'm sort of dead inside. I love Esther, but I just couldn't react to her disappearance like everyone else. Then there's Yvonne. I love her dearly but can't express it. Our sex life is non-existent. She's terribly patient and...almost *too* understanding. You know what I mean? If she would only hit me, then I might get aroused. God, I must be getting like my father!"

Maurice shook his head.

"No, you're not. Don't clone yourself with him. What you describe sounds pretty normal under the circumstances, as if you're afraid of your feelings, afraid you can't handle them. And that's because, especially now, you're full of strong ones. See? Ordinarily you lock them in, though now you're so full of them, and they're so strong, that you've turned in upon yourself and tried to deaden them. But if you don't allow them out you won't experience the love within and behind them – the love for Esther and Yvonne. Follow any feeling you have to its ultimate source and you'll find love there. Your world of feeling is uniquely yours, foreign to outsiders, so at root only you can do anything about it. It's not dead, just locked in by you, like mine was locked in by me. Because I did that, my feelings couldn't integrate and let me honour myself, love myself with self-esteem. Not a narcissistic love, but a love for oneself as a valid, whole person first before one can truly feel love for others. The love is innately there, just locked."

He paused to relight his pipe, wondering if a question would be posed. It was, hesitantly.

"And you *did* unlock it?" Ian feared to ask this, yet desperation drove him, mingled with a logical curiosity he could always retreat behind if the answer looked tough.

"Yes," said Maurice simply.

"…Well?" Then, without response from a man who had become distant, Ian dared further – a slight catch in his voice: "How?"

Maurice was silent, surveying his friend. He could see the build-up of eye-moisture; and now, over curiosity, he heard desperation win, crying out:

"For God's sake man! You've gone so far. It's like a joke without a punch line."

"It's no joke Ian. It's a story, and my answer."

Ian nodded, staring open-mouthed. "Yes? Go on."

"Okay." The sigh given was deep rather than long. "But I'll need to talk a little about the time in my life just before we met. You'll have to bear with me. It'll clarify things for you maybe."

Ian nodded again. He did want to understand, more than ever. Hope at last gleamed in his eyes as Maurice began.

"As you already know, Maples had been empty for ten years before I decided to make the pilgrimage back here again. My mother had left a clause in her will stating that until twenty years had elapsed after her death I was prevented from selling the house. In retrospect I believe she was afraid that Keith might find some way of getting his hands on it although I can't imagine quite how. Still, I could let it out or live in it myself. At that time I didn't want to do either of those options, therefore I had the house shut up under dust covers, gave the keys to the estate agent who was supposed to keep an eye on the place, and wandered off.

"I was totally aimless, living from hand to mouth in a variety of dingy bed-sits, trying to paint, managing to sell the odd canvas here and there, suffering from fits of depression and low self-esteem. I finally had a nervous breakdown, ending up in a psychiatric hospital where I was already known, I might add. But I knew I had to get out of there or die.

"I also knew instinctively that other people, however kind and well meaning, couldn't help me because they didn't know the real me. The *ME* in here." Maurice thumped his chest. "How could they? Therefore, nobody could help me *except* me. I felt it was wrong to listen to an outsider's advice but was sure that Maples could help in some way. Therefore, I made my way back here, broke in, and lived rough for a week or so until dear old Mrs Pope discovered me. Sunk in my misery I'd completely forgotten that I'd agreed with Hartley Staples' suggestion that it would be a good idea to increase my sparse funds by renting out the house, and that a family called Latimer were about to be my first tenants!"

Ian gave a small smile. Maurice continued:

"Somewhere in the house I knew the secret to overcoming my low self-esteem lay hidden. I wandered from one empty room to another, seeking clues. They seemed to lie among the echoes, in the dust and cobwebs, in the whispered snatches of conversation I kept 'hearing'. All the while I was summoning the courage to enter my mother's study where I had suffered the worst humiliations."

He glanced again at Ian whose gaze hadn't left his face, his hand gripping the arm of his chair.

"When I finally went in, the first thing that struck me was how small it seemed. Everything was shrunk: Mother's influence had gone, completely gone. I felt a weight fall from me. But my amazing discovery was that the lost boy I had once been was still there, feeling unloved, rejected. He had been hidden there for a decade. I don't know quite how to put this, but he seemed to run towards me and I gathered him up and hugged him close. He was the answer to overcoming my low self-worth, the answer I had been seeking all those years. I had left him behind ten years before without saying good-bye. But we were now whole, integrated. I was starting to be in control of my life."

"I then met you and knew what I wanted to do. I knew that I wanted to keep the house more than I'd ever wanted anything. When your parents moved out, as they inevitably would, ·I would move in and perhaps open an art school. Your sister, of course, also had ideas later along the same lines; and the rest, as they say, is history."

There was a long silence after Maurice finished speaking. He had said far more than intended; tears were running down his cheeks and he brushed them away.

"Maurice.. I…" Ian's voice was hoarse. "I want to go home."

"Yes, Ian, that would be best. It's where you belong at the moment. Wake Yvonne and Esther now and the three of you go back to the Gallery. When you are ready, talk to them if you can. Try to tell them how you really feel. You have two fine women in your life. They love you very much. That love will make up for any lack of understanding on their part. But the three of you do need some time on your own. Take the phone off the hook and forget the outer world."

Ian got unsteadily to his feet and made for the door, then turned back and crossed over to Maurice, laying his hand on the other's shoulder. He could feel the man shaking. "I think I might know where my lost boy is," whispered Ian. "I left him in the gardens here. I'll find him one day and then I'll be all right, won't I?"

Maurice patted his hand, unable to answer. He felt very, very tired.

Christopher did not appear that day after all. In the end it was almost a week before his somewhat battered old Vauxhall car nosed its way up Maples' drive. Maurice made no attempt to hide his relief for the respite: he needed the break, suddenly feeling his age. Christopher, unable to prevent a hint of self-importance sounding in his voice, had rung to say he was busy liaising with old chums in the Force in order to nose around where strictly he had no right to be.

Nothing had been seen or heard from Ian, Yvonne or Esther since their abrupt departure. 'A good sign,' reckoned Maurice to himself. In reply to their friends' anxious enquiries he strongly advised leaving them alone. He stressed how crucial it was for Ian's recovery that they had time to themselves – crucial too if a rebonding of the trio was to take place.

It was a grey, drizzling day when the group of friends finally met in Maples' sitting room, having just been treated to one of Christine Pope's superb steak and kidney pies, so satisfying that everyone was surreptitiously undoing buttons. Keith was seated self-consciously but proudly among them. No longer on the fringe, but on a sofa between Martin and Megan.

'H'mm,' he mused, 'after all I said to Maurice about leaving Maples for the last time, here I am back again.' Moreover, he savoured a new feeling of belonging. Everyone needed to feel wanted. He experienced a new sensation of warmth toward all those gathered round him.

Lamps were alight and the fire was cheerful in the grate as Chris rubbed a finger across his moustache and cleared his throat.

"Ask questions if you want to," he urged, but once he started talking all were held by the unfolding tale.

First, however, he explained that he had seized an opportunity to interview Jensen and Jean Preston, and had chatted over a pint with Gordon Preston one evening in 'The Globe'. Marsden was too distraught to see him; indeed, alerted by his state of mind, the prison staff had put him on a 'suicide watch'. Megan drew in a sharp breath at this snippet.

Maurice looked across at her. Of course, he must have been blind. He knew she had a boyfriend in the village and Simon must have been the man. Megan was now a most attractive young woman and they were probably lovers. Poor girl, he thought compassionately, her loyalties must have been tugged both ways during the past week. Still, time enough for that later. He began to concentrate on Christopher's narrative.

"I'll start by filling in a few gaps for you about Antony Jensen. I imagine you are all curious about this guy. Well, Jensen is a greedy, volatile, forceful man, with the dubious reputation of being an expert safe cracker; a man who has already spent a quarter of his seedy life in prison. Like many habitual criminals he was sick and tired of being inside, but wasn't prepared to give up his nasty ways. Dreamed of carrying out that last really big job – then he could retire to Spain, etc. etc. His sister, Jean Preston, has spoilt him since he was a baby. I truly believe that after her house, he was the only thing she ever really loved.

Fifteen years older, she had brought him up after a fashion when their mother was killed and the father took himself off. In return, Jensen, in his strange, warped fashion, was fond of her. Always gave her a cut of the proceeds from each of his robberies, enabling her to buy something for her precious house. She was damned crafty though. Never told him about her legacy. She let him think she'd had to wheedle a mortgage from a bank. Many years ago she married, purely for convenience's sake, Gordon Preston, who had a job in the wine and spirits trade at that time. He was also fond of her, although for the life of me I can't quite think why. Anyway, when he finally became landlord of 'The Globe', she was already used to plenty of freedom; as a consequence she was only there for part of the year. Preston employed a couple of local girls to help him when he was on his own. He never asked questions, preferring not to know where she went. However, to state that he was surprised to learn about the house in Larkhill Road is putting it mildly!

"One evening last summer 'Lady Luck' seemed to be smiling on Jensen. Although Gordon hated the man there was no way he could prevent Jensen from visiting Jean. Therefore, brother and sister were closeted together in the back parlour – the room with the bead curtain – when Keith walked into the bar and ordered a pint. Jensen could hardly believe his eyes. An ex-con here in the 'Globe'. And, better and better, Preston seemed to know him, which meant he wasn't simply a casual passer-by. Even though Keith had aged considerably during the eight years since they had last met. Sorry, Keith!" Keith grinned. "Anyway, Jensen recognised him as the man considered to be a top expert on fine jewels. The germ of an idea began to grow in his devious mind. This could be the 'big job' of his dreams.

"Jean, of course, knew all the gossip about everyone in the village. People working in pubs always do! Folk like nothing better than to dish the dirt on their neighbours. Therefore,

Jensen soon learnt that Keith was the half-brother of Mr Caton who owned the big house on the edge of the village. Keith was rumoured to be from the wrong side of the blanket. He visited Mr Caton from time to time and was said to live somewhere in London. Maurice Caton was a well-known artist. 'Never heard of him,' Jensen had sneered." It was Maurice's turn to pull a face. "Keith was known to be fond in an avuncular way – definitely no funny business – of the young teenage daughter of Mr Caton's close friends. Jensen swooped upon this piece of information, so Jean told me. It seemed as if it could be the tit-bit he was looking for. And yes! Keith came in most evenings for a lager.

"Jensen had chuckled. He had this man over a barrel. If, as he shrewdly suspected, Keith was going straight, then he now had a useful lever in his hand to send him crooked. And yet another stroke of good fortune had fallen in his lap. A stupid young fool named Simon Marsden owed him a packet of money. Jensen was working as a legitimate loan shark at the time. Marsden had even handed over the deeds of his farm. And the farm turned out to be right here in this God forsaken hole of a village, and the chap fancied himself as a racing driver. The pieces were falling into place one by one – or so he fondly imagined. If he couldn't put a job together with everything handed to him on a silver plate, then he didn't deserve retirement in Spain.

"Jensen began his campaign of intimidation, trying to pressurise Keith, but he had badly misjudged his man. Keith was indeed truly fond of Esther, and despite being frightened was prepared to put up a fight to protect her." Keith's face reddened at this remark. "Jensen went ahead and laid his plans, which included kidnapping. Marsden was his lackey and will come to deeply regret his part in the whole sorry tale. He is basically a nice enough fellow, but weak, very weak. I should think he will go inside for six months and will certainly lose the farm." Maurice saw Megan clench her hands tightly together and her face lost some of its healthy colour. "Marsden had let slip to his tormentor that he often saw Esther waiting for the bus into town. 'Right,' said Jensen, 'use your charm to persuade her into accepting a lift. Let me know when she is on board and the job can be carried out that night.'

"We have since discovered" kept up Christopher "that Jensen had an accomplice working in an extremely high class jewellers; a female accomplice, high up in the company, well thought of, etc. etc., who would arrange to have the security alarm system turned off. She turned out to be a damned attractive woman, well educated, good figure…"

Chris's voice tailed off, and he paused, looking round at his friends.

"D'you know I will never understand, words fail me, what a super woman like that would see in an uncouth man like Antony Jensen. She was his 'bit on the side'. But she could have attracted any man she wanted. And yet I've seen the same thing happen time and time again."

He shook his head in disbelief.

"Passion," announced Joanna suddenly. "Passion. Quite simply that. Some women would sell their souls for it. If he provided – how can I put it delicately? – what she needed in bed, then that would blind her to everything else. All scruples would fly out of the window."

She laughed. "Don't all stare at me. I'm not speaking from personal experience! Sorry, Christopher, carry on."

"Thank you, madam. Well! I did ask. That was most illuminating."

Joanna stuck out her tongue at him, and there was general laughter.

"To continue," went on Christopher, "although I've almost finished my tale. I'll return to the day of the kidnapping. As we

224

know, Marsden seized his opportunity and picked up Esther.

He then rang Jensen to say the job was on, who in turn alerted his sister who had been poised to drive to her house at a moment's notice."

"The rest I think you probably already know. Thanks to the tenacity of the Private Eyes, Jean's hideaway was tracked down, where the police swooped and picked up the gang. And a more amateurish attempt at burglary I've yet to see." Keith nodded agreement. "So Jensen, who sweetly imagined himself to be halfway to his life of luxury, is now being held on remand and will probably go to prison for, at the least, three years. Serve the bugger right. Kidnapping and attempted burglary are not treated lightly by the courts. Well, I think that about covers it. A rather sad tale I think, especially where Jean Preston and Marsden are concerned."

★

There would probably have been a complete silence after Christopher leant back in the chair, certainly everyone appeared subdued, but that fact would never be known. Joanna had taken matters into her own hands by emitting a sharp shriek. Startled eyes looked at her in alarm and Martin jumped to his feet.

"What is it, pet? It can't be the baby! It's not due for nearly another three weeks. It's not that, is it? Oh, say it isn't. Or shake your head if it isn't, if you can't speak!"

But instead Joanna nodded a vehement 'yes', rubbing hard at the small of her back, her face pale and sweating. John Dean felt the cold hand of fear squeeze his heart, remembering his own wife and their small, sickly son in similar circumstances many years ago. 'Stop thinking like that,' he admonished himself, 'everything is different nowadays. Start sending Jo some good, strong thoughts right this minute.'

Calm, capable Megan moved smoothly into action. Kneeling on the carpet beside Jo's chair, she gently took over the massage of the painful back. She tilted her head to focus on Martin.

"Go and ring the hospital, Martin. Tell them exactly what's happening – that Jo's in a lot of pain, and that you'll be bringing her in straight away."

"Thanks, Megan," whispered Joanna, "you are helping my back. The pain is quite bad but I haven't got tummy contractions yet." She managed a weak smile. "See where passion has landed me!" The younger woman giggled.

Martin hurried out to the hall to obey instructions. 'Marvellous, bloody marvellous,' he muttered. 'I'm the chap who's supposed to stay calm in any emergency and here I am quivering like a jelly. Stop it, Hurst, for Pete's sake. Pull yourself together, man.' However, when he finally got through to the hospital he had great difficulty in preventing himself from shouting at the girl on the end of the line. He decided that she must be a half-wit.

In the sitting room the four other men were hovering in the background feeling 'de trop', only too relieved that Megan had taken charge.

"Keith," she said quickly, "go to the kitchen and ask Christine to make a hot water bottle to help relax Jo's back. I don't think she'll have gone home yet. And explain to her what's going on.

"Yes of course Megan."

Keith was half way out of the door before she had finished speaking, almost bumping against Martin on his way back. He opened the kitchen door assured of a warm reception. Since he had saved her beloved girl, he was now a hero in Christine Pope's eyes. Her back was towards him, bending over the sink, swilling away the last of the soap suds. He suddenly wondered what it would be like to cheerfully look after others, to care for their physical well-being, to want to make them comfortable. Oh yes of course, she was paid for the job, but he knew she didn't do it for the money, it went much deeper than that. He shook his head slightly, moving over to stand beside her. She jumped.

"Lor, Keith, you didn't 'alf startle me. Are you all ready for a pot of tea now, and I've made some scones. I'll bring it through in 'alf a mo'."

"No.. well, yes.. that is, it might.. no, what I really came for was a hot water bottle.. but.."

"A 'ot water bottle! What are you on about? What d'you want that for? Are you sickening for summat. Yer look rather flushed, 'ere let me feel your fore'ead."

"No! No, Christine." Keith was exasperated. "It's not for me. It's for Joanna, to help the pain in her back. It began suddenly."

"For Jo? Why, 'as she started the baby?"

When Keith agreed that it rather looked that way, even though he didn't know much about such things, he found himself being brushed aside while Christine filled the large kettle and placed it on the Aga.

"Why didn't yer say so in the furst place?" she grumbled.

"I did but you thought…"

He could have saved his breath since the bustling woman wasn't listening. She was searching for a hot water bottle, producing a running commentary at the same time.

"Reminds me of me furst, my Alan, 'e gave me pains in me back summat terruble. 'ours and 'ours 'e were."

Keith felt distinctly uncomfortable and hoped that no more details of Christine's sufferings were about to be revealed. He began to edge out of the door but found Christine following him.

"Oi must come and see what's what. The poor lamb. She needs someone to 'old 'er …'and wiv all you men around."

Keith thankfully made his escape by slipping into the dining room. It struck cold in there after the heat of the kitchen, and a faint whiff of steak and kidney pie still clung to the air. He found Maurice, John and Christopher already in situ. Walking up and down the room, hands in pockets, they nodded somewhat sheepishly at him as he joined them on their walkabout.

"How's Jo now?" he asked.

"Much the same, I think," replied Maurice. "We simply felt in the way."

"Apparently," supplied John, "the hospital advised Martin to call Doc Wendell out first, before carting her off in the car in case it's a false alarm. He shouldn't be too long."

"Aah."

A quarter of an hour later the doorbell rang perfunctorily, footsteps crossed the hall and went into the sitting room. Alec Wendell's rich brogue could be heard reassuring. A few minutes passed, then Martin put his head round the door.

"Everything is okay," he beamed. "Alec says I should be a father by later tonight. I'm taking Jo in now. I'll keep in touch."

"Give Jo our..." started John. But too late; Martin had already gone.

Left behind, the four men began to visibly relax. Christopher switched on the table lamps; John carefully prodded the dying fire back to life; Maurice drew the heavy brocade curtains across the cold windows. A brief knock at the door heralded the arrival of Christine carrying a substantial mahogany tray laden with the promised tea and scones. Megan followed close on her heels. Life was getting back to normal again.

Tea appreciated, Maurice withdrew to his sanctum – his usual habit at this time in the afternoon. He was acutely aware of a sense of relief washing over him. Fond though he undoubtedly was of Joanna, he was nevertheless heartily glad that she and her pains had retreated to a hospital. He would prefer that the mysteries of women and childbirth remained a closed book to him. Part of the allure of women was their air of secrecy and romance.

Moreover, just at this precise moment he was experiencing a turmoil in his own life. He wanted Maples to himself again, empty of people with all their various problems, even if only for a short while. He felt no guilt at this admission. He had always been a most private person – so shy at one period in his life that he would cross the road rather than have to speak to an acquaintance. Despite this agony, for many years now he had generously opened the doors of his home to diverse personalities, every room filled with an assortment of activities.

Seized with a now pressing need to close up the house, to move away he knew not where, or even cared, he sat in his armchair trying to calm his churning emotions. This was something to be considered extremely carefully; a decision to be reached on his own. There was no one he could consult since they were all interested parties. And this was certainly not the moment to be hasty in thought, word or deed. He was tired, a bone weary tiredness that follows emotional strain. He would retire punctually and see how life appeared in the morning.

It was his habit to awake early, anticipating the coming day with all the excitement of a small boy. After all, who knew what might lie ahead? This particular morning was no exception. Then memory flooded back in. He lay on his side in bed watching the tops of the tall pines that surrounded the house slowly reveal their shapes against the dark grey clouds. The answer to his dilemma was clear. He knew he would feel diminished if he parted company with any one of his friends. They seemed vulnerable, leaning on each other for care and support; a family in the truest meaning of that word: people who lived together because that was what they wanted. In his own way he had drawn them under his roof and, yes it was true, he had helped bring out the best in them. He savoured the exaltation of contentment which arose from a job well done.

But the fact that he needed a break could not be denied – a short holiday on his own. Everything else could wait – Ian and his problems, Joanna and her baby, Megan's love life. He sat up in bed, grey curly hair tousled. After breakfast he would catch the train to Cornwall. He knew a tranquil seaside port with a quaint, old, comfortable hotel where he would be well looked after. He could wander the sandy coves, the narrow, steep byways and the harbour, with his sketch pad. He needed the feeling of isolation that one could find in that remote county. Eager not to waste a moment, he was out of bed searching for his suitcase before the household was astir.

CHAPTER FIFTEEN

Once or twice in a lifetime a special magic may creep over the horizon, heralding hope and joy for the future.

For Jean Preston, stumbling out from the grim court chambers, blinking in the sunlight, magic indeed had been at work. She felt dazed. No one could suggest that there was anything beautiful about that building, but something rare and beautiful had taken place inside it. Her house, her precious home, was safe. It was hers again.

A frizzle of people had been squeezed in the sombre court room. She took a good look at them when she climbed into the dock. Such diverse expressions on their faces – some hard and accusing, some holier-than-thou, a few – a mere handful – appeared sympathetic. She scanned them more carefully. No, no sign of Gordon. Well, what could she expect? She certainly didn't blame him. No doubt he would be wanting a divorce next. She sighed. There had been plenty of time to think, sitting in a dingy remand cell. She had treated him shabbily – a wife in name only.

Then her heart lurched. Seated in a corner of the dusty room was Mr Caton. How embarrassing! Without knowing why, she respected him. She had never spoken to him, but watching him walk past 'The Globe' she knew he was a gentleman in every sense of the word. She felt ashamed that he should see her here. But why *was* he here? Not idle curiosity, she would stake her life on that. To her surprise he smiled and nodded when he caught her eye. She flushed and dropped her gaze. He had an odd effect on her, just like that girl Esther; she wanted to be near them. It was all very confusing.

The magistrate entered, accompanied by two minor acolytes, and after some bowing and scraping Jean was asked the usual questions: name, address and occupation. She flicked a contemptuous glance at her legal aid solicitor, who was preparing to open the proceedings. With his round, baby face and habit of picking at his nails, he reminded her of a grubby schoolboy. They had only met once, so he didn't know her and there was little, if anything, he could submit in her defence. His name was Carter or Cartwright, something of the kind.

'Hm', she thought, 'the day of reckoning has come, my girl. You were weak. You were greedy. You let Antony have his own way far too much. But at least you did try to make the girl feel at home – you did do that. And you would never have done anything to harm her. But no one knows anything about that either.'

But here she was wrong. She heard her solicitor call Mr Caton to the stand. Jean leant forward, gripping the rail in front of her. Now she was for it. The artist stepped down from his seat and entered the witness box.

Maurice answered the obligatory enquiries and then stood, quietly waiting. The magistrate peered at him from over the top of his glasses, reminded of how his wife had persuaded him to buy one of Caton's paintings. He had been pleasantly surprised by both its high quality and reasonable price. So this was Maurice Caton. Looked a decent, normal enough fellow. But what was his connection with the accused? He consulted his papers. Oh yes, the daughter of Caton's friends had been the kidnap victim. Therefore, his deposition might add interest to this case. He sat back in his chair and prepared to listen.

Mr Cartwright was already on his feet, brushing specks of dandruff from his jacket, eager to begin.

"Mr Caton, standing in the dock is a woman who it is alleged held hostage the teenage daughter of good friends of yours. Yet, in spite of her actions you have come here today, entirely of your own free will, to speak on her behalf. Could you please explain your reasons to the court?"

"Certainly. To put it in a nutshell I feel strongly that every human being deserves a second chance in life; that nobody should be arbitrarily punished simply because of the dictates of a man-made law. Mrs Preston did wrong, yes of course, but she was motivated by good intent. Moreover, she has admitted her guilt, and by pleading guilty has spared young Esther Latimer the ordeal of giving evidence."

A murmur had spun round the court at Maurice's phrase '…motivated by good intent'. The prosecuting lawyer, a Mr Briggs, jumped up.

"Could the witness kindly clarify his remark about good intent? How exactly did Mrs Preston demonstrate this? She was merely out for what she could get. Where was the good intent in that? The whole idea is absurd."

"Mrs Preston thought, albeit mistakenly," replied Maurice, "that by aiding and abetting her brother in his planned crime she was helping him fulfil his dreams of a life of luxury." His voice rose slightly. "All her life has been devoted to helping him achieve his desires. Her actions were wrong, but I repeat were motivated by good intent – a good intent that sprang from love for that wayward brother. I feel she needs the chance to right that wrong. Therefore, I am here to ask the court to give her that chance. After all, she presents no danger to anyone, and would not repeat her mistakes. She needs an opportunity to be of use to the community which she could not do if locked behind bars. She has a home…"

"I protest, Your Worship," objected Briggs. "She may well have a home but I understand that debts have been incurred while she has been on remand. Why should the taxpayer have to foot the bill?"

"Exactly what are these debts referred to, Mr Briggs?" enquired the magistrate.

"If Your Worship would turn to your file, page ten, you will see that there are listed unpaid rates, gas and electricity bills, plus several hire purchase agreements for furniture etc."

"Pardon me, Your Worship," interrupted Cartwright, "but if you would care to turn to page twelve, you will see that all the debts referred to have now been paid. There are no monies outstanding, none at all."

"I still don't understand," protested the magistrate. "How did these debts come to be paid, Mr Briggs? First you say there are monies outstanding, but now I can clearly see that there are not. An explanation if you please."

The unfortunate man was shuffling through the pages of his file, looking somewhat flustered.

"I'm sorry, Your Worship, but I don't have one at this stage."

"Pardon me again, Your Worship," spoke up Cartwright, "but I think I can explain matters. Mr Caton, would you please give the bench an answer."

"It was I who paid all Mrs Preston's debts," said Maurice.

The magistrate stared in amazement. He was beginning to be more than a little bewildered by the artist's replies.

"*You* paid them, Mr Caton. *You* paid this woman's debts! But.. in Heaven's name why?"

Maurice looked calmly at the puzzled man and stated:

"Because she is a fellow human being, and therefore worthy of help. I've more than enough money for my needs and it gave me pleasure to help her in this way. I would also like to point out that I am here today at the instigation of Esther Latimer, who came to see me saying how much she wanted Jean Preston to be able to keep her home. We had a long talk and it was decided that I would make myself available to speak on Mrs Preston's behalf."

"I see," said the magistrate. "Well, thank you for your frankness. The world would be a more straightforward place to live in if everyone was as clear as yourself. Mr Briggs, do you have any questions for this witness? No. Right then, Mr Caton, you may stand down. Mr Cartwright, do you have any more witnesses? No. Well then, Mr Briggs."

"I call Jean Preston to the stand."

Jean did not hear her name called the first time. Her tear filled eyes were following Maurice as he made his way back to his seat. No one had ever been that kind and considerate to her in her whole life. Then she heard her name being called sharply, and was directed to go into the witness box.

"Jean Preston," said Briggs, "you have fully admitted your part in the robbery and kidnapping for which you are on trial today. Have you anything you wish to say in your defence? Remember these were serious crimes. Take your time."

Jean had donned her best suit and white silk blouse for her court appearance to try to create a good impression. Besides she always found that clothes, the right clothes, gave confidence. But the suit had become creased and she stood trembling slightly trying to smooth out the wrinkles with her hands. She felt so lonely. She glanced around the room again, avoiding Maurice, and then settled her eyes on the magistrate. He looked a kind old boy; he gave her encouragement to speak out. She cleared her throat, still gingerly palming her skirt.

"Well, sir," she began. "I'm very sorry for what I did. I've had time to think about all that. I was only trying to help Antony – my brother that is – only I know now that I wasn't helping him at all. I should have stopped him. But you see I've always done what he wanted ever since Mum died and Dad went off with some woman. I know I spoilt him. But I'd never have hurt the young lady, Miss Latimer, or allowed anyone to hurt her. She was nice. I liked her. And I want to thank Mr Caton for what he's done for me. No one has ever done anything like that before..." She had to pause and swallow hard. It was very quiet in the room now. "But I know I've done a great wrong and will have to be punished. I know that. That's all I have to say, sir, except I hope the young lady can truly forgive me."

"Thank you, Mrs Preston," said Briggs. "You may sit if you wish while their Worships decide on sentence."

The magistrate and his two minions huddled together on the bench, whispering. Jean shut her eyes, unable to bear to watch. How long a sentence would she get and how would she be able to bear life in prison? And her house – would she ever see it again, or would it have to be sold? At last the three men perched above the chamber of the court-room broke away from each other and the old chap addressed her:

"Jean Preston, your actions were wrong, very wrong, but we are of the opinion that you understand and are truly repentant. You have people, good people, prepared to stand by you it seems, and you will need good friends at this difficult period of your life. We have also taken into account your previous clean record, although we rather think you have in the past turned a blind eye to your brother's criminal activities. That must stop; indeed, I strongly advise you to sever all connection with him for your own good. Do you think you would be able to support yourself?"

"Oh yes, sir. I can always get work in a pub. I have worked in them all my life."

"And what about your husband? Are you still in touch with him at all?"

"No sir. But I don't blame him. I have not treated him right.

He was always very generous to me with money and such like. I didn't deserve him."

"I see. Quite. Well, taking all these different factors into consideration we sentence you to three years on probation. However, you must clearly understand that if you appear here again, then you will undoubtedly receive a custodial sentence. Do you understand?"

"Yes, sir, and thank you very much."

"Good luck to you. You are free to go."

A brief chat with her probation officer – a nice young woman who reminded her a little of an older version of Esther – and then she was out in the sunlight, a free woman. Darn it though, she had probably missed Mr Caton and she did want to… No! There he was, standing at the bottom of the steps. She hurried down and stood in front of him.

"Mr Caton, I did so want to.."

Maurice stopped her by putting a finger to his lips, looking benevolently down into her flushed face.

"No need, no need, Jean. You get yourself sorted out and one day, when you are ready, come and have tea and a chat at Maples. Meanwhile, there is someone waiting to see you."

With that, Maurice patted her shoulder and walked briskly away.

Jean turned round, quite unable to recognise anyone. To the left of where she was standing there was a small paved square with a few wooden benches. A half-hearted attempt had been made to enliven some straggly flower beds with gaudy bedding plants. An eddy of warm wind blew a scattering of crisp and sweet packets against her shoes, but overall the area was quite clean. A few yards away a man stood up from one of the benches. With the sun shining directly in her eyes Jean couldn't see him clearly. He moved toward her and said:

"Hello there, Jean. I'm truly glad you are free again."

Jean felt her face grow hot. Gordon was here after all. She felt absurdly pleased. After many years of thinking he was a dull stick with not an iota of imagination in him, she was suddenly overwhelmed to see his familiar, stocky figure. The last few weeks had helped her to value what was truly of importance in her life. Tears could no longer be restrained and she sobbed on his shoulder.

"Oh, Gordon, I-I've b-been such a fool, such a b-bloody f-fool. And… and everyone has been so kind to me. Mr C-Caton, Esther – everyone. You have n-no idea. And now y-you're here and I don't deserve…" Words refused to come as emotion took over.

Gordon fumbled in the pocket of his jacket and managed to locate a clean handkerchief. He handed it to his wife and she blew her nose.

"Look here, old girl," Gordon unconsciously dropped into the affectionate phrase he hadn't used for a long time. "You look tired out. There's a cafe just across the road – I had a cup of coffee in there while I was waiting. It's quite clean and you could do with some hot food inside you."

Jean nodded and Gordon tucked her arm in his and guided her through the traffic. When he pushed open the cafe door for her and the smell of cooking assailed her nostrils, she realised how hungry she was. Gordon found a table and suggested:

"Why don't you slip to the Ladies and freshen up. You'll feel better."

Luckily there was no one in the loo and she was able to wash her face and comb her hair without being observed. Back at the table Gordon was already pouring out a cup of tea, stirring in her usual three lumps of sugar. She sipped gratefully, beginning to relax and take in her surroundings. The cafe was half empty, and the whoosh of steam coming from the expresso coffee machine sounded loud but friendly.

' "Are you hungry, dear?" asked Gordon. "What about some fish and chips?"

To her surprise Jean found she did have an appetite when they arrived, together with another pot of tea.

"Feeling better?" Gordon's open, honest face looked anxious as he leant across the table.

Jean looked down at her empty plate. "Why are you being so good to me? I don't understand. I've treated you badly. I know that."

"I've always been fond of you. I don't know why. I just am."

He hesitated, trying to make up his mind about something, and then went on:

"Look, Jean, I've been thinking. I know it's early days for you, but have you any idea what you are going to do next? I mean, where are you going to go? And where will you live?"

Jean shook her head dumbly, and spread her hands open on the table. The man gently took hold of one, causing Jean to look up in surprise. He continued:

"I'm leaving 'The Globe'. I've surrendered the licence. The brewery have found a youngish couple to take over almost straight away."

Jean's eyes filled with tears once more.

"Oh no, not that. You love the place, and the village, not to mention the regulars."

"But don't you see? It means nothing to me without you there. I know what you are going to say – you were hardly ever there anyway. That's true. I admit that. But at least I knew I would see you from time to time. Now – well, I just don't know."

Jean fell silent for a moment or two, then asked:

"Now it's my turn to ask what *you* are going to do? How will you make a living? You have been in the brewery trade for almost all your working life. I can't imagine you doing anything else. I simply can't."

"Well, that's as maybe, but I'm going to have a damned good try. I'm not that stuck in my ways. Take a good look around you, Jean. Yes, at this cafe and tell me what you see. You've an eye for detail."

She swivelled in her chair and gave the room a long, hard appraisal. She saw about a dozen red plastic topped tables, all with the usual cruet sets and sauce bottles carelessly pushed together. There was a warm, steamy atmosphere and the few customers dotted about appeared to be familiar with the overweight, red faced woman behind the counter. The room was reasonably clean although the carpet was splattered with grease stains. She glanced out of the window. Good position – no doubt about that; close to the centre of town which meant a steady stream of people continually passed by. No immediate competition as the nearest restaurant was roughly five hundred yards further on. Certainly not enough thought had been given to making full use of the locale's natural advantages. The interior could be made much more enticing.

Gordon raised his eyebrows in enquiry.

"I don't quite understand," protested Jean, "why you are asking my opinion, but since you are, I reckon that in the right hands the cafe could be a little gold mine. It needs a thorough re-vamp of course, and a good idea would be to give it a theme. I can't think of one off the top of my head, but you know the sort of thing I mean."

Gordon grinned.

"The person doing the re-vamp might well be me."

"You!" exclaimed Jean. She frowned. "I don't understand."

Her husband rubbed his hands together, smiling broadly. "When I was in here earlier there were no customers and I was able to chat to the owner – two-ton Tessie behind the counter. She is selling up apparently and has given me first refusal. She quoted a reasonable figure and I've enough money saved to buy it outright. But – and here comes the big but – I'll need a partner. It would be too much for one person to run efficiently on their own. So, how about it?"

"What *me*?" Jean was amazed. "I'd have thought you'd be glad to see the back of me by this time."

"You haven't been listening, dear. I have just been at pains to explain how much I miss you – being with you. You and I together could be the team to turn this cafe into a gold mine. What about a country and western theme with checked tablecloths, really clean and starchy, with good quality hamburgers to eat, best sausages and folk music playing quietly in the background. We both like that sort of thing. Perhaps we could call it the Big 'G'!"

"Oh, I do like the sound of that," Jean's eyes sparkled. "And you could dress like one of those old fashioned ranchers with a thin black tie and a – oh, what's it called – a cum-cummer..?"

"A cummerbund," supplied Gordon.

"Yes, that's the word."

Jean took another look round and made up her mind.

"Gordon, I'd really like to be in on this project. I'm a town person who never seemed to fit in a village. I really didn't like 'The Globe'."

"I know. It was short sighted of me to expect you to. But does this mean that you are saying 'yes'? That you will join me?" Gordon sounded wistful.

"Yes. Yes, please! And I'll work hard, I promise. Really pull my weight. But something has only just occurred to me. You will need somewhere to live, won't you, or is there accommodation overhead?"

"Well, no there isn't. T-T-T did tell me that much. But for the moment, that is the least of my worries. I'm more interested in buying the cafe and getting started on that."

Jean felt shy and hesitant as she broached a sensitive issue, but one that had to be faced.

"As you know, Gordon, I've a house. I feel ashamed now that I never told you anything about it. There's been so much I've kept to myself. Anyway, it's quite big enough for two people and I'd really like you to see it. Maybe you could.. ..I've the key right here in my bag."

"Oh no, I don't want you to feel I've been pressurising you when you are at a low ebb. That wouldn't be fair."

"But you haven't, you haven't. You've done far more than I deserve – far more than most men in your position would have done. I know that only too well. And I want you to know that I'm having nothing more to do with Antony. I made such a mess of trying to look after him. Please at least come and see the house."

"Put like that, then I'd really like to. I have to admit to being extremely curious about it. I keep trying to imagine you living somewhere I've never seen."

And so this somewhat ill-assorted couple, as so many couples are, left the cafe together and started out for Larkhill Road. They didn't know what the future held for them of course, determined simply to hold fast to the lifeline that fate had thrown them.

For a while life carried on fairly smoothly at Maples.

Another new intake of students arrived. The speed with which they settled down no longer surprised their mentors; indeed, they had come to expect nothing else. Through many years only one young man had proved unsettling enough to be sent home. Occasionally, a smaller quota of young people arrived than the usual eight, but everyone involved in the undoubted success of the venture had been pleasantly surprised that there was endless talent available, combined with a keen as mustard desire to put it into action. Still, as John Dean triumphantly declared:

"There's an awful lot of untapped, unlocked creativity out there in the world and we're the people and the place to turn the key and set it free. And I also believe that these kids really appreciate how damned lucky they are."

Joanna and Martin's announcement that they had begun house hunting caused a minor stir, but they noticed that not one of their friends put up too much of a protest. They grinned to themselves. This decision was a right one. The safe arrival of their lusty son, James Maurice, had brought matters to a head. His seeming increasing need to exercise his lungs at more and more frequent intervals was starting to build an imperceptible tension within the household. Maurice thought him a grand little chap but close proximity for any length of time caused strain. Privately he considered the baby would be far more interesting four or five years hence. Add to this the fact that Esther and Christine spoiled him at every opportunity, and Martin began to think he would soon have a young delinquent on his hands. It was high time to move on.

Martin's job as liaison worker between the youth centre at Lewisham and Maples meant a good deal of driving, therefore a house somewhere between the two was needed. They quickly found what they sought in the shape of a semi-detached, two bedroomed, hundred year old cottage complete with gables and a large, overgrown garden. Oddly enough, what clinched matters came in the guise of a dear old lady, Mrs Roberts by name, who lived in the adjoining cottage. She had popped round to meet them when they were having a second look. She could be a story book character with her soft white hair and rosy cheeks, romanticised Jo.

Apropos the baby's screams, wonder of wonders Mrs Roberts was almost stone deaf, and quite refused to wear a hearing aid. Her daughter told them at a later date that her mother was afraid that the aid would get lost inside her head and begin sending signals to aliens! Her deafness was sad for her but marvellous for them, since they would have no worries about James yelling. Apart from that one quirk she was perfectly 'compos mentis', and most knowledgeable about plants and vegetables and gardening in general. When Jo and Martin finally moved in they devised a sign language with her, and the three of them got along famously.

The village postmaster lost no time in relating the tale of the ghost who supposedly haunted the cottage. It was of a sweet, young girl who died of scarlet fever, and apparently had been seen on the staircase and in the garden. However, Martin sensibly concluded that if she was sweet and young, then she would hardly wish them harm. Moreover, in all the happy years they lived in the cottage, not once was she seen or heard. In time, one of their two grandchildren did say she thought she heard merry laughter – but who can say…?

Back to the present. Minds made up and offer accepted, they then had to wait for the conveyancing wheels to turn. They did, but oh so slowly! Still, the day finally dawned when the removal van arrived and they were gone, leaving a strange quiet behind them.

★

Joanna's departure meant significant changes in Megan's life. At the age of twenty-seven she was now in complete charge of the day to day running of the household, in addition to being Maurice's right hand woman where the students were concerned. At least the busy days helped her to sleep at night instead of tossing restlessly among crumpled pillows, glad to see the dawn, for Simon Marsden was the problem that brought about her insomnia.

She knew he needed her support but simply wasn't sure whether she had the necessary mental strength. Her early life had been so traumatic, humiliated by abusive parents, that she felt ill equipped to help another. Yes, she loved advising the students with practical problems but that was quite straightforward; and she had seemed to know instinctively how to ease Jo's pains when she had started early labour, but these things did not impinge on her own emotional space which she kept fiercely private. Simon drained her energy and that frightened her.

When they had first met in the village a couple of years ago she had been flattered by the attentions of this good looking man. He had been her first lover and she imagined herself 'in love' with him. She had daydreamed of living with him, helping to run the farm. Now she realised that the idea only had appeal because it meant she could stay close to her beloved Maples. Christopher was right, of course, in his brief summing up of Simon's character: "He's weak, very weak". This had become painfully obvious to Megan whenever she visited him in prison. He seemed unaware and uncaring of the perilous nature of his position, showing no concern about the loss of the family farm which involved three loyal workers being out of a job: men with families to support.

One point in his favour was his genuine remorse for exposing Esther to such an unpleasant experience. Even so, Megan had firmly resolved to be a friend, nothing more. When Simon kept whining: "You *will* wait for me, won't you, Megan? Then when I've made some money again we can get married." She answered with a resounding: "No! No! Friends only, Simon." He would just sadly shake his head looking like a bewildered small boy. However, with her mind made up, and new daily challenges to meet, her whole demeanour brightened. She had an important role to fill, she had her music to play and teach, she had her youth and vitality – life was sweet and good. She would stand by Simon as a friend but that was all.

Maurice waited, watching her arrive at her decision with relief. He felt she was worthy of a much stronger life partner when, or if, the time was ready. He had worried that she might throw herself away on Simon, in a relationship where she would undoubtedly be the prop. The man had formed his reality and would have to face his problems in his own way.

Meanwhile, it was heartening to see the young woman's eyes sparkle, a spring return to her step, and to hear her sing as she performed her duties. It came about that Megan stayed single all her life, no lovers but always plenty of good friends.

Maples' local railway station was almost deserted this early on a fresh April week-day morning. In actual fact the word, station was rather a misnomer – a 'halt' would be a more accurate description. Keith knew that Megan would have willingly driven him to a station eight miles further up the line but he rather liked this country halt. On the wild flower bedecked grassy bank opposite he could see several rabbits cropping the grass, long ears continually alert for any danger, and off in the distance a field of sheep, many lambs among them.

He was returning to London after the Easter holiday. Since his somewhat ridiculous outburst at Christmas telling Maurice how bored he was by the countryside, he now knew that to be untrue; at the time, he had been dissatisfied with himself. Certainly he would always be a Londoner at heart, but there were plenty of other places to visit and appreciate. He had kept it a secret for the moment, but he was seriously considering indulging in a coach trip to Italy – he had all the details in his breast pocket. A journey across Europe down to Florence, it sounded so romantic. He had read and re-read the brochure. All his life he had never been abroad, for one could hardly count a day trip to Calais. It was time he began to explore. And he must move out from his seedy flat, having been too lazy to bother before. He wanted to invite Maurice for the day; this time he was sure he would come. Keith was already planning the meal. Since the 'Esther episode', as he privately referred to that extraordinary experience, he felt more of an equal. He could hold his head high. He was 'somebody'.

He looked at his watch. Five more minutes before the train was due. He looked round curiously at his fellow travelling companions, one or two more having drifted on to the platform since his arrival. There was an elderly couple in almost matching tweed suits and hats, the only difference being the woman's skirt. They appeared contented with each other's company. A twelve to thirteen year old schoolboy, cap pushed right to the back of his head, was trying to catch up on his homework. Keith recognised the tell-tale signs with a grin of sympathy. Then there was a young chap in his mid-twenties, wearing a cheap, bespoke suit, avidly reading a tabloid paper. Who else? Ah, yes, someone to avoid – a young mother with an infant in a folding pram. After a day spent in the company of Joanna's baby he had had enough of screaming.

An extremely tall, thin man had just parked his car and was coming through the barrier, showing his season ticket to the collector on the gate. The man must be at least 6'6". Keith had always considered extremes of anything awkward, and shuddered at the idea of having to have clothes personally tailored. Still, the man looked 'moneyed' so it probably wasn't too much of a problem.

The train was signalled and could be seen approaching off in the distance. Then suddenly it had arrived and all was bustle. Keith chose a compartment away from the baby and the train moved off, gathering speed. He gazed eagerly out of the window, revelling in the sensation of fast movement. It was soothing. Damn! He had that indigestion spasm again. It must have been that second cup of breakfast coffee which he knew he should have refused. Fumbling in his pocket he tried to locate his Setlers tablets. The pain struck again, sharper, more suffocating this time. He doubled over, struggling for breath. What the hell was happening? From far off he could hear a woman's voice asking anxiously: "Are you all right? Can we be of help?" It must be Mrs Tweedy. Silly woman. Of course he wasn't all right. He shouted at her: "No! I feel ill. I need help." But she couldn't seem to hear him. He shouted once more. He could just see her shaking her head but her shape was growing dim. Then he could faintly hear a man's voice. "Let me see him. I'm a doctor." His eyesight cleared slightly. It was the bean-pole man, and he was lifting Keith's legs up on the seat and taking his pulse. 'I wonder,' imagined Keith, 'if he has to have his white coats tailored or does he just wear ordinary ones above the knee?' But he really didn't care. He felt deliciously drowsy. So drowsy…so drowsy he was…he was floating and he felt warm and comfortable. The train must have entered a tunnel because he was spinning down it… spinning… spinning… out into space.

That same morning Maurice had time to spare between art classes. Fresh air, blue skies and sunshine beckoned through the windows – he would stroll down the front drive to the gates. It was too early for the bluebells but the daffodils and narcissi were in full and glorious bloom. He wanted particularly to mull over in his mind thoughts that had lain there since his visit to the Latimer family three days ago. Ian still felt embarrassed about coming to Maples, therefore Maurice had boarded the familiar bus for his journey to the Gallery.

On arrival, he had found two or three would-be customers in situ, wearing that rather bemused expression folk adopt when wandering round art galleries and museums. Yvonne, managing to appear both efficient and attractive in a rose coloured wool suit, was seated behind her desk, writing an invoice. She gave Maurice a welcoming smile and he winked. Striding to the back of the room, he opened the door that led to the family flat above, giving a quick ping on the discreet brass bell as he did so. Esther was expecting him and was leaning over the bannisters to greet him with a kiss on the cheek. Looking at her, he could see at a glance that she had fully recovered from her ordeal.

"You'll stay to lunch, won't you Maurice?"

"Try and stop me," he twinkled, "as something smells good in the kitchen."

"I'm trying out a new recipe," she announced proudly.

Maurice wondered if he had been a trifle rash in agreeing to lunch. Past experiences with Esther's 'new recipes' had found them to be mysteriously burnt. Too late now, for she was disappearing back into the kitchen. He turned toward the sitting room, a cosy, welcoming family den directly over the downstairs Gallery with a matching, elegant bow window. Ian got to his feet on Maurice's entrance, and the two men took stock of each other.

"You look much better, Ian. Very much better, old chap."

"I feel much better. I really do." came the firm reply.

Maurice sat down, saying with a grin that Esther was trying out a 'new recipe'. Ian rolled his eyes in mock horror and they laughed together. Esther, listening at the door, was delighted to hear her father's familiar laugh, so long silent, and darted back to the kitchen with a light heart. She would surprise them!

Yvonne slipped into the room, perching on the arm of her

husband's chair. They wouldn't be interrupted since the Gallery was now empty, and she had locked the main door. There was a small silence broken by Ian.

"Maurice, I never thanked you for all you did to help me that evening when I was nearly going out of my mind. I was in a terrible state. You are the truest of friends – really you are. I did give careful thought to all you said about not involving outsiders for help, but succumbed when a good friend of ours suggested a hypnotherapist who had greatly helped her. I simply didn't feel confident enough to go it alone, even with Yvonne's help." He squeezed his wife's hand.

"For Pete's sake, don't apologise," protested Maurice. "It is simply my personal preference. Each one must find the way that is right for them. Do you feel like telling me what happened, because it would be obvious to a blind man that something definitely has? Something positive. Or would you rather keep it to yourself?"

"No…no. We want to talk it over with you, to share. It's why we asked you to come. I have had three sessions with the therapist, whose name is June." Ian's face was flushed and excited, his head relaxing back against Yvonne's arm. "The first one was taken up with telling her something of myself and my problems. To my surprise she suggested we try hypnotism at the next session – I hadn't expected that so soon – and to my even greater surprise found that I was a natural subject. I regressed back to my arrival at Maples at the age of thirteen, to our meeting in the farmer's field. I became aware of my young self, crossing that field until I reached your tent. I was aware of the water-colour you were working on at the time – you remember, the view of the village church?" Maurice nodded. "I was marvelling that you could make it look easy. I felt an envy which I had suppressed. I watched myself making a decision – albeit unconsciously – that I could never be as good as you, bypassing the fact that I was only thirteen and that you were a grown man; an experienced artist. But I desperately *wanted* to paint. Yes I had talent, but that wasn't enough for me. It had to be greater than *yours*. I had made two decisions, strong decisions, which were pulling me in opposite directions.

"When I 'came round' June said she was pleased with the results of the session. She had explained to me before we began that she was hoping for an abreaction, which means resolving a neurosis by reviving forgotten or repressed ideas of the event first causing it. Sorry for the techno-speak but I did want to make it as clear to you as possible. Anyway, June, as I have already said, felt the results were better than she had hoped for and suggested that we carry on in the same way the next time we met."

Maurice was filled with curiosity, remembering his own sessions with various therapists. "How did you feel after this experience, Ian? I mean were you apprehensive about what might come floating up to the surface?"

"No, I wasn't. Not at all. I simply wanted to *know*. I felt a whole wodge of stuff was moving out of the way. I felt physically better, too, for the first time in ages. I was ready to face anything if it was the truth.

"Anyway, still feeling pretty fit, back I went for the third session. This time I came forward to a few weeks prior to my accident. Once again I found I had been suppressing feelings of unworth, of loneliness. I felt I would never make the grade as an artist and began to panic. I was quite unconsciously making these decisions. I found my right hand was becoming weak and shaky. Here was a way out, although the weakness passed. Then came the night of the accident, and I know now, can face now, that I had let that car hit me. It was going to solve all my problems. But being able to admit to that stark fact, I can live with myself and.. and.. begin to get to know myself, perhaps even one day love…"

His voice faltered, his eyes bright with unshed tears. Maurice leant across and patted his knee while Yvonne gently squeezed his shoulders.

…By that precise moment in his reflections, Maurice had reached the large double wrought iron gates of Maples which were standing open. He had barely noticed the flowers he had meant to admire, so absorbed had he been with his thoughts. He was rudely jolted back to the present by the sudden arrival of a police car which swung into the drive, pulling to a halt when the driver spotted him.

Maurice's stomach performed an unpleasant somersault and his heart began to thump, believing the police only called with bad news. What could it be this time? Was it Esther again? Or was Keith in some kind of trouble? He was aware of the policeman's approach and made an effort to pull himself together.

The young constable said casually: "Sorry, sir, I didn't mean to alarm you. I'm looking for Maurice Caton, Mr Maurice Caton. Do you happen to know where I might find him?"

"I'm Maurice Caton. What is it you want with me? Has something happened? Tell me quickly."

"I do have bad news, I'm afraid Mr Caton. I regret to have to tell you that your brother, Mr Keith Dunsett, died this morning."

"Died! You're mistaken. You must be! He can't have died this morning because I only saw him then – at breakfast. He was planning to return to London by train."

"Before I say any more, it would be better if we went up to your house, Mr Caton. You will be more comfortable there." Showing his warrant card, he said he was P.C. Jennings.

Still shaken, Maurice allowed himself to be driven to the house. They went into the sitting room, by which time he had managed to regain a little of his usual composure.

He asked in a quiet voice:

"Please tell me exactly what has happened."

"Your brother collapsed and died on the train, Mr Caton. A doctor, one of the passengers, attended him and said he died quickly and peacefully. He didn't suffer at all. Most probably a heart attack, the doctor reckoned. Did he have a problem with his heart?"

"Not that I was aware of." Maurice rubbed his chin. "He did look rather tired now I come to think of it, and he did keep complaining of indigestion. Where is he at the moment, Constable? Will I be able to see him?"

"Yes, of course. We do need someone to identify the body, you understand? He is in the local mortuary chapel."

Only last evening Keith had been seated, laughing and talking, in this same armchair and now... Maurice felt a lump come up in his throat. He coughed.

"Will you excuse me for a few minutes? I must tell my assistant the news and where I'm going" He stood up, feeling oddly detached. The policeman rose to his feet.

"Take your time, Mr Caton."

He watched Maurice slowly leave the room head down, and begin to mount the stairs. This man was genuinely upset.

Five minutes later Maurice was back, having changed his paint spattered trousers. He left behind a weeping Megan in the kindly care of John and Chris. A strangely quiet knot of students had gathered on the landing as word spread. The two men went out to the car and a thought struck Maurice as he climbed in.

"Were there other people with him besides the doctor? I mean other passengers?"

"Yes, sir. Everyone was kind and helpful, especially an elderly couple who had noticed him on the platform."

Maurice fell silent, and the policeman wisely left him to his thoughts.

'I'm glad he didn't die alone,' reflected Maurice to himself. 'I'm glad he had other people near him. He might have been frightened on his own, but I do wish I could have been with him nevertheless.'

Officialdom was found to have a most human, sensitive side. Maurice was left alone with his brother to make his private farewell. Keith's face looked serene, younger somehow, the worry lines smoothed. Maurice realised, then, that Keith would not have wanted to grow old. This was the best way. He touched his hand lightly and left the room, knowing that only the physical body lay there. Keith's spirit was free.

Later that evening, in his room, Maurice looked at some of Keith's personal belongings given to him by the police. There was a wallet with a small amount of money, a watch, a comb, a notebook indicating that he, Maurice, was next-of-kin, a railway ticket and, most intriguing of all, a brochure describing a coach tour to Florence. Keith had pencilled in some dates when he was obviously considering setting out. How extraordinary. Maurice sat on the side of his bed, the pamphlet in his hand, staring at it. He would have enjoyed going with him, showing him corners of that beautiful city where the tourists were almost unknown. Perhaps they could have travelled to other countries together.

He wept then for the brother he was only just beginning to know. He wept for the precious hours that had been wasted.

★

The village church was preparing for its annual summer jumble sale. Even though Maurice heartily disliked communal events, this occasion he turned to his advantage. By nature a hoarder, unable to throw anything away, he was always delighted to have an excuse to clear his squirrel-like accumulation from numerous cupboards and drawers while, at the same time, feeling virtuous that he was helping some distant 'good cause'. Before long clutter would build up again, but for a month or two he would endeavour to remain organised.

John Dean had amazed him one year by announcing that he had absolutely no jumble. When asked why, he replied in his quiet, self-effacing manner: "Well, you see, Maurice, I always have a monthly sort out, and take anything of worth to the local charity shop." Initially dumbfounded by this exemplary behaviour, the answer was unsurprising when Maurice recalled John's ultra tidy house. It was in keeping with this neat, kindly man.

Aware that another day or two would find the usually mild mannered vicar, flanked by his band of helpers, marching in military style up the drive, intent on plunder, Maurice decided that this year he would tackle the bookshelves in the sitting room. Here was a classic example of his most squirrel-like behaviour. Books of every size were squeezed tightly together, with the overspill lying on their sides in higgledy-piggledy fashion on top. The collection represented Maurice's eclectic taste in reading, from Dickens to Dostoevsky, Emerson to T.S. Eliot, Hardy to Hemingway. Over the years he had been given books as gifts – some of them so entirely unsuitable that he never read beyond the first few pages. Yet he still found space for them somehow. He held the view that if someone had been creative enough to attempt to write a book, then regardless of the sentiments expressed within the covers, the book itself should be treated with respect.

But space had now run out; its zenith had been reached! Drastic measures were required. First, he would pack up all the paperbacks he didn't like, especially biographies of men and women he would never wish to meet since they radiated unpleasantness. Somewhere, too, there lurked an absurd book entitled 'Cooking for One' whose complicated recipes would leave a clutter of dirty pans in their wake as though cooking for six. Yes, he'd be glad to remove that particular book out of his life.

He selected two stout cardboard boxes from the lobby and approached the task with determination. The sitting room was filled with sunshine with one golden shaft playing over the shelves, exposing a thick layer of dust. Maurice lifted out one book and myriads of dust particles danced in the light. He sighed and went in search of a duster.

An hour passed. Very slow progress made. The trouble was he couldn't resist dipping into every book he selected. Extracting with difficulty another paperback, he found something caught behind – something that crackled like old parchment. He removed with care a thin, yellowed book which must have slipped down behind the one in front. Mystified, he opened the pages, and to his amazement found it to be a diary written in his mother's hand.

Where had it come from? And how did it get there? He didn't remember it at all. Wait a moment, though. A picture memory was forming. He was back in the summer-house nearly thirty years ago. He could even smell the dust – more acrid than the dust in this room. He could see the fat spider scuttling behind the two old deck-chairs. Something was lying on the floor – this slim book which he had mistaken for a volume of poetry, picking it up to tuck under his arm. Not bothering to look inside since his mind had been preoccupied with other matters, he did remember bringing it with him on return to the house later that evening, after the departure of Doris Pope and the police.

He re-opened the pages, almost reluctant to read the faded words; already having a shrewd idea what he would find, he felt like a voyeur. But read he must – not now, later, in the summerhouse where she would have sat writing. He put the book away in his studio and quickly finished filling the boxes, no longer interested in reading anything else. He dragged them back to the lobby and washed his hands.

Supper finished, he made his way to the summer-house while it was still light. He opened the door and went inside, sitting down in a deck-chair. While lighting his pipe he lay the book on his knees. One fact puzzled him: how had it lain unnoticed on the floor for the ten years following his mother's death?

And what was it doing in the summer-house anyway? Surely she would have kept it hidden in her room?

The answer came immediately. She must have known how ill she was, how weak her heart, perhaps even that she was dying. She would have come here in the evenings, bringing the diary with her – the journal of her passionate love affair all those long years ago. She would have sat here, once again keeping tryst with her ardent lover, remembering tender caresses and words of arousal. Her weak eyes might have thought she saw him approaching once more through the dusk. Probably, one night pain struck, and she had to hurry back to the house, never to return. The book would have slipped from her lap in the haste of her flight, to be ignored when the house and gardens were shut up after her death.

Maurice took a deep breath and began to read. He was right, of course. She had poured out her heart in a torrent of words, her normally repressed, cold nature seeking release. He found it too intimate to continue. It was meant for no one's eyes but hers. He was just about to close when suddenly his own name leapt out at him. Faint though the ink was on this page, he could make out the words.

'Maurice is out there in the garden, watching me. He thinks he cannot be seen but I know he's often there. Oh, what is the matter with me? I long to call him to me, to sit him on my lap and talk to him. I know I am distant and harsh with him, but I simply cannot help myself. Why can't I behave like any normal mother? What makes me turn against him? He is a talented boy, whose interest in painting I should be encouraging, not sneering at. And now this great love I have for Alec makes me deliriously happy. I should be sharing that happiness, but I am selfish and want to keep it all to myself. Forgive me, my son, for wronging you. I hope that one day you too will find happiness.'

Maurice flicked through the rest of the journal but he could not find another reference to himself. He put the fragile book carefully in his jacket pocket and sat for a long time deep in thought. Poor Mary Caton. When love had finally filled her empty heart, guilt made it impossible for her to share that joy with her son. How little we know of each other's secret yearnings.

He had forgiven her many years ago, but he did want her to know that she had brought him happiness. She had given him a great treasure – Maples, the house where he had learnt to love and be loved in return.

Lightning Source UK Ltd.
Milton Keynes UK
UKHW02f1315131117
312671UK00006B/109/P